D0400714

In a South Carolina nursing home, a lost world re-emerges as a disabled elderly woman undergoes newfangled brain-restoration procedures. At a deluxe medical spa on a nameless Caribbean island, a middle-aged woman hopes to revitalize her fading youth with therapies that combine cutting-edge medical technologies, holistic approaches, and the pseudo-religious dogma of Zen-infused self-help. And in a mill town, an adolescent girl is unexpectedly inspired by the ravings and miraculous levitation of her fundamentalist friend's weird grandmother. These are only a few of the scenarios readers encounter in Julia Elliott's debut collection, *The Wilds*. In these genre-bending stories, Elliott blends Southern gothic strangeness with dystopian absurdities, sci-fi speculations with fairy-tale transformations. Without abandoning the tenets of classic storytelling, Elliott revels in lush lyricism, dark humor, and experimental play.

the Wilds

the Wilds

Stories by JULIA ELLIOTT

 TIN HOUSE BOOKS / Portland, Oregon & Brooklyn, New York

Published by Tin House Books, Portland, Oregon, and Brooklyn, New York Distributed to the trade by Publishers Group West, 1700 Fourth St., Berkeley, CA 94710, www.pgw.com

Library of Congress Cataloging-in-Publication Data

Elliott, Julia (Fiction author)
  [Short stories. Selections]
  The wilds : stories / by Julia Elliott.
     pages cm
   ISBN 978-1-935639-92-3 (paperback)
   I. Title.
   PS3605.L4477A6 2014
   813'.6--dc23
                                    2014011906

These stories appeared, sometimes in slightly different form, in the following publications: "The Whipping" in the *Georgia Review* and *Best American Fantasy 2007*; "Rapture" in the *Georgia Review*; "Jaws" in the *Mississippi Review*; "Organisms," "The End of the World," and "Feral" in *"Conjunctions"*; "Regeneration at Mukti" in *Conjunctions* and *The Pushcart Prize XXXVII: Best of the Small Presses*; "The Wilds" in *Tin House* and *Fantastic Women: 18 Tales of the Surreal and Sublime from Tin House*; and "LIMBs" and "Caveman Diet" in *Tin House*.

First US edition 2014
Printed in the USA
Interior design by Diane Chonette
www.tinhouse.com

FOR MY PARENTS

CONTENTS

Rapture

Brunell Hair lived in a lopsided mill house with her mama and her uncle and her little withered-up critter of a grandmaw. In honor of her eleventh birthday, she was having a slumber party, but so far, only my best friend, Bonnie, and I had showed. Our mothers had had some kind of powwow, during which they'd smoked cigarettes and worked themselves into a tizzy over how vain and selfish we were getting, finally declaring that sleeping over at Brunell's house would be just the thing to "teach us a lesson" about how fortunate and spoiled we were. Truth told, we wanted to see Brunell in her natural habitat. We wanted to see the creepy troll-child's lair, witness the antics of her Jesus-freak mother, spy on her uncle, who'd appeared in several television commercials, and see her Meemaw speak in tongues.

Brunell's mother, who wore hideous dresses and sported an old-fashioned mushroom cloud of hair, was making hamburger patties. The other two family members were holed up in their rooms, Meemaw praying for the soul of her gay son, the uncle just sitting up there enduring the prayers she threw at him, sighing every five minutes over the man in California who'd broken his heart. According to Brunell, ever since Meemaw's husband died, the woman did nothing but pray and eat candy and watch the TV she'd won at a church raffle. According to Brunell, although her mother could spit her share of prayers at the sins of the world, she stayed busy while doing it. She kept a spotless house, vacuuming their pink wall-to-wall carpet three times a week and scrubbing their kitchen until it gleamed.

❦

Huddled out back behind a clapboard shed, smoking the cigarette butts that Bonnie and I had stolen from our mothers, we tried to teach Brunell to French inhale. Scrunching her angelic frog-face, Brunell blew out a smoke cloud that'd definitely not laced her lungs.

"You're not really smoking," said Bonnie.

"Smoking is a sin." Brunell tried another puff.

"Whatever," said Bonnie. "Where's your uncle?"

"He's in Mama's room. Mama's bunking with Meemaw. I can't take her sleep talk. Gives me nightmares."

"What does she talk about?" asked Bonnie.

"The Rapture," said Brunell.

"The Blondie song?" I said.

"The end of the world, stupid."

Though I knew about the book of Revelation, I'd never heard the end times referred to as the Rapture before. Now I couldn't help but picture Jesus cruising down to Earth on a glittery gold escalator, his white robes spattered with disco light. Two angels hovered above him, twirling a mirrored ball. Down in the pulsing city, Debbie Harry waited in a red convertible Corvette. All decked out in ruby spandex, she winked and blew Jesus a kiss. The Son of God hopped into her car and they drove off toward the beach, the wind mussing his hippie hair into a wild, Mötley Crüe mane.

❦

While her mother slaved over a skillet of french fries, Brunell played her uncle's commercials on the VCR he'd brought from California. We watched Uncle Mike, named for the archangel Michael, make out with a cheerleader in a Big Red commercial. We watched him carve into a bar of Irish Spring soap while perched on the back of a black stallion. We sighed as Brunell's handsome uncle portrayed the dangerously masculine essence of Oleg Cassini cologne: he drove a Rolls-Royce, played polo, flew his private jet to an exotic beach, where he dallied on a yacht with a chick in a French-cut bikini.

"Goddamn," said Bonnie, who liked to make Brunell cringe. "He's fine as all get out."

"He's gay, so he wouldn't look twice at you."

"Maybe he hasn't met the right woman." Bonnie tossed her hair.

"First of all," I said, "a training bra doesn't make you a woman. Secondly, when you're gay, you're gay."

"Who said?"

"My mama."

"He might be bi," said Bonnie.

"Brunell," I said, "is he gay or bi?"

"He's gay, but Meemaw's been praying for that to change. She's been praying for a good Christian woman to come along and lead him down the path to holy matrimony. If her prayers worked only halfway, I reckon they'd turn him into a bisexual."

"I do hope the Lord has answered her prayers," said Bonnie. And she solemnly walked over to the picture of Jesus that hung above their TV. She knelt before the handsome, blond Messiah and pretended to speak in tongues.

❦

There he was, Uncle Mike, the epitome of male hotness and urbane stealth, curled on his bed like a panther in repose. We crowded around the keyhole, fighting each other for a decent look. Whereas Brunell was a sickly little bug-eyed thing with splotched skin and crazed blond frizz, Uncle Mike was dark and piratical, his hair a fountain of black silkiness, his lips pouty yet strong. How was this creature sibling to Brunell's homely mama? What was he doing in this podunk town? He was God's Gift to Women, yet queer as a three-dollar bill. And now the demigod rose from his bed to pace around the room in tight black jeans and a flowing shirt. He sneered at himself in the mirror. He plucked a magazine from a stack and then tossed it haughtily onto the floor. Rummaging through his suitcase, he pulled forth a bottle of Jack Daniel's.

Bonnie giggled, and Brunell pinched her. Through the open hall window I could hear a mockingbird going to town. Every year spring came to Whitmire, South Carolina, with its riot of flowers and bees, promising a larger world. For a while, summer would live up to this promise. But soon the dog days would descend and trap you in a bubble of gaseous heat. Amnesia would set in, wiping out all dreams of escape until autumn pricked you out of your stupor.

❦

We sat before our hamburgers, awaiting the appearance of Meemaw and Uncle Mike. A Garfield cake, positioned center-table, depicted our favorite obese feline reclining pasha-style on a sofa, a thought bubble betraying his cynicism: *So it's your birthday? Big deal.*

Brunell kept glancing at the presents stacked atop the refrigerator. We sneaked french fries every time her mother turned her back, even though the food had not been blessed by the sanctimonious Meemaw, who, Brunell had informed us, possessed mysterious powers. Meemaw could, for example, "talk off a wart." When a pea-sized growth had sprouted on Brunell's thumb, her Meemaw had cut a potato in two and set the pieces down on her Bible. She'd mumbled some holy gibberish over the spud, rubbed her grandchild's wart with one half of it, and then buried the untainted piece in their backyard. Two days later, Brunell's wart turned black and fell off.

According to Brunell, her grandmother's powers had grown stronger after her husband died. Meemaw could stop bleeding and scare the fire out of burns. Meemaw had put a hex on Uncle Mike's boyfriend just last month, causing him to run astray. Because the faith-healing power passed on to the firstborn child, Meemaw had summoned her eldest to her bosom. And there he was now, Uncle Mike, strolling into the kitchen in a black dress shirt that probably cost a hundred dollars. It was as if some sexy nocturnal creature from a Night Flight video had crawled out of the TV into Brunell's humble abode.

"The birthday girl," he said, tousling Brunell's weird hair. "And who are these lovely ladies?"

"Lil and Bonnie," Brunell said, casting a sour look at our beaming faces.

Uncle Mike acknowledged our sophisticated maturity with a nod. Then he sat down at his place and removed the meat from his bun.

"Trying to lay off the red meat," he said to Brunell's mother.

"It won't hurt you," she said.

"I'll just have some lettuce and tomato on mine."

"That don't make sense. Mama said you look too skinny. Mama said you might be sick."

"Mama hasn't been reasonable since Daddy died," said Uncle Mike, "and you know it."

According to Brunell, Meemaw's husband had been a gambler and a drinker, a handsome man who'd doted on her. According to Brunell, he was clever with his hands, built sweet little birdhouses and hand-carved chests, planted five-acre vegetable gardens and raised bees. Meemaw had kept his corpse in her house for three days before Brunell's mama dropped by for a visit, discovered what was up, and called the hospital.

"Well, speak of the devil," Uncle Mike said.

There she was, the infamous Meemaw, a scrunched piece of woman in a tangerine pantsuit of stretch polyester, a gleaming black brooch pinned among the ruffles of her lime blouse. She sported a Washingtonian cap of white hair, which gave her tobacco-cured face a stately quality. A few gray whiskers twitched around her fuchsia lips as she smiled.

"Happy birfday, Brunell," she said.

"We were waiting for you to say grace." Brunell's mama eyed the food. "The fries are getting soggy."

Meemaw gazed heavenward and swayed on her black Reeboks. Then she closed her eyes in prayer.

"Heavenly Father, bless this child on her eleventh birfday. Give her the strength to resist the loins of Satan. Lead her not into the snarls of temptation, to citified evils, the stink of cigarettes, booze, and fornication . . ."

"The food, Mama," said Brunell's mother.

"Thank you Jesus for sending my son back to my bosom. Thank you Lamb for washing away his vile, polluted sins with your blood. Thank you for cleaning the stinking sulfurous slime from his nasty . . ."

"Mama, please."

"And thank you for these victuals. We thank your heavenly self for these hamburgers and french fries, ketchup and mustard, lettuce, tomatoes, and buns. We thank you for the sweet tea and Mr. Pig. We thank you for all the . . ."

"Mama."

"In the name of Christ's ruby wounds, amen."

Meemaw sat glaring at her hamburger, took a dainty bite off a french fry, and placed the rest of the morsel on the edge of her plate.

"You got to eat more than that," said Brunell's mother.

"Not too hungry. Just came down for the fellowship of loved ones. Don't know how much longer I've got on this earth."

"Really, Mama," hissed Uncle Mike. "Cut the melodrama. I saw the candy wrappers in your trash can." Turning to Bonnie, he said, "She gorges on sweets all day and spoils her appetite."

"Candy's about the only thing I can keep down."

"You ain't go die, Meemaw," said Brunell.

"Everybody's go die, sweetheart," said Meemaw. "And I will rejoice to join my dear departed husband before our Messiah's golden throne."

They went on like this the whole supper. Uncle Mike rolled his eyes while Meemaw described obscure aches in her heart, intestines, and joints. Uncle Mike snorted when she suggested that he join her adult study group at the Greater Zion Tabernacle. Uncle Mike fumed as she rhapsodized over the godly beauty of Tonda Lark, an unmarried woman at their church who craved the firm, guiding spirit of a man's Christian love. When Meemaw whipped out her pocket Bible and read—*thou shalt not lie with mankind, as with womankind: it is abomination*—Uncle Mike threw down the wadded-up ball of his napkin and fled the kitchen.

❦

While "Love Is a Battlefield" blared from Uncle Mike's fancy boom box, I flew across Brunell's carport on wheels of fire. Uncle Mike had moved the cars to the road so we'd have a place to skate, and the gorgeous man stood under the dogwood looking sad. He toked on a Benson and Hedges, took sips from a flask when he thought we weren't looking. He brooded and sighed as the wind had its way with his dark mane. Though the angle of the sinking sun brought out his crow's feet and made it obvious that his hair was dyed, Uncle Mike resembled an ageless warlock, and I wondered if it was true that he was heir to Meemaw's powers.

"How old is your uncle?" we asked Brunell for the hundredth time.

"Older than he looks."

She smiled like a possum and told us about her great-granddaddy, the hexmeister from Dutch Fork who'd worn a badger-tooth talisman and could control the wind and rain. His fruit trees had buckled from the weight of their yield. His hens had laid two eggs a day. The hexmeister had died at age 106 with a scalpful of raven-black hair.

Brunell whipped around on the new roller skates Uncle Mike had bought her in California, bragging about her great-granddaddy. Her old skates were those strap-on doohickeys from the 1960s, and her new ones were nicer than ours. But Bonnie and I strutted our stuff in Gloria Vanderbilt jeans while Brunell sported Kmart Wranglers. Whereas we wore authentic Izods, Brunell donned the sad dragon insignia from Sears. We flipped our stylish home perms, sculpted with electric rollers and frozen to perfection by generous gusts of Aqua Net, well aware that Brunell could barely run a brush through the clumpy flaxen afro she called hair.

Poor Brunell. When she'd unwrapped those skates, she'd nearly gone into a conniption, emitting a series of demented rodent squeals. She ignored her mama's gift (a butt-ugly corduroy jumper) and didn't look twice at

Meemaw's (*The Rainbow Study Bible*, its passages color-coded to highlight specific themes, and every spoken word of God underlined in gold). I'd gotten her the "Sweet Dreams" single by the Eurythmics, which had shot to the top of the charts that year, but the girl had no record player. She did, however, spritz herself all over with the Love's Baby Soft perfume Bonnie'd bought.

And then she slipped on her new skates and rolled out into the spring air, the sky a pink mess of ruptured clouds, two beams of light reaching down to Earth like the headlights of God's Cadillac.

$$ \psi $$

"Meemaw can see into the future," said Brunell. "She claimed Uncle Mike would arrive home on a Thursday, and he did. She said two young harlots would come to my slumber party, one redheaded and one brunette, and here you are. On a rainy Sunday morning three years ago, she dreamed that a flaming arrow pierced my Pawpaw in the heart. That night he died of cardiac arrest."

We'd rolled our sleeping bags out in the living room, even though it was only 8:36 PM, and we planned to stay up all night. We'd turned off all the lights except one lamp, which enveloped Brunell in an otherworldly glow. In dim lighting she looked almost pretty, like some big-eyed elfin princess who lived in a cave. We were girls, without breasts or blood, huddled in a cloud of Love's Baby Soft. Hyped up from too much sweet tea, we whispered of supernatural mysteries, hoping to spook ourselves into an exalted state of fright.

"Meemaw's got Uncle Mike trapped in a spell," Brunell rasped.

She looked oracular, kneeling on her Holly Hobbie sleeping bag in a white nylon nightgown, and we wanted to believe her.

"How?" we breathed in unison.

"I'll show you," she said. "At nine o'clock, Meemaw'll go to the bathroom to do her thing: take out her teeth, wrap her hairdo in toilet paper, clean off her makeup with cold cream. We can sneak into her room, but we'll have to be super quiet."

"What about your mama?" said Bonnie.

"She'll be in the kitchen, working a Bible crossword."

"How do you know?"

"I just do."

Brunell flashed her cryptic possum smirk and then she looked solemn. We watched the clock in silence, listening to the house creak as Uncle Mike paced upstairs. On the stroke of nine, we heard Meemaw get up and walk to the bathroom.

We tiptoed up the narrow stairs.

In the eerie silence of Meemaw's room, which smelled of White Shoulders dusting powder and seemed to belong to another century, we stood before a kind of shrine. On a small carved-wood table tucked behind a chest of drawers, Meemaw had placed Uncle Mike's high school picture dead center, encircling it with black chicken feathers and painted bones. In the photo, a pimpled young hippie who refused to meet the camera's eye appeared to be gazing down in bewilderment at what looked like a withered alligator foot, which Meemaw had positioned just beneath the silver picture frame. The old woman had sprinkled salt and some kind of dried herbs around the edge of the table. She'd glued various magazine shots of Uncle Mike onto a piece of notebook paper and taped the collage to the wall. Two bowls of water stood on either side of the gator claw, a weird tidbit of flesh afloat in the middle of each.

"Chicken hearts," Brunell whispered. "The most magic of the giblets."

Bonnie, standing there in her Garfield nightshirt, couldn't help but giggle, even though she was scared shitless.

"What's up, ladies?" a deep voice asked.

It was Uncle Mike, leaning against the doorframe in a black bathrobe, his hair slicked wet and glowing in the light. From where he stood, he couldn't see Meemaw's freaky shrine.

"Nothing," said Brunell. "We were gonna say good night to Meemaw."

"Ah, youth," said Mike, looking us over, "so effortlessly ethereal. When you reach middle age, you try to look nubile. When you get old, you struggle to pass as human."

"What the hell does that mean?" said Brunell.

"Nothing, Tinker Bell. Don't pay attention to your uncle's depressive rambling."

"Are you drunk?"

"A mite tipsy. Now really, what're you girls up to?"

"Tell him," Bonnie whispered.

"Shhh," hissed Brunell.

"Don't worry." Uncle Mike sneered. "I know all about Mama's little art project."

"Aren't you scared?" said Brunell.

"I'm terrified, actually, but not of her."

Uncle Mike tittered and walked over to the shrine. He pulled something from his robe pocket and waved it in front of our eyes like a magician: it was a Smurf pencil eraser. He placed the object smack dab in the center of the magical objects, right between the gator claw and the picture frame.

"Ogligattavato gucci Smurf," Mike chanted.

Chuckling, he regarded us with his beautiful, exhausted eyes.

"See, girls, the spell has been broken. Now, don't worry about me. Go back downstairs and have your slumber party. Gorge yourselves on cake while you still can. Stay up giggling until your abs ache."

"We will," said Brunell, "but . . ."

"Shhh," whispered Mike. "I hear the matriarch gargling her Listerine, which means we have exactly three minutes to make our escape."

☙

It was 10:10 PM—at least eight hours to go until the sun came up. We were cocooned in our sleeping bags, Brunell scanning *The Rainbow Study Bible* for the juiciest passages, namely those highlighted in gray (Sin) and brown (Evil). In her croaky voice, Brunell read choice bits aloud:

"Leviticus 20:16: 'And if a woman approach unto any beast, and lie down thereto, thou shalt kill the woman, and the beast.'

"Deuteronomy 25:11–12: 'When men strive together one with another, and the wife of the one draweth near for to deliver her husband out of the hand of him that smiteth him, and putteth forth her hand, and taketh him by the secrets: Then thou shalt cut off her hand, thine eye shall not pity her.'

"Ezekiel 23:19–20: 'Yet she multiplied her whoredoms, in calling to remembrance the days of her youth, wherein she had played the harlot in the land of Egypt. For she doted upon their paramours, whose flesh is as the flesh of asses, and whose issue is like the issue of horses.'"

"Excuse me?" said Bonnie.

"This is boring," said Brunell, snapping the Good Book shut. "Let's watch a movie on Uncle Mike's VCR."

Uncle Mike had a stack of videotapes we'd never heard of. We narrowed it down to the three most titillating titles—*Blade Runner*, *Liquid Sky*, and *The Elephant Man*—and after debating the potential of each, finally settled on *The Elephant Man*.

"Great," said Bonnie when the film started up, "it's black and white. Was this shit made in the 1950s?"

"Shut up," I said. "Just watch the movie."

And we did, remaining speechless as the gut-wrenching tragedy of John Merrick unfolded. Because he had a weird disease that made his head look like a giant piece of cauliflower, the world treated him like a freak and an idiot even though he was a regular nice guy inside. Underneath that cloth sack he wore over his head, underneath the deformed skull and the huge bunions that grew upon it, John Merrick was a poetry-reciting sophisticate, sensitive and gentle. Just like the rest of us, all he needed was love.

By the time he exclaimed "I am not an animal" to the homicidal mob that had unmasked him at the train station, we were all sniveling. When he collapsed in exhaustion and was carried back to his room at the hospital, we cried harder. When his best friends took him to the opera and the poor, dying man stood in the royal box to receive a standing ovation, we wept with our whole bodies. Even after the Elephant Man had died, and his soul had soared up into the starry heavens, where a woman's floating face informed him that he would live forever, we wept. We sobbed as the credits rolled on a black background and eerie space music played. We cried after the tape had ended and the screen had turned to fuzz.

Burrowed deep in our sleeping bags, we lay in the half dark, nestled in the exquisite sadness the movie had mustered, a kind of moist emanation that hovered in the room. No one spoke. We didn't need to: our minds had fused into a single entity.

My tears were just starting to dry when I spotted something moving in a dark corner, a small figure in fluttery clothes. I thought our strange mood had summoned some supernatural creature, and I was scared. As much as I pitied the poor Elephant Man, as much as I loved him, I wasn't ready to look into the face of whatever being rustled in the darkness. It stood there, making a sound like crackling cellophane, which blended with the TV static. And then the creature stepped into the gray light of the television—hunched, clad in flowing nylon, lumpy-headed, its mouth open in a toothless snarl.

It was Meemaw in her nightwear, her skull mummy-wrapped in toilet paper she'd secured with a hairnet to protect her wash-and-set. Meemaw, her face shiny with cleansing grease and spotted from countless cruel summers. Meemaw, right fist lifted in wrath, clutching a rubber Smurf.

She sat down on the couch and placed the Smurf beside her on the cushion.

"Harlots," she hissed.

Her small frame shook. She reached into the pocket of her housecoat and pulled out a penny candy, unwrapped it, and popped it into her mouth. She frowned as though butterscotch were bile.

"You don't know what you're messin' in," she said. "Powers bigger than you."

"We didn't do nothin'," Brunell rasped, but Meemaw didn't seem to hear her.

"Twelve generations," she said. "Twelve generations brought over the sea. My daddy gave it to me and now it's time to give it to Michael. I ain't got long."

"You ain't go die," said Brunell.

"Shush, child. Your flesh will melt like dirty snow."

"But we didn't *do* nothin'." Brunell sat up in her sleeping bag and crossed her arms.

Meemaw groaned. She clutched her bosom and gazed up at the ceiling fan. A great shudder contorted her body. Her little feet kicked, sending one of her purple bedroom slippers flying.

"Aw crap," said Brunell. "She's got the Holy Ghost on her. We'll never hear the end of it now."

From the depths of Meemaw, a strange voice came bubbling up: the voice of a primordial masculine spirit, the voice of Darth Vader.

"Roboto bulch," said Meemaw. "Booboo kakopygian bog."

The TV light cast Meemaw in a ghoulish glow. Eyeballs rolled back, she swayed and twitched and vomited her guttural language, words scraped up from her ancient guts. Dark fumes spurted from her. She seemed to be summoning things. I glanced around the room, thought I saw bats flitting in corners. My sleeping bag was damp with sweat and I couldn't move.

Meemaw stopped babbling on the stroke of one, just as the clock on the shelf above their space heater emitted a single moan. Her eyeballs resumed their customary position. She sat on the plaid couch panting, and then wiped a strand of brown dribble from her chin.

She reached into her pocket, pulled forth a Tootsie Roll, opened the sweet, and set it on her tongue to melt.

Sucking her candy, Meemaw grunted softly. She smoothed her housecoat and patted her hairnet. She looked us over as though she'd forgotten we were there.

"Jezebels," she mumbled.

Her voice sounded normal now, albeit scratchy and faint, worn down from whatever thing had rocked through her, scaly and slimy, born through her prehistoric throat.

"'And the woman was arrayed in purple and scarlet,'" said Meemaw, "'decked with gold and precious stones and pearls.'"

Meemaw ate another Tootsie Roll and told us about the Whore of Babylon, who laughed like a monkey and slurped fornications from a golden cup. The Whore rode a seven-headed dragon bareback and caressed the beast's spine with her private parts.

Meemaw leaned into the TV light. She told us she had a secret that was about to bust her heart wide open. She grinned.

"I'm a prophet," she whispered. "And every single night Jesus gives me dreams."

She told us the Messiah would arrive this December in a spaceship so big its shadow would darken the entire state of South Carolina. He'd land in the Blue Ridge

Mountains and set up his golden scales on top of Caesars Head. He'd take away the righteous, leave the sinners to wallow in the dung heap they'd made of planet Earth.

Meemaw leaned back on the couch, tucked her legs up under her bottom like a little girl.

"Covered in festering sores," she said, "the sinners will suffer one thousand plagues."

According to Meemaw, locusts would devour all crops. The seas would turn to blood, a trillion dead fish afloat. And the great Beast of the apocalypse, a kind of *Tyrannosaurus rex* with thirty-six heads and three hundred horns, would roam the earth, blasting fiery halitosis at every sinner he stumbled upon, scorching their bodies with third-degree burns. Flesh would fall from their bones. Skeleton people would run howling across the ashen fields.

"People will eat each other," Meemaw said, "mothers will eat fathers and fathers will eat mothers. Children will gnaw upon the rancid hides of their parents. Parents will eat the sweet fat boiled from their babies' bones."

Meemaw teetered forward and her whiskers caught the light. Her eyes were bright, swimming with fever.

"Dragons," she croaked, "will burrow in the poisoned seas."

Meemaw went on and on, prophesying until she was hoarse. She filled the room with horrific visions that left us deeply freaked, though we didn't want her to stop.

Drunk on sweet terror, shivering in our sleeping bags, we followed her every word, delighting as the tales grew stranger.

She described the filthy, outsized lusts of the Beast, who had a member like an oak trunk and who copulated with his harem of stinking she-dragons. Though the dragons were vile reptiles, they possessed the fatty teats of sows. Their young sucked blood from their mothers. They smacked their lips and had incestuous intercourse with each other until the world was full of dragons, so many dragons that swarms of flying serpents blotted out the sun.

Eyes squinted in the dim light, we saw them—the pterodactyl flocks darkening the sky, the hordes of naked people running helter-skelter upon the barren earth, their scorched hides festering with open sores. We smelled the sad acrid scent of burnt hair, the turnip-green stench of unwashed bodies, the blunt black reek of smoldering tires, for there was no wood left upon the planet, and the sinners sat around fires of trash, roasting the radioactive carcasses of dogs.

"Meanwhile," said Meemaw, "the chosen will walk in robes of flowing satin, rose petals strewn upon the pure diamond floor of Christ's spaceship. Their beds will be stuffed with doves' feathers and covered in satin quilts. Upon each bed, a snow-white baby lamb will rest, its eyes as blue as summer skies. And angels will bring the chosen little cakes to eat and nectar in golden cups."

Meemaw smacked her lips. She could taste the nectar, she said. Sweeter than all the best drinks put together—Dr Pepper and Pepsi-Cola, Mello Yello and Mountain Dew, grape Kool-Aid with five cups of Dixie Crystals sugar. Each room on the spaceship would be equipped with a whirlpool Jacuzzi. And behold—when the aged and infirm dipped their withered limbs into these fragrant holy waters, washing them clean with the Lamb's blood, they'd pull those limbs out, young and radiant again.

Meemaw retrieved a Hershey's Kiss from the pocket of her robe and held the twinkling sweet up to the light of the television.

"Lovers will be reunited," she said, peeling foil to reveal the fat droplet of chocolate. "They'll revel in their rosy flesh. Amen."

She popped the candy into her toothless mouth, closed her eyes in reverie as the morsel dissolved upon her aged tongue. Meemaw moaned and swayed, and then, in the faintest of whispers, just a scratch of voice that floated like a dandelion seed upon the air, Meemaw described heaven, a warm green planet wrapped up like a birthday present in white mist. The streams were clear and sweet as Sprite, with goldfish flapping in the bubbly waters. Lush trees grew, velvet-leaved and heavy with glowing fruit. A zillion colorful birds darted in the fragrant air. Soft fluffy animals tussled in dappled shade. The lion lay down with the lamb. And shining insects buzzed in the air, no mosquitoes among them, no wasps or hornets or other stinging pests. The bees had no poison in their bodies, freely offering their honey up to man. And the cows and nannies and mares gave suck, sweet flowing milk that tasted like melted ice cream.

Her mouth wrenched open in a beatific grin, Meemaw rocked on her haunches. She said Christ's spaceship would land in a flowering field. The angelic bodies of the chosen would be personally escorted by Jesus to paradise, where there was no sickness, no aging or bodily wounds. If you cut yourself, the flesh mended in seconds, no scabs or scars left behind. You could chop off your head one hundred times with a machete and it would always grow back, more beautiful than before. There was no hunger, no thirst, no wrath, no jealousy. There was no lust, for each would have his perfect mate, a beautiful fair creature shining with celestial light. Meemaw's husband would be there, of course, looking like he did at age nineteen, his hair thick as a stallion's mane, his lips sweet as summer plums.

"Naked like Adam and Eve," rasped Meemaw. "Wives with husbands young again, in the pleasant afternoon shade."

She closed her eyes and sat there smiling. Her cragged hand skittered like a crab to the pocket of her housecoat to pluck a sweet—a piece of hard candy. Meemaw pulled forth Starburst Fruit Chews, Rascals and Pop Drops, Sparkies and Skittles and Dots. She smacked and she smiled and she beamed. And then, as dawn broke and lavender light came gushing through the polyester sheers, Meemaw's skin glowed through her nylon nightwear. For about ten seconds she floated, her harrowed buttocks hovering one inch above the stained sofa cushion.

And then the old woman fell to Earth. She sank into the couch. Her head wobbled on her neck as she fell asleep.

🌿

The sun was coming up. We could see the brass-framed portrait of Jesus. We could see the pink wall-to-wall carpet and Brunell's mother's collection of Care Bears lined up on a mounted shelf. We could see Meemaw, by all appearances an ordinary grandmother, innocently napping on the plaid couch, and it was hard to believe that this tiny little woman in a housecoat and bedroom slippers had just described the end of the world.

Still drunk from her visions, we left Meemaw crumpled on the couch, for we could hear Brunell's mother clattering pots and pans. We drifted toward the primal sweetness of frying bacon, toward the bright kitchen, where Uncle Mike sat weeping at the Formica table, his hair slicked back in a tight ponytail. Our first impulse was to rush in and pet him all over with our small, silken hands. We wanted nothing more than to kiss him on his wrinkled brow and stroke his hair, the gray roots of which were clearly visible in the morning light. But we hung back in the darkness of the dining room to watch and listen.

"What most disappointed me," said Uncle Mike, wiping his eyes with a dish towel, "was that he ran off with that rich asshole, that he wasn't the boy I thought he was."

"You're better off without him," said Brunell's mama, hunching over the stove.

"And to come home to find Mama off her rocker," said Uncle Mike, "after not sleeping for a week. That was just too much."

"It might be that Alzheimer's."

"It's not Alzheimer's. Just old-fashioned craziness, aka mental illness. Whether it's biological or cultural, I don't know, but either way . . ."

"She's had a hard time lately, what with Daddy gone and all. Plus, Reverend Dewlap took away her Sunday school class. He never would let a woman preach, and that's what she's always wanted to do."

"And you're baffled by the patriarchal oppression of the church?"

"Reverend Dewlap's a good man. You should come to church with us today. He might be able to help you."

"Help me?"

"Make life a lot easier for you."

"If you're implying what I think you're implying, then I'm disgusted with you."

"Don't take it personal." Brunell's mother turned from the stove, waved her spatula in the air fairy-wand-style. "We all have our crosses."

"My sexuality is not a cross," said Uncle Mike. "And if you don't want me to lose my shit, I suggest that you drop the subject."

"You're the one who was talking about your friend."

"Boyfriend," said Mike. "Boyfriend, okay? And I would think that I could discuss my relationships with my own sister. We used to talk a lot in high school, remember? When you used to sneak out with Bill and come home wasted and Mama lashed out at you. You would come to my room crying, remember? Of course, I'm a fool to try to talk to you now that you've been brainwashed by snake handlers."

"We don't handle snakes."

"Whatever. Brunell's the most reasonable person in this house."

"She's just a child. And speaking of children, we ought to keep it down. We got kids in the house. Nice girls."

"By which you mean middle-class."

"What's that got to do with it?"

"Dear God." Mike sighed. "Let's just drop it."

"Girls!" Brunell's mama yelped.

When we strolled into the kitchen with our smiles of fake innocence, both adults greeted us with fierce, clenched grins. We reveled in the exquisite alchemy of bacon coated in the artificial-maple runoff from Bisquick pancakes. We drank glass after glass of Mr. Pig. We devoured the remnants of the Garfield birthday cake and ate every last Pop-Tart in the house. Uncle Mike, pretending to recover his spirits, tucked his sadness into a corner of his heart and chatted with us about Duran Duran. When he started up on California, Brunell's mama went upstairs to get ready for church.

Uncle Mike said we'd love the Venice Beach boardwalk, where fine ladies like ourselves roller-skated in string bikinis as palm trees swayed in the warm wind. There were break-dancers and snake charmers, mimes and jugglers, ancient movie stars with Latin gigolos and beribboned poodles that smelled of death. As Uncle Mike described the ecstasy of sipping a tropical cocktail on a beachfront cabana while sea winds tousled his hair, he reminded us of Meemaw, his grin crooked, his face lit up like a jack-o'-lantern. He, too, seemed to float in his chair for a minute as visions of paradise spewed from him—the swarming stars, the crashing waves, the tan men in white shorts who smelled of cocoa butter. A boy whisked by on a glittering ten-speed. A bodybuilder the color of roasted liver flexed his rippling pecs. An escaped pet parrot swooped down from a coffee-shop awning, landed on Uncle Mike's shoulder, and said, "I love you."

As Uncle Mike imitated the mechanical croak of the parrot, a light beam bounced off the refrigerator and shot directly into his forehead, where it left a small, red welt. A great twitch shook him. His pale skin glowed like the moon.

And Brunell's mother shrieked.

☙

Meemaw sat scrunched on the sofa, dead, her eyes jacked open wide, her hands crimped up like bird claws. Her skin looked dark and moist, vaguely congealed like canned ham. Just as Brunell splashed a glass of water in her mama's face to rouse her from her fainting fit, just as Uncle Mike came to from the sudden seizure that had sent him collapsing into a La-Z-Boy recliner, Bonnie and I caught sight of our mothers cruising up the driveway in a white convertible LeBaron. As they climbed out of the car, they looked two-dimensional, light and unencumbered, like magazine women. Bonnie's mother wore tight Calvin Kleins with a cotton sweater draped over her back like a cape. Her hair was honey blond, colored by Tina at Cut-Ups and styled to look wind-blown and free. My own mother wore hers in a sleek wedge, not a speck of lipstick on her mouth, though she did accessorize her linen tunic with a string of wooden beads. They traipsed up the stepping-stones that led to Brunell's front door with its BLESS THIS HOME knocker. Through the window we could see them—laughing like heathens, reveling in harlotries as they prepared themselves for the sight of Brunell's poor mama in her sad polyester dress.

Brunell's mother sat up and picked at her ruined hairdo. Her jaw muscles jerked her mouth into a snarling grin. She stood erect, smoothed her Sunday frock, and answered the door.

"Hi," said my mom chirpily, perhaps sarcastically, and I wanted to slap her in the face.

"I hope the girls behaved themselves," said Bonnie's mother, winking wryly, craning her neck to catch a glimpse of the living room.

"Like little angels," said Brunell's mother. "Do come in. You'll have to excuse my mama, she just . . ."

And then the taut musculature of her smile went slack. Her lips writhed as she unleashed a primal howl.

"No need to make excuses." Uncle Mike pulled himself up from his chair and wiped a tear from his cheek. "Our mother just passed away."

"My God," said my mom, who now looked terrified. "I'm so sorry. I don't know what to say."

Mike smiled darkly. "I know. Sympathetic platitudes never cut it, do they?"

"I hope the girls weren't in your way," said Bonnie's mother.

"They're fine." Mike took hold of my shoulder and pushed me toward the door. "Wonderful girls."

"Yes," Mom piped. "Let's be going."

As we stumbled out into the sunny day, I felt a tug in my gut, a visceral longing for the magical dusk of Brunell's living room, which smelled of strawberry air freshener and the dark, turbulent vapors of the Holy Ghost. Just before the door closed on its own like a haunted house prop, I caught sight of Brunell, hunched and sniveling, falling into her uncle's manly embrace. Uncle Mike's hair, popped free of its ponytail, cascaded over his shoulders.

꙳

To take our minds off death, Bonnie's mother suggested a shopping trip to Columbia. As we drove out to Dixie

City Fashion Mall, our mothers kept glancing back at us, scoping our faces for signs of trauma. Bonnie and I exchanged looks but said nothing. We kept the rich darkness fermenting inside us, like wine to savor in illicit sips. We sprawled in the backseat, staring up at the cryptic convolutions of clouds, our eyes awash with mystic light. The clouds were thick, the color of smoke, as though the whole world were on fire. I could see hosts of dragons slithering in the froth, their damp, gray scales blending with the mist. I could see sparks of light like silver flashes of wings. I could see angelic multitudes, their faces crumpled in wrath, gearing up for the final battle. I could see a near-naked Jesus nailed to a cross, his long hair fluttering in the wind. Skinny and ripped like Tommy Lee, he wore nothing but a loincloth, and his eyes gazed right into my heart.

When a drop of rain hit my cheek, I imagined that it was a drop of blood. I stuck my tongue out to taste the holy wine. But then, with the press of a button, Bonnie's mother eased the LeBaron's top back up. She trapped us in the sterile air-conditioning, Neil Diamond whining on the radio. When the DJ decided to torment us with a double shot and "Sweet Caroline" came on, we couldn't take it anymore. Smirking knowingly at each other, Bonnie and I sang "Rapture." Trying to warble like Debbie Harry, we belted out her visionary lyrics, reveling in the thought of strange funky beings sweeping down from space to wreak havoc on planet Earth.

The men from Mars would startle disco dancers out of their comatose trances. They'd stomp around the crowded cities, terrifying twenty-four-hour shoppers and devouring cars. They'd fill our tired old world with blissful panic. Businessmen would cast off their suits like werewolves and flaunt their hairy bodies. Housewives would hop astride their brooms and fly laughing through the electric air. Schoolchildren would turn into ferocious wild animals and romp ecstatically in patches of forest behind their suburban homes.

But then, growing bored with human beings, the spacemen would fly back to their cold red planet. Things would return to normal: the men marching to work in their suits, the housewives furiously sweeping, the schoolchildren squirming in cold, metal desks.

The spacemen would leave us earthbound and restless, dissatisfied with everything, watching the sky for glints of ominous light.

LIMBs

On a gauzy day in early autumn, senior citizens stroll around the pear orchard on robot legs. Developed by the Japanese, manufactured by Boeing, one of the latest installments in the mechanization of geriatric care, Leg Intuitive Motion Bionics (LIMBs) have made it all the way to Gable, South Carolina, to this little patch of green behind Eden Village Nursing Home. And Elise Mood is getting the hang of them. Every time her brain sends a signal to her actual legs, the exoskeletal LIMBs respond, marching her along in the gold light. A beautiful day—even though Elise can smell chickens from the poultry complex down the road and exhaust from the interstate, even though the pear trees in this so-called orchard bear no fruit. The mums are in bloom. Bees glitter above the beds. And a skinny man comes toward her, showing off his mastery of the strap-on LIMBs.

"Elise." He squints at her. "You still got it. Prettiest girl at Eden Village."

She flashes her dentures but says nothing.

"You remember me. Ulysses Stukes, aka Pip. We went to the barbecue place that time."

Elise nods, but she doesn't remember. And she's relieved to see a tech nurse headed her way, the one with the platinum hair.

"Come on, Miss Elise," the nurse says. "You got Memories at three."

Elise points at the plastic Power Units strapped to her lower limbs.

"You're gonna walk it today," says the nurse. "I think you got it down."

Elise grins. Three people from the Dementia Ward were chosen for the test group, and so far, she's the only one with nerve signals strong enough to stimulate the sensors. As she strides along among flowers and bees, she rolls the name around on her tongue—Pip Stukes—recalling something familiar in the wry twist of his mouth.

※

For the past few months, nanobots have been rebuilding Elise's degenerated neural structures, refortifying the cell production of her microglia in an experimental medical procedure. Now she sits in the Memory Lane Neurotherapy Lounge, strapped into a magnetoencephalographic (MEG) scanner that looks like a 1950s beauty parlor hair-drying unit. As a young female therapist monitors a glowing map of Elise's brain, a male spits streams of nonsense at her.

"Corn bread," he says. "Corn-fed coon. Corny old colonel with corns on his feet."

Elise snorts. Who was that colonel she knew? Not a colonel, but a corporal. She once kissed him during a thunderstorm. But she was all of sixteen and he was fresh from Korea, drenched in mystique and skinny from starving in a bamboo cage. Elise vaguely recollects his inflation into a three-hundred-pounder who worked the register at Stukes Feed and Seed. Pip Stukes.

In a flash, she remembers the night they ate barbecue together, back when the world was still green, back when Hog Heaven hung paper lanterns over the picnic tables and Black River Road was dirt. After wiping his lips with a paper napkin, he said, *You ought to be my wife* in his half-joking way—and she dropped her fork.

"Look," says the female therapist. "We've got action between the inferior temporal and the frontal."

"Let's try another round," says the male, the one with the ponytail so little and scraggly that Elise wants to snip it off with a pair of scissors.

"One unit of BDNF," says the female. "And self-integration image therapy with random auditory sequencing and a jolt of EphB2."

The boy clamps Elise's head into a padded dome, and the room gets darker. She hears birdsong and distant traffic as a screen lights up to display a photo of a couple, the girl decked out in a wiggle dress and heels, the man slouching beside her in baggy tweed, his face obscured by a straw hat. At first Elise thinks they're walking on water, but then she realizes they're standing at the edge of a pier, a lake glinting all around them.

Something about the lake makes her gasp, and Elise wonders if the young woman in the photograph is her daughter, though she's pretty sure she never had a daughter—so maybe it's her mother's daughter, which means she and the girl are the same person.

"We've got action all over," says the female therapist, "mostly in the temporal and right parietal lobes."

"Emotional memory and spatial identity," says the male, tapping a rhythm on the desk with his fingertips.

Elise glares at him for breaking her stream of thought, then looks back up at the image, noting a streak of silver in the upper-right corner.

"Boat," she whispers.

And then she sees him clear as day: Pip Stukes at the wheel of the boat, his hair swept into a ducktail by the wind.

☙

In the pear orchard, Elise takes long strides, easy as thought, around the bed of mums. Scanning the lawn for Pip Stukes, she notes a cluster of wheelchair-bound patients idling at the edge of the flower bed, two women and a sleeping man, his shoulders slumped forward, his chin resting on his chest.

"Hey, good-lookin', what you got cookin'?" Pip Stukes struts toward her on cyborg legs. The skin around his eye sockets looks delicate, parchment shrunk down to the bone. While one of his eyes shines as blue as a tropical sea, the other is frosted with glaucoma. But Pip still flirts like a demon, sadness nestled under the happy talk.

Elise blushes, and Pip laughs, stands with his hip cocked.

"Pretty day for a walk." He holds out his arm and she takes it.

He leads her into a stand of planted pine. Interstate 95 drones, but Elise thinks she hears a river. Looking for a thread of blue, she gazes through the trees, but all she sees is the blurry outline of a brick building. A crow flutters down in a shaft of green light. And Pip turns to her with an aching look from long ago.

"Elise."

She studies him, mentally peeling back layers of wrinkled skin to glimpse the shining young man inside. She thinks he may have been *the one*, the dark shape in the bed beside her when she came up gasping from the depths of a bad dream.

She practices the phrase in her head first—*Are you my husband?*—but her lips twitch when she tries to say it.

"What?" says Pip.

And then a male tech nurse, alerted by their RFID alarms, rushes into the patch of woods to retrieve them.

❦

Elise sits by the lake on a towel in early spring, delighted to see that she's young again. As the sun sinks behind the tree line, she shivers, waiting for someone. She spots a wet glimmer of motion out past the end of the pier, a lithe young man doing tricks in the water. He crawls dripping from the lake, a merman with seal-black hair and familiar green eyes. As he inches toward her, his tail, a long fishy appendage glistening with aqua scales, swishes behind him in the sand.

Elise wakes, panting, in her semielectric bed. She reaches into the dark, claws at the aluminum railing. She's cold, her blanket wadded beneath her feet. And her roommate moans, a steady animal keening. The night nurse drifts in with pills in tiny cups. Though Elise can't see her, she knows her voice, low and soothing like a sheep's. The night nurse fixes her blanket, checks her diaper, gives her a drink of water, and then slips out of the room. Now her roommate's snoring. The air conditioner hums. And Elise lies awake, thinking about the beautiful swimmer from her dream.

Elise can smell the stuffiness of Eden Village Nursing Home only when she returns from being outside for a while. It's as if they've shellacked the floors with urine and Lysol. And in the cafeteria, some gravy is always boiling, spiked with the sweat and waste and blood of the dying, all the juices that leak from withering people—huge cauldrons of gravy that emit a meaty, medicinal steam.

Now that Elise can walk, now that she's thinking a little faster, she feels up to exploring. She wants to find the room where Pip Stukes lives, ask him point-blank if he's the man she married.

Someone's approaching down the endless hallway, a speck swelling bigger and bigger until it transforms into a nurse, a boy with a golden dab of beard.

"Looking for the Dogwood Library?" he says. "Elvis and the Chipmunks?" He points toward a small corridor, then shuffles off into nonexistence.

Peering down the passageway, Elise sees a parlor: wingback chairs, sofas, a crowd of patients in wheelchairs. She wills her strap-on LIMBs to move and, after a heartbeat pause, lurches down the hall. Over by a makeshift stage, the wheelchair-bound patients watch some middle-aged men set up equipment. A few people with LIMBs weave among the furnishings. Elise recognizes a tall woman with bald spots and a stubby old man with big ears. She creeps behind a potted palm to watch Elvis and the Chipmunks take the stage. Three large plush rodents sporting high pompadours, they jump into a brisk, twittering version of "Jailhouse Rock." Elise is about to leave in disgust when she spots a man slumped in a wheelchair, dozing, his face so familiar that the shock of it interrupts the signals pulsing from her brain to her legs and into the sensors of her Power Units. She collapses onto a brocade couch. Sits there wheezing in the blotchy light. Then she calms herself and looks the man over. She remembers the hawk nose, the big, creased forehead.

The Chipmunks croon "Love Me Tender" in their earsplitting rodent way, and Elise snorts. The man in the wheelchair had a great voice, could play guitar by ear. All those summer evenings they spent on the porch have been streamlined into archetypes and filed away in different sections of her cerebral cortex. And now the memories come trickling out. She remembers the sound of the porch fan and the smell of the lake and the feel of his hand on the back of her neck. She recalls swimming under stars and singing folk songs and drinking wine until their heads floated off their necks.

Elise steps around a coffee table heaped with *Reader's Digest*s. She studies the pink bulges of the man's closed eyes, the blanket draped over his legs, the big, fleshy head, humming with mysterious thoughts. The mouth is what strikes her hardest, the lips full, just a quirk feminine. When he opens his eyes and she sees the strange green, she knows it's him, the man who once kissed her in a birch canoe, moonlight twitching on the water.

"Who are you?" she says, the words pouring miraculously from her tongue.

He studies her, and she fears he's been drained dry, all of his memories siphoned by therapists into that electric box, where they bump around like trapped moths.

He makes a gurgling sound, small and goatish. His left eye is blighted with red veins. His hands rest on his knees, and she wonders if he can move them at all.

"Are you my husband?" she says.

The man's tongue pokes out and then retreats back into the cave of his mouth. He grunts. His left hand closes into a fist.

"I thought you were dead," she says.

"Bwa," he says, but then a nurse seizes his wheelchair, jerks him around, and trundles him off toward the corridor. Elise staggers in a panic and her LIMBs malfunction, leaving her crumpled on the carpet as the Chipmunks mock her with "Heartbreak Hotel."

She pulls herself up, squats, then stands, wills her legs to move fast, and they do, speeding her along like a power walker, but then a CNA with dyed black hair stops her. Scans her tag, beeps the Dementia Ward, and shuffles her back to the place she's supposed to be.

Hands folded in her lap, Elise slumps in the MEG scanner. Groggy from an antipsychotic called Vivaquel, she's having a hard time concentrating on what the therapists are saying.

"Barbecue bubba," says the boy. "Magnolia, moonshine, ma and pa."

"Very original," says the girl. "How about some limbic work? Aural olfactory?"

"Whatever," says the boy.

"Doo-wop and gardenias." The girl giggles. "Who the hell makes this shit up?"

Elise wishes they'd quit flirting and get on with it. She has half a mind to tell the boy that he'd be attractive with a decent haircut, but she doesn't. She sits with her arms crossed until the boy slips in her ear buds and clamps a plastic cup over her nose. In minutes Elise smells sickly sweet aerosol air freshener. She coughs, and they lower her olfactory levels. As the Everly Brothers croon "All I Have to Do Is Dream" in their wistful Appalachian twang, she can't help but sway to the music, breathing in a whiff of synthetic cherry, the exact scent of a Lysol spray that was marketed in the 1980s.

"She doesn't like it," says the boy.

"She's responding," says the girl. "Look at her amygdala. It's glowing."

Elise recalls a cramped hospital room that smelled of cherry Lysol, the green-eyed man hunched in a bed, looking at the wall. He dove into the lake one summer night and bashed his head against a rock. Now his legs wouldn't work right and he refused to look her in the eye. She held his balled fist in both hands and squeezed. The doctor said his motor neurons were damaged, compromising his leg muscles. The doctor went on and on about *partial recovery* and *physical therapy*, but the man didn't seem to be listening.

Elise remembers the smell of the man and the way he cleared his throat when he got nervous. She remembers how his silence filled the room every time he heard a motorboat fly by on the water. Stiffly, they'd wait for the sound to fade, and then pretend they hadn't heard it.

※

She wakes up with his name on her tongue: Robert Graham Mood, otherwise known as Bob. In the depths of her Vivaquel nap, she saw him, swimming in the lake's brown murk, down near the silty bottom. Enormous primordial catfish flickered through the hydrilla, and Bob fed them night crawlers with his hands. Right where his sick legs used to be, Bob was growing flippers, two stunted incipient fins sprouting from his knees.

This merman *was* her husband, Elise realized, and he was swimming away from her, toward the deepest part of the lake, where the Morrisons' pontoon had sunk during a severe thunderstorm. The whole family had drowned: mother, father, three sons. And scuba divers swore they'd seen ghosts slithering near the wreck, glowing like electric eels.

Elise rolls onto her side. Her room has a window, but an air-conditioning unit blocks the view. And now a tech nurse is here to attach her LIMBs to her scrawny legs. As he hooks up her sensors, he doesn't say one word, doesn't make eye contact: he might as well be tinkering with an old lawn mower.

※

Out in the pear orchard, Pip Stukes comes strutting, does a little turn around a park bench, and stoops to pluck a fistful of chrysanthemums, which he presents with a debonair smirk.

"Thank you," says Elise, shocked when the words pop out of her mouth.

"So you *can* talk!" says Pip. "I knew it. I could tell by the look in your eyes. I knew Elise Boykin was in there somewhere."

Elise Mood she wants to say, but keeps her lips zipped. Elise Boykin married Bob Mood, but Pip Stukes refused to honor her changed name.

"Have you seen the goldfish pond?" Pip extends his arm, and she takes it in spite of herself. Curls her fingers around his bicep and gives it a squeeze, surprised by the wobble of muscle encased in the sagging skin. They amble over to the pond, which is tucked behind a stand of canna lilies.

"Watch this," says Pip. He pulls a plastic bag from his pocket, shakes bread crumbs into his hand, and flings them into the water.

Elise concentrates on the oblong circle of liquid, eyeing it like an old queen gazing into a magic mirror. She sees a glimmer of orange, and then another, and another: six fish flitting up from the black depths. Lovely, greedy, they pucker their lips to suck up bits of bread.

Pip laughs and slips his arm around her, a gesture so familiar that she mechanically follows suit, twining her arm around his waist. She ought to pull away, but she doesn't.

She studies his profile and sees him as a younger man, after his grandfather died and left him the money, after the Feed and Seed shut down and he took up jogging. He'd run by her house at dawn, handsomeness emerging from his body in the form of cheekbones and muscle tone. Meanwhile, Bob slumped, staring at the TV—a man who used to hate the tube. Called it "the idiot box," "the shit pump," "opiate of the masses." But now he said nothing, just eyeballed the screen, silence filling the house like swamp gas.

She took up smoking again, would slip down to the dock and sit with her feet in the water. She's the one who checked the catfish traps. She's the one who picked the vegetables that summer and trucked them to the market. She still sold her chowchow and blueberry jam and eggs from the chickens whose house needed a new roof. She sold azalea seedlings to the Yankees who were buying up every last waterfront lot on the lake. After Bob's accident, they'd sold fifty acres of their land, the woods shrinking around them, big houses popping up in every bay.

One day in July she took a break to go swimming. Just before Bob's accident, she'd bought a French-cut one-piece that now seemed shameless—too young for forty-three—but she was alone in the cove. She dove into the water and swam out to the floating dock. Let the sun dry her hair, which had darkened to auburn over the years. And then Pip Stukes whisked by in his new motorboat, a dolphin-blue Savage Electra. He looked sharp in aviator sunglasses, slender and tan, a cigarette clenched in his teeth.

Elise eats every bit of her supper, fast, even the creamed corn. Remembering the ears of sweet corn Bob used to roast on the grill, she swallows the filthy goop. Smiles at the CNA when he sweeps up her tray. Sits waiting in bed, listening to her roommate smack up her gruel. Then she stands and teeters toward her LIMBs, which rest against a La-Z-Boy. Panting, she sits in the chair and grapples for one of the units, grabs it by the upper thigh and drags it to her, shocked by how light it is. She's been watching the tech nurse, knows exactly how to strap the contraptions onto her legs, fastens the Velcro and then a hundred little metal snaps. She stands up. Takes a test run around the room. Pokes her head out into the hall, looks both ways, and then lurches into the white light.

Since most of the Dementia Ward nurses are in the dining room with patients, Elise has a clear shot down the hall. She makes it all the way to the main desk without incident, then stops, baffled, trying to remember which passage she took the time she came upon Robert Graham Mood. She recalls a different kind of fluorescent light, bluer than usual, a lower ceiling. *That's the one*, she thinks, the one with the green wall. Elise ambles down the hall, finds the library. Over by the front desk, a solitary CNA reads a magazine.

Elise recognizes the corridor down which that bitch of a nurse took her husband, a man she thought was dead. She ambles down the hallway, peeks into dim rooms, sees lumps curled on beds, aged figures zoned out before televisions. When a wheelchair emerges from one of the doorways, her heart catches, but it's not Robert Graham Mood. She keeps walking as though she knows where she's going, nods whenever she passes a nurse. The hallway narrows. At the end of the hall, she spots a nurses' station around the corner, the CNA at the desk bent over a gadget.

Elise squats, scampers like a crab around the desk, almost laughing at the ease of it, and enters the little hall where the severely disabled are stashed away. She sniffs, the burn of disinfectant stronger here. And then she peers into each room until she finds him, three doors down on the left, her husband, Bob, drooping in his wheelchair before a muted TV.

She remembers that summer—when the stubble on his face grew into a dirty beard and his sideburns fanned into wild whiskers. Jimmy Carter was floundering, the oil running out, those hostages still rotting in Iran. And Bob, TV-obsessed, sat wordless as a bear. Soviets in Afghanistan and J. R. Ewing shot and Bob's legs as weak as they were the day before. She couldn't keep up with the okra picking. Blight had taken the tomatoes. One of their hens had an abscess that needed to be lanced. It wasn't Bob's sick legs that had pushed her over the edge, but his refusal to talk about the details of their shared life.

Elise steps between Bob and the TV, just like she did that day in July when she'd had enough of his silence.

His eyes stray from the screen—still the strange green, steeped in obscure feelings.

"Robert Graham Mood," she says. And he blinks.

"Elise." His voice rattles like a rusty cotton gin, but to her the word sounds exquisitely feminine, the name of some flower that blooms for just half a day, almost too small to see but insanely perfumed in the noon heat.

"How long have you been here?" she asks.

He looks her up and down.

"You're my husband?" she says.

"Yes," Bob rasps. The air conditioner drones and they stare at each other.

Elise is about to touch his arm when a CNA rushes in, smiles, speaks softly, as to a cornered kitten, and takes her firmly by the arm.

When Elise wakes up from her Vivaquel nap, a boy looms over her—Robert Graham Mood, a sleek young stunner with red hair. She frowns, for Bob's hair had been black, his lips plump and just a tad crooked. She thinks she may be dead at last, Bob's golden spirit hovering to welcome her to the next phase.

"Mom," says the boy.

When her eyes adjust, she notes lines around his eyes, the bulge of a budding gut. Not the father but the son.

"Just give her a few minutes," says the nurse. "According to the neurotherapists, she's made enormous strides. Her roaming incident shows some planning, thinking ahead, which indicates enhanced semantic memory."

"And you think she knows he's my father?"

"She knows he's somebody. Found him halfway across the complex. I had no idea they'd even been married."

"They still are, technically, you know."

Elise snorts at this, but nobody pays one bit of attention.

"Of course. Very odd, though it happens from time to time. Married people in different wings. We don't do couples at Eden Village."

"It really didn't matter until now," says the boy, sinking into the chair by the bed. "I didn't think the therapies would lead to anything, with her so far gone. But still, I figured *why not?*"

Elise claws at her throat, her tongue as dead as a slab of pickled beef. She knows the boy is her son, but she can't remember when he was born or how he got to be grown so fast.

"Mom," says the boy, that familiar tinge of whininess in his voice, and it comes to her: her son home from college for a few days, pacing from window to window, restless as a cooped rooster. He said the house felt smaller than he remembered. Stayed out on the boat all day with the spoiled-rotten Morrison boys. Acted skittish when he came in from the water, pained eyes hiding behind the soft flounce of his bangs. He'd gone vegetarian, looked as skinny as Gandhi, and she fed him fried okra and butterbeans.

As the two of them sat at the kitchen table making conversation, Bob's silence leaked from the boy's old bedroom like nuclear radiation from a triple-sealed vault—the kind of poison you can't smell but that sinks into your cells, making you mutant from the inside out.

"Bye, Mom." The boy pats her crimped hand. "I'll be back soon." And they leave her in the semidarkness, window shades down, unable to tell if it's night or day.

※

The therapists have strapped her into the MEG scanner and popped in a retro-TV sense-enhanced module. While they play footsy under the desk, Elise turns her attention to a montage of *The Incredible Hulk* episodes, breathing in smells of Hamburger Helper and Bounce fabric-softening sheets. She never cooked Hamburger Helper; she never wasted money on fabric softeners. She never sat through a complete episode of *The Hulk*, but the seething mute giant reminds her of Bob, who watched it religiously after his accident. She remembers peering into his room, standing there in the hallway for just one minute to watch the green monster rage. Then she'd close the door, drift out into the night with her pack of cigarettes.

Now the screen goes dim and Elise hears crickets, smells cigarette smoke and a hint of gas. Pip's boat had a leak that summer, and everything they did was enveloped in the haze of gasoline. What did they do? Zigzagged over the lake. Dropped the anchor and sat rocking in the waves, drinking wine coolers and watching for herons. Then they'd drift up to this island he knew. The first time Pip took her to his secret island—the one with the feral goats and rotting shed—she drank until her head thrummed. Bob had not said one word for sixty-two days. Each night before bed she'd stick her head into the toxic glow of his room to say good night, and he'd grunt. She kept track of the days. Ticked them off with a pencil on a yellow legal pad.

He sat there glued to the TV, waiting for news on the hostages, wondering if Afghanistan had turned Communist yet, trying to figure out who shot J. R. She even caught him watching soaps in the middle of the day—*like sands through the hourglass, so are the days of our lives*—foolishness he used to laugh at. Now he sat grimly as Marlena mourned the death of her premature son and her marriage to a two-timing lawyer fell apart. The dismal music, the tedious melodrama, and the flimsy opulent interiors sank Elise into a malaise. And she'd leave Bob in the eternal twilight of the TV.

Out in the humming afternoon heat, Elise had started talking to herself. *Goddamn grass,* she'd hiss. *Bastard ants.* One day, in the itchy okra patch, where unpicked pods had swollen into eight-inch monsters, where fire ants marched up and down the sticky stalks, crawling onto her hands and stinging her in the tender places between her fingers, Elise ripped off her sun hat and shrieked. Then she stormed inside and changed into her swimsuit. Without looking in on Bob, she grabbed her smokes and jogged out to the cove, walked waist-deep into the water while taking fierce drags. *Fuck,* she hissed—a trashy cuss she never indulged in. And then she felt drained of wrath.

She tossed her cigarette butt and swam out to the floating dock, where the water was cooler. Pip Stukes came knifing through the waves, skinny again, his sunglasses two mirrors that hid his sad eyes, and Elise crawled up into his glittery boat. She swigged wine coolers like they were Cokes and laughed a high, dry laugh that was half cough. She lost track of herself: let another man kiss her on an island where shadowy goats watched from the woods. She stayed out past dusk and got a sunburn, a bright red affliction that she didn't feel until the next day.

When she came in that night, Bob didn't ask where she'd been. Didn't say one word. Just kept clearing his throat over and over, as though he had something stuck in it—a bit of gristle in his windpipe, a dry spot on his glottis, acid gushing up from his bad stomach. He cleared his throat when she served him supper (one hour later than usual). Cleared his throat when she changed his sheets and punched his pillow with her small fist. Cleared his throat when she quietly shut his door, and kept on clearing his throat as she brushed her teeth and crawled into the bed they'd shared for twenty years.

Elise's skin blistered and peeled. For several nights she lay in bed rolling it into little balls that she'd flick into the darkness. And then, one week later, her skin tender, the pale pink of a seashell's interior, she went off with Pip Stukes again.

※

"I figured out how they catch us," whispers Pip.

Elise widens her eyes. As they take a turn around the birdbath, she scans the crowd for wheelchairs. They sit down on a concrete bench.

"Feel that bump on your arm?" Pip slides the tip of his index finger over her forearm, stops when he reaches that hard little pimple that won't go away. Maybe it's a wart. Maybe it's a mole. Elise doesn't know what it is, but she blushes when he touches the spot.

"Microchip," he says. "My son put one in his dog's ear. A good idea. Except we're not dogs."

Pip laughs, the old, dark laugh that lingers in the air. Elise can't remember Pip's children. And what about his wife? He must have had one. But now she's unsettled by his eyes, the clear one at least, which drills her with a secret force while the other stares at nothing.

Something about his laugh and fading smile, something about the slant of light and the wash of distant traffic remind her—of what, she's not sure, not until the blush spreads from her hairline to her chest, not until she sees Pip walking naked from the lake, sees the scar on his chest, the sad apron of belly skin, relic of his previous life as a fat man. And then she remembers. He did have a wife, a girl named Emmy from Silver. They'd had two boys and divorced. Emmy had kept the house in Manning, and Pip moved out to the lake house, free to whip around on the empty water.

For two months they boated out to the little island almost every afternoon. Got sucked into the oblivion of the dog days: shrieking cicadas and heat like a blanket of wet velvet that made you feel half-asleep. It was easy to sip wine coolers until you couldn't think. Easy to swim naked in water warm as spit. In September they finally went to his lake house, a fancy place with lots of gleaming brass, the TV built into a clever cabinet, a stash of top-notch liquor behind the wet bar. Showing her around, Pip pointed out every last effect, all bought with his grandfather's money. Something bothered her: the way he slapped her rear like a rake on *Dallas*, the way he smoked afterward in the air-conditioned bedroom. Hiding his saggy gut under the sheet, he kept checking himself out in the mirror. He ran his fingers through his gelled hair.

As Pip went on about the Corvette he wanted to buy, she thought about Bob, how, in the past, he was always quietly tinkering with something. And then poor Pip started up on Korea, told her about coming back home after starving in that bamboo cage, eating for a solid year in a trance, waking up one day to the shock of three hundred pounds. He'd lost the weight and gotten married. But then he gained it back, got divorced, lost it again—his whole life staked to that tedious fluctuation.

That night when she got home, Bob turned from the television and spoke to her.

"Look at this joker," he said, pointing at Ronald Reagan, the movie star who was running for president, the one who looked like a handsome lizard.

The next day Bob bathed himself and rolled out onto the screened porch. Watching the lake, they shelled field peas all morning. She knew that Pip would come flying out of the blue in his boat, and when he did, Bob cleared his throat and said nothing.

Pip's boat appeared every afternoon for the next week. They'd hold their breath and wait for the high whine of his motor to fade.

Bob started doing his leg exercises, made an appointment with the hotshot therapist in Columbia. In two years he could get around the house with a walker. By Reagan's second term he was ambling with a cane. He took care of the chickens, started dabbling with quail. And every year they sold more land, acre by acre, until all they had was their cottage—mansions towering on every side, the lake a circus of Jet Skis, houseboats so big they blotted out the sun.

Bob and Elise got old on the lake, their son breezing in twice a year to say hello. And they planned to die there, right on the water, even though the place was turning to shit.

❦

Elise fingers the scab on her arm. It's been a week since she gouged the microchip out with the sharp scissors she nabbed from the Dementia Ward desk. All this time she's kept the fleck of metal in her locket and nobody's said one word. The nurses know better than to touch her locket, a thirtieth-anniversary gift from Bob—not a heart, like you'd expect, just a circle of gold that opens via a hinge, a clip of Bob's gray hair stuffed inside as a sweet joke. *To thirty more years of glorious monotony,* Bob said, and they laughed, opened another jar of mulberry wine.

A tech nurse escorts Elise out to the pear orchard. Just as soon as she's released into the flock of seniors, Pip Stukes comes swaggering across the grass.

"Hey, good-lookin', what you got cookin'?"

Elise takes his arm as usual and they promenade across stepping-stones, over to their favorite bench. Pip talks about his son, who dropped by this morning with Pip's grandbaby, now a grown girl. He talks about the artificial bacon he had for breakfast and the blue jay that perched on his windowsill. Then he goes quiet and just stares at her, filling the space between them with sighs. It's warm for November. The mums have dried up and the pear trees drop their last red leaves. When Pip leans in to kiss her, Elise embraces him, keeping her lips off limits while hugging him close enough to slip the microchip into his shirt pocket.

She sits back and smiles. It feels good to be invisible.

"You remember that island?" says Pip.

Elise nods, touches his cheek, stands up on her robot legs, and then walks off into the canna lilies. Behind the dead flowers are two big dumpsters and, if she's calculated correctly, a door leading into the Dogwood Library.

※

When Bob wakes up, she's standing there in a shaft of late-morning light, a small-boned woman wearing strap-on plastic Power Units like something from the Sci-Fi Channel, her gray hair cropped into an elfin cap.

"Elise," he rasps.

"Bob," she says.

His thick lids slide down over watery eyes.

"Bob?" she says. He shifts in his chair but won't wake up.

She checks his pulse, grabs his blanket from the bed, and tucks it around him. Makes sure he's got on proper socks under his corduroy slippers. And then she rolls him toward the door.

Though Elise has spent many an afternoon wrinkling her nose at the smell of chickens, she isn't prepared for the endless stream of barracks southwest on Highway 301: three giant buildings as long as trains and leaking a stench so shocking she can't believe it doesn't jolt Bob from his nap. Mouth-breathing, she hustles to get past the nastiness, fingering the button that operates his chair, kicking it into high gear, the one the nurses use when they're in a tizzy.

She's been walking for an hour, on a strip of highway shoulder that comes and goes, smooth sailing for a mile and then she'll hit a patch of bumpy asphalt and veer onto the road. A number of motorists have passed—mostly big trucks, pickups, the occasional SUV—and she worries that some upstanding citizen has already called Eden Village. She expects a cop car to roll up any minute. Expects to see the officer put on his gentle smile, the one he uses with feeble-minded people and lunatics, geezers and little children. She would prefer a back road, some decent air and greenery, but she knows she wouldn't remember the way.

If she recalls correctly, 301 is almost a straight shot to the water. Though her legs don't hurt, her shoulders do, an ache that dips into her bones. Her fingers cramp as they grip the handles of Bob's chair. And she's too thirsty to spit. She imagines sweating glasses of sweet tea, cold Coca-Cola in little bottles, lemonade with hunks of fruit floating in the pitcher. She remembers the time she took Bob to meet her grandmother. They drank from a pump on the old wraparound porch, drawing cool springwater up from the earth. She recalls sipping from the garden hose and tasting rubber. Remembers the special flavor of Bob's musty canteen, the one they always took camping. She and Bob once hiked up Looking Glass Rock, crouched under a waterfall with their mouths open, taking giant gulps, the whole mountain wet with dew. Hosts of tiny frogs clung to the stone, suckers on their toes.

When they get to the lake Elise will roll Bob to the end of their old pier. It'll be dusk by then, she thinks, catfish crowding in the shallows. She wants him to see water on every side when he wakes up, vast and black, with the sky in pink turmoil, as though it's just the two of them, out there floating in a little boat.

Feral

That autumn a pack of feral dogs swept into our school yard, barking and keening and charging the air with an electrifying stench—wild festering creatures, some bald with mange, others buried in clumps of matted frizz, or hobbling on three legs, or squinting through worm-eaten eyes. Rip Driggers was on the porch of my portable, cooling off after a laughing fit, and he came scrambling through the door, waving his fists and spitting, "Dogs, dogs, dogs, hundreds of 'em—craziest mutts you ever saw." We were into the sluggish haze of afternoon, picking at a Dickinson poem, the room smelling of sour socks. My dozing seventh-graders dashed from their seats to the windows. The dogs were their salvation, mongrel hordes pouring in from strange, magic parts of the earth.

The animals skittered around the playground, yapping at each other, squirting piss onto swing sets, sniffing each other's piss, pissing on each other's piss, snorting at each other's anuses, and snarling. They threw themselves into tangles of squealing and flew apart again.

The principal emerged from the cafeteria, peered at the dogs, and then hurried back inside. A minute later his nasal drone issued from the PA system: "A collection of stray canines has entered our playground area. Teachers and students must not leave the main building or their portable classrooms. Please check to make sure all doors are closed and locked."

I stood at a window watching the wild beasts prance in the sun.

In less than fifteen minutes a fleet of SUVs glittered in the school's front drive. Mothers sat idling, but no one could leave the school yet, even though the dogs had moved down to the soccer field, even though the ASPCA, the Humane Society, the police and fire departments had all been called, even though the soul-stirring, apocalyptic wails of multiple sirens announced that authority figures were speeding nigh.

❦

Suddenly I'd found myself past thirty, shacked up with a fussy bald man nine years my senior who enjoyed monitoring every facet of our household—finances, thermostat, hot-water heater, water and electricity usage, lawn maintenance, and pest control. His brain had become a grid of interlocking systems. His eyes were shrinking into beads as the years went by—he who had once been a luminescent lover, a beautiful, pale trembler with long, flowing hair. I didn't know how this had happened. But now he sat by our sliding glass door, clutching his Beeman air rifle, some of his old pluck surging back as he scanned the yard for curs.

"The bastards," as he called them, had chewed our plastic garbage cans to shreds, had consumed every edible morsel in our trash, had strewn the remaining filth far and wide. The hunger-crazed beasts came in the night and gobbled up anything vaguely organic—sprouting potatoes, blood-smeared butcher paper, old leather slippers—and then they puked; they ate their own warm puke; they ran in crazy circles, pausing to deposit steaming mounds of crap onto our green lawn—usually a masterpiece of emptiness now polka-dotted with yellow nitrogen stains.

The previous week the dogs had sprayed our garage with their spicy pee and sent my husband into a tizzy. He removed every object, pressure-washed the area with bleach water, and then slathered key spots with Get Serious! pet odor and pheromone extractor. At night he slid his recliner close to the sliding glass door to keep his vigils. While consuming exactly three Budweisers, he'd brood in the dark with his gun, waiting for that moment when the brutes would come whirling into his floodlit territory, rearranging the molecules of air with their yipping and fried-egg stink. BB pellets did not kill the dogs, who did not seem to remember from one night to the next that they'd been shot, but the yelp of a struck dog made my husband smile. And he, a passionate advocate for gun control, kept threatening to buy himself a serious firearm.

I watched TV alone. Each night the news spouted facts about dog packs. Feral dogs, fast becoming a worldwide menace, dwelled in condemned buildings, junk-car lots, sewers, and abandoned strip malls. They invaded human territory to scavenge and hunt. They killed in teams, herding livestock, cats, and rodents into corners, where they tore them into bite-sized chunks. The American pet craze had led to an epidemic of abandoned dogs. A rash of dog-fighting rings had flared in rural ghettos. And the repressed wolfish instincts of domestic dogs had been coaxed out, had transmogrified into weird new breeds.

The fighting champions of packs naturally ruled over the ex-pets, also over the bait dogs—smaller, wimpier dogs once bred to rile the fighters. You could recognize a bait dog by its shabby condition, its downtrodden vibe and crippled state: etched with scars, half-blind, riddled with abscesses and often lacking a limb, it slunk and whined around the glorious, snapping fighters—sinewy beasts with bear claws and yellow shark teeth. Some of the more splendid alphas had long incisors like baboons'. Others had needle claws that retracted into their toe pads like those of cats. Legions of freakish specialists had stepped out of the woodwork to describe these evolutionary quirks of reverted dog species, and they, along with innumerable dog-bite victims, bewildered farmers, and owners of dis-membered cats, were always being interviewed on TV.

My favorite dog specialist was an evolutionary ecolo-gist who'd written his dissertation on the mating habits of wild primates that had forgone foraging to scavenge human food. He'd made his mark with a documentary on a troop of hamadryas baboons who spent their days picking through the rubble of a Saudi garbage dump. And now, back in the States, Dr. Vilkas had become in-terested in what he called "de-domestication." He wore army fatigues. He shot his own footage with a digital Minicam. Half artist, half scientist, he looked a little wild himself, peering through unkempt black hair with an unnerving set of mismatched eyes—one blue, one green. Though an American citizen, Dr. Vilkas had a trace of an accent, trilling and growling, and the way he pronounced his z's made me blush.

He sported bite-proof arm and leg bands and drenched himself with special pheromones to keep his beloved dogs from attacking him. He skulked among them, filmed them eating and coupling and suckling their scraggly young, filmed them squealing in the throes of birth and barking with joy as they sabotaged a dumpster or disemboweled a rat.

Dr. Vilkas followed dog packs as they migrated among urban dead-zones, blighted farm belts, and dying towns. Our own town fit the usual profile: failing schools, rinky-dink chicken farms, and closing plants, an obese and debt-strapped populace who fed on processed food, their offspring suffering new configurations of hyperactivity disorders and social dysfunction, children who gobbled generic methylphenidates and performed miserably on standardized tests.

Dr. Vilkas gave no instructions on how to deal with the dog epidemic. He eluded authorities who solicited advice on how to hunt down and exterminate the dogs. Though he seemed to know something about the dogs' roaming and sleeping patterns, he remained tight-lipped on these subjects while talking about the social habits of the dogs: their complex hierarchies, mating strategies, and choreographed hunting tactics; their territorial urination, sensitivity to pheromones, body language, and variations of barking.

Howl, growl, yowl, snarl, yap, yip, woof. Each vocalization meant something, and domestic canine pets could pick up some of these messages. When a reporter asked Dr. Vilkas how frequently pets were tempted away from domestication into wildness, the specialist warned dog owners to keep their animals secured. And though he encouraged them to invest in sturdier leashes and to read books on canine psychology so as to recognize signs of restlessness, he couldn't disguise his excitement over the thought of tame animals lured from their lives of monotonous sycophancy by the siren calls of ferals. His strange eyes shone. He gazed longingly at the horizon, where a chemical plant huffed filth into the sky.

🌿

Outside, the autumn afternoon swelled golden, and the children squirmed in their desks. They looked grubby, their clothes rumpled, their hair greasy. I assumed their parents were distracted by the dog epidemic—everyone was. Because the students gabbled of nothing else, most teachers had given in to their obsession. We designed dog-themed lesson plans. The principal arranged for specialists to speak in the auditorium. Some even made classroom visits. Earlier that day, in my world history class, we'd watched a film on the history of canine domestication, learning that around a hundred thousand years ago, the first dogs had split from wolf species, emerging from forests to lurk near human territories—not put off by Homo sapiens' decadent stink, eventually creeping up to human fires, dazzled by smells of roasting meat. In a time-lapse sequence, a wolf morphed into a German shepherd, which morphed into a collie, which morphed into a teacup Chihuahua, sending the children into howls of laughter.

But now in English class a warm miasma of boredom settled on my students. Eyelids fluttered. Heads drooped. The restless among them jogged their knees, tapped their pencils, and glanced toward windows. Tammy Harley, swatting the air in front of her frown, said that Bobby Banes had cut one. A sly smile smoldered on Bobby's freckled face—poor little Bobby, whose father hosed down the gut room at the poultry plant with scalding bleach water. And then three football players blasted long farts, timing their stunt with hand signals. Children covered their noses. They gasped and pretended to faint. Several cheerleaders scrambled from their seats to the air-conditioning vent, stood panting over it, screaming "Pigs!" and rolling their mascara-crusted eyes.

My heart beat faster. I shivered. I felt a tingling sensation in my spine. Suddenly, I could detect the salty, rank smell of dogs and I wondered if some of the animals had been sleeping under my portable classroom. Seconds later, Tonya Gooding spotted a dog pack leaping from the trash-strewn copse that separated our school yard from a Burger King parking lot, splitting the day wide open with its barking and feral verve.

"Damn!" she cried. "Looks like they flying."

Though I motioned for the kids to keep their rears glued to their seats, all but Jebediah Jinks, a preteen preacher with eleven siblings, flew to the windows. I took my usual station at the door, sniffing what was now almost palpable in the air.

"Does anybody smell that?" I asked my students.

"Smell what?" said Tonya Gooding.

"'As dead flies give perfume a bad smell, so a little folly outweighs wisdom and honor,'" Jebediah preached from his desk. "A sign of the end times. A plague like frogs or locusts, except only with dogs, or like them swine Jesus put the demons in. We got war, we got AIDS and hurricanes, we got terrorists and obesity and homosexuality and dogs. You think God's trying to tell us something?"

The other kids just tittered.

And the dogs came romping and snarling, tussling and woofing: mongrels big as panthers and little as squirrels, balding curs with skin like burnt cheese, mutts with lions' manes, canines with dreadlocks matted over their eyes. Short dogs waddled on stumpy legs. Tall dogs loped like spooked gazelles. And the big, rangy fighters led the pack, nipping their inferiors.

"'The dogs shall eat Jezebel,'" croaked Jebediah, ogling Tammy Harley's leopard-print miniskirt. "'He that dies of Ahab in the city the dogs shall eat; and he that dies in the field, the birds of the sky will devour.'"

Then I saw Dr. Vilkas sprinting from the woodlet after the pack, camera hoisted, lank hair streaming. My heart lurched. My ears burned. I stepped out onto the porch and locked the children inside. I could barely hear their muffled screams, so loud was the clamor of dogs. The air smelled of Fritos and urine. And hot winds blew, as though the mongrels had brought their own weather. I gripped the railing and watched Dr. Vilkas creep up on a skirmish between two alphas.

In the middle of the playground, two gape-mouthed fighters were hurling themselves at each other—a liver-colored pit bull against a spotted mastiff. I could hear the clack of their teeth. The dogs growled, retreated, and flew together again, lifting a cloud of orange dust. Dr. Vilkas stood two yards from them, squinting into his camera. When the dust cloud dispersed, the triumphant pit bull was dancing around the fallen mastiff. But then the creature stopped cold, sniffed the wind, and looked right at me. As though fired from a cannon, it flew toward my portable, leapt over a stunted juniper, and landed in the sad little place right below my porch where my children had spit a thousand loogies.

The dog snarled at me. When it opened its rank maw, I gasped at the sight of its jumbled teeth. Its slimy bug eyes watched me. Breath flowed from the beast in thick wheezes. The animal growled. I fingered the keys in my pocket, backing toward the door. The children, watching this spectacle from within, yelled and pounded on the windows. And Dr. Vilkas scrambled toward me, holding some object in both hands, his camera, I thought, figuring he'd film my disembowelment.

I dropped my keys, heard them clatter against the wooden porch and bounce onto the ground. The pit bull's neck hackles shot up. Its gums quivered. The creature sprang three feet into the air, then fell on its side, flopped around in the dust, and rolled into a motionless heap.

"You okay?" Dr. Vilkas stood beside the dog.

"Did you kill it?"

"Stunned it with a portable electrode dart." Dr. Vilkas waved his newfangled aluminum gun. "The animal will revive in five to ten minutes."

"I'm glad you didn't kill it."

"Really?" He smiled. "You know it's illegal to shoot them with real guns."

"I know. Actually, my . . . I mean, someone I know bought a tranquilizer gun."

Dr. Vilkas fixed me with his mismatched eyes. His gaunt cheeks were scruffed with faint stubble. He had a beautiful mouth, wide and full. He stooped to pluck my keys from the ground.

Sirens took the air again and the dogs started howling. The pack scrambled east, as though fleeing the sun. The fallen pit bull let out a little croak and twitched its hind legs.

"Better get inside your classroom," said Dr. Vilkas, "before this beast revives."

I slipped back into my portable, where the children had turned off the lights to see better.

They cheered for me. Girls pressed in to hug me, wet-eyed, smelling of french fries and imitation designer perfumes.

❦

I found my husband on the back stoop, hunched over his new tranquilizer gun, three beer cans methodically crushed and stacked at his feet, ready to be boxed and hauled to the scrap-metal recycling center.

"You're almost an hour late," he said.

"Emergency meeting," I said. "The dogs came back to school today."

For some reason, this made my husband frown.

"You left three lights on. The kitchen faucet was dripping. You forgot to padlock the garbage cans."

"We had a meeting before school and one after—about the new safety procedures. And then the dogs came, so the meeting was delayed."

"I needed you here. I wanted to run through the drill."

"Drill?"

"With the cages. Remember? We've got to get the fallen dogs into cages within twenty minutes. That's how long the tranquilizer darts last, on average, and for some of the larger species, who knows what our window of op will be."

"Why don't we run through it now?"

"Because it's dusk. The dogs always show up at dusk, or else after midnight. Haven't you noticed that?"

My husband was sporting hunting chaps. He wore his new HexArmor bite-proof gloves, purchased on the Web from a veterinarian supply emporium. He'd bought a pair of dog-kicking boots, with treads for running and steel toes, and I'd seen him practicing, kicking logs, smashing the snouts of invisible monsters. But now he slumped on the bottom step—all dressed up for our drill, and I'd stood him up.

I patted his scalp. I sniffed the air for whiffs of wild dog. My husband, perpetually congested from allergies, could never smell the animals coming, could never sense the bustle in the air, the electromagnetic hullabaloo that made my spine buzz and brought a pleasant fizzle of panic to my heart, even before the animals tumbled into my field of vision like a promise kept.

"The dogs won't come tonight," I said.

"How do you know that?"

"Feminine intuition."

"Whatever."

"I think I may have a more developed vomeronasal organ than you do."

(I smiled as I said this, but I half believed it.)

"What the fuck is that?"

"Pheromone detector, a throwback organ maybe, deep in the nose."

Some people had sensitive ones, moist and throbbing and bristling with neurons, while other people's were all dried up, almost nonexistent.

I opened the sliding glass door.

"It's like half the population has lost its sense of smell," I said.

"The air conditioner's on, you know."

"But it's getting cool. Why don't we open some windows?"

"How many times do I have to explain? We live on low land. Moisture breeds mold and mildew. This house was not designed for the open air. In this humidity, without air-conditioning, it would rot away in no time. Do you know what that would do to our property value?"

"It would plummet?"

For some reason, this made me laugh. I knew all about humidity and its effects on our house—this was one of those conversations we had over and over for ritualistic, perhaps even religious, purposes. My husband kept a humidity meter posted above the kitchen bar, and sometimes, when he felt especially restless, he'd roam the house at night with his integrated, probe-style thermo-hygrometer, sticking its supersensitive bulb under chairs and beds, sliding it into drawers and cabinets, sometimes crawling into our shower to monitor subtle changes in the closed-off air. Snorting to himself, he'd jot data in his notepad. I'd even seen him thrust the bulb into his own nostrils and ears, smiling slyly, the way he used to when our love was a living creature, breathing in the room with us.

I closed the sliding glass door. I went to check my e-mail.

There was a message from our principal with an attachment that contained a list of experts willing to make classroom visits. I scrolled to the bottom of the page, where I discovered the e-mail address of Dr. Ivan Vilkas, evolutionary ecologist and forerunner in the burgeoning field of de-domestication.

Dr. Vilkas was scheduled to visit my world history class. My students fidgeted and fussed. Whispery agitation erupted in problem areas. Gobs of slobbered paper flew from certain mouths, smacked against the napes and cheeks of certain targets. It was a hot muggy day, our air-conditioning system on the blink. And the children's sweat smelled peculiar, as though spiked with new combinations of minerals. Their lips looked redder than usual. Most of the kids needed haircuts. And Jebediah Jinks would not stop mumbling biblical gibberish—he might've been speaking in tongues for all I knew. Girls snorted and giggled. And an ugly plot seemed to be brewing among the football players—they whistled ostentatiously, cracked their beefy knuckles, and smiled.

We were discussing an archaeological excavation in Iran, where a tomb containing both human and canine remains had been discovered, the dog skeleton curled in a jar, the man buried with daggers and arrowheads.

"This means that he was an important man," I said. "And that the dog was probably a pet."

"Or he might have eaten it," said Rip Driggers. "My daddy says Chinks eat dog. Maybe they eat mutts in Iran too."

"But why would they put a dog skeleton in a jar?" asked Tammy Harley.

"Maybe it was a cooking pot." Rip snorted.

"Gross," said Tonya Gooding. "You're one sick puppy."

"And you're a biatch," snapped Rip. "Ruff-ruff."

"Watch the language," I said. I could no longer send Rip outside to calm himself. The principal's office was swamped these days, delinquents clogging the hallway outside his lair. All I could do was move troublemakers to unpleasant areas of the room, make them clean the dry-erase board, deny them time on our virus-wracked Dells.

Just as it began to rain, Dr. Vilkas arrived, his knock quick against my hollow aluminum door. I found him grinning on my little porch, spattered with drops, clutching his laptop and a tangle of cables.

"PowerPoint presentation," he said, tapping his computer.

"It's that guy," said Rufus Teed.

"I saw you on television!" said Tonya Gooding.

We had thirty-five minutes left until the class ended and my planning period began, so we hustled to get his laptop hooked up to my digital projector. As we searched for the right cable, rain beat against the flat, tar roof of my ancient portable. The children murmured and sniggered and pinched each other. Cryptic underground smells oozed up from the vents. Dr. Vilkas asked me to cut the lights, and I stood in the humming darkness with my arms crossed over my breasts.

"Well, now," he said, flashing his first slide (a diagram of the canine nasal system). "We don't have much time, so I'm going to jump right in."

Dr. Vilkas rubbed his palms together and smiled at the students, his chin receding.

"While the human nose contains about five million scent receptors," he began, "the average dog snout boasts over two hundred million."

After pausing to let the drama of his opener sink in, he launched an incomprehensible lecture, describing the receptor neurons and olfactory epithelium of the vomeronasal organ, its dark, squishy, fluid-filled sacs, its mucus-slaked cellular microvilli, which absorbed innumerable odor molecules. As he descended deeper into thickets of technical jargon, his sentences became endless, his accent heavier.

The children could not take their eyes off the odd man. One by one their mouths popped open. They sat stock-still in their cramped desks. By the time the bell rang, Dr. Vilkas had not progressed past his first slide. Rather than darting from their chairs, the students filed out slowly, glancing back at the evolutionary ecologist before slumping out into the drizzle.

We stood alone in the dark room.

"I had a film I wanted to show them," Dr. Vilkas said.

"That's too bad," I said. "I would have loved to see it."

"Well, you could. I mean, we could watch it right now. If you're free."

The classroom smelled pungent, with a trace of something coppery that I could almost taste. Who knew what chaos of desperate, pheromonal signals my poor caged students pumped out, day after day, in our dank little portable as the beauties of the world glimmered beyond their reach in the mythical places they watched on screens. We sat in their tiny desks toward the back of the room, in the territory of the football players, where a turbulent energy still seemed to hover.

The film, a montage of hundreds of individual canines caught in the act of sniffing, had no sound. We watched one silent dog after another thrust its snout toward this or that reeking object: a pile of dung, a dead cat, a battered Nike tennis shoe. We watched dogs take long, contemplative whiffs of each other's anuses. We saw them snorting hectically at each other's genitals. Male dogs patrolled invisible borders, adding their own messages to the mix. Female dogs snuffled their fragrant nurslings. Old dogs nosed their bodies all over for signs of doom.

Halfway into the film Dr. Vilkas started talking about the different kinds of pheromones: territorial scent markers creating boundaries, alarm pheromones warning of looming dangers, male sex pheromones conveying the special genotype of each species, female sex pheromones announcing optimum fertility, and then there were comfort pheromones, released by nursing females to calm their worried young.

"The world is a tempestuous tangle of significant odors," said Dr. Vilkas. "And humans are blunt-nosed fools."

"Is it possible for us to pick up some of the dogs' messages?" I asked him. "Without knowing what we're picking up?"

"We don't really comprehend the human vomeronasal organ," he said. "Scientists are just beginning to understand a little about human pheromones, how they give us very particular impressions about each other."

The film ended and the room went dim, gray storm air glowing outside the windows.

"Sometimes," I said, "before a dog pack appears, here at school or at my house, I get this special tingling feeling."

"Where?"

"I don't know. In my brain, my spine. The nervous system, I guess. I don't know if I really *smell* anything at this point."

"Very interesting," he said, rising from his desk. "I have an appointment, but I'd like to talk more about this . . . phenomenon. We could . . . I don't know."

"Meet somewhere?"

"Yes, we could do that."

Dr. Vilkas walked to the media cart and closed his laptop.

"Like for coffee, maybe," I rasped.

"Or maybe we could conduct some tests, scientific experiments with the dogs."

Dr. Vilkas dropped one of his cables and picked it up, put it down on the media cart, shook my hand with his hot hand, tucked his laptop under his army jacket, and walked out into the rain.

ψ

"Late again," said my husband, who held a baggie of fetid meat in his hand, bait for the new leghold traps he'd positioned in shallow trenches around our yard. We were standing behind the garage, beside our new aluminum garbage cans, a hot spot for canine activity.

"The dogs," I said.

"Did they come to school today?" he asked.

"No. But we had another meeting. Working out the kinks of certain safety procedures."

"What kinds of safety procedures?"

"Rabies prevention."

"Which involves?"

"You know, detection. Symptoms. Vaccination. Rabies is a virus."

"Duh."

"And we've got something this Saturday, something on crowd control."

"I thought you were going to help me install the electric fence."

"An electric fence won't keep them out."

"How do you know? Intuition?"

"No. Actually, a dog expert who spoke at school said so."

Suddenly I felt very alert. Wind blustered through the trees, shaking drops from leaves. Something zinged up my spine. I thought I smelled Fritos.

"I know you think I'm crazy, but I feel like they're coming," I said. "I really do."

"It's too early. They always come at dusk."

"At school they usually come in the afternoon. I'm going inside."

"Plus, they've never come when it's this wet out," my husband called after me.

I was jogging toward our house. The mist felt good on my skin. I thought I heard my husband laughing at me, or maybe I heard a braying dog. By the time I reached the back porch, they were already streaming into our yard. My husband yelled, ran around the side of the garage, scrambled into the closet where he kept his power tools, and shut the door. He was safe, so I could laugh triumphantly on our back steps, one foot from the door but still outside in the electromagnetic air, my head thrown back, my neck muscles rippling, a long liquid howl shooting out of my throat.

The dogs didn't plunder or linger, but tumbled right through, a stinking river of fur and clamor that flowed around our side yard, dipped down into the gulch that had just been cleared for a vinyl-sided mini-McMansion, and disappeared. I couldn't tell whether they'd gone west or east, and with my heart still thudding, I ran inside to e-mail Dr. Vilkas.

"A fluid progression?" said Dr. Vilkas.

"Yes, beginning at the crown, dropping to the top of my nape, moving down my spine, and then, well, from the coccyx to the pubic bone, an, um, quivering in between."

"In between?"

Dr. Vilkas was smirking. I'm not sure if he believed me, and perhaps I did exaggerate, but he was also tipsy, slurping exotic liquid from something called a Scorpion Bowl—gin, rum, vodka, grenadine, orange and pineapple juice—a drink that'd arrived with a flaming crouton afloat in the middle of it, making him giggle and rub his palms together. There was a straw for each of us, and I'd taken more than a few nervous sips. We sat alone, deep in the interior of the Imperial Dragon, a strip-mall restaurant with several windowless rooms, the inner room a jungle of plastic vines with two golden bulldogs cavorting by a miniature waterfall. We dined in a gilded gazebo. Pentatonic lute tunes flowed from speakers. The air-conditioning, set low, smelled moldy.

Dr. Vilkas tore a chicken wing apart and gnawed gristle from bones. The way he hunched over his food reminded me of a praying mantis, his face an uncanny blend of ugly and beautiful. He had long eyelashes and greenish temple veins. Soft lips and sunken cheeks. And then there were his eyes—one a crisp arctic blue, the other a woodsy green—burning above his receding chin.

"It could be a reaction to the overwhelming flurry of pheromones the dogs put out. Have you always been this sensitive?"

"Sort of, but this is different—like something in my brain's opened up."

"Is there any chance you're pregnant?"

For some reason, in this red-lit, windowless room, with Dr. Vilkas's head hovering two feet from mine, the word *pregnant*, applied to my own body, evoking my invisible husband, uttered with a guttural dip toward the word's heavy, eggy letter *g*, brought a hectic flush to my face.

I wondered if Dr. Vilkas would've asked this question in the businesslike bustle of a coffee shop, or at school, in the fluorescent brightness of my portable.

"No," I mumbled. "I mean, probably not. I seriously doubt it. Though I guess it's not impossible."

My cheeks felt hot. I vaguely remembered having sex with my husband once in the last month, late one night on the couch, struggling to concentrate, fidgeting to achieve a comfortable position, the television buzzing on mute.

"I don't mean to pry into your private life, but pregnancy would explain an intensification of olfactory perception."

Dr. Vilkas smirked again. He smiled at the oddest times, undercutting the professionalism of his words.

I imagined him scrawny and naked, moving toward me with the purple heat of his erection, his chest narrow, hairless except for a few wisps around his nipples, his thighs shaggy, his fingers splayed to clamp my shoulders, to hold me steady for a proper mount. I saw myself drawing my knees up. I could smell the bleach in the motel sheet. And there would be other smells, intimate and bodily, pumped from his glands and blending with odors of feral dog.

His breath would also have an odor, a mix of food and toothpaste and the health of his mouth, bacterial colonies, his tongue and gums seething with organisms, infinitesimal animals bursting with the drive to swarm. The room would reek of his equipment, plus the ghostly effluvia of inhabitants past—layers of eagerness and disappointment, ecstasy, bitterness, rage—feebly radiant but there, almost pulsing.

His wallet on the nightstand. His underwear on the floor.

"I've got to go," I said, pulling cash from my purse, stacking it in front of me, wrinkled and grubby with the sweat of a million human hands.

❦

"What?" said my husband, for I had kissed him on the mouth; I had probed with my tongue until tasting the animal depths of him, hoping to pull this part of him out into the waning day. But he fiddled with his electric fence, which had a short, and I was tipsy, my heart getting ahead of itself, red leaves fluttering down from the maple trees.

"You've been drinking," he said.

"Just a cocktail," I said, "with a few of the teachers, after the workshop. But look at me now: I'm home."

I was pacing in little circles around him.

"And we should do something," I said. "Go somewhere, maybe?"

"Where?"

"I don't know. A walk?"

"What about the dogs?"

"Take your stun gun. That would be fun."

"I don't feel like it," he said. "I'm kind of involved with this. And it's about to get dark." He turned back to the manual that had come with his electric-fence system.

"Well, I'm going," I said, taking big strides away from him. I was crossing the street now, dipping into the gulch where the mini-McMansion had sprouted up overnight. I looked back, half expecting to see my husband scrambling after me, but apparently the idea of wild dogs tearing me to pieces didn't bother him, or perhaps he hadn't even seen me stalking across the street with my fists clenched.

I started to run. I jogged into the scrap of woods where a doe had been killed by a dog pack just last week, hunted and cornered and stripped of flesh, her bones cracked open and scattered. It was getting dark, and the terror I felt was like a ringing in my blood, an addictive stirring of something I hadn't felt in a long time, ancient feelings pouring from deep nooks of my brain. I could run forever, I thought, and I kept going, scrambling up a weedy hill until I reached the top. I watched the sun sink into the pond of an empty golf course, and then I sat in the dark for a spell, wondering what to do.

❦

The next week a cold front came, and my students arrived bundled, their winter things musty from summer storage, their eyes lit with the false promises of different weather. The old heat pump groaned. Smells of burnt dust floated up from the vents. The children were squirmy. And my mind kept going blank. The words on the pages of my books would blur, and I'd squint up at the children's faces, forgetting why I was confined with so many restless young mammals. Each day I turned off the lights. I showed them films about dogs—*Benji, Lassie, Cujo*—making their minds converge into a single entity—gray, staticky, amorphous— and their bodies sit still.

I saved *Cujo* for after lunch, the most difficult period, and it seemed that the reign of terror held by the crazed slavering dog would never end, that Cujo had always ruled the endless afternoon with his fury and red snap-ping mouth. But then, by two o'clock on Friday, the dog lay dead. His exhausted hostages were finally crawling from their dusty Ford Pinto into the harsh summer sun. My students were finally filing out into the cold bright day. And Dr. Vilkas was finally standing outside my portable, hunched in his army jacket, his face freshly shaven and vulnerable looking, like the skin of a baby mouse. The wind flapped his hair, and I could see the crow's feet that etched the corners of his eyes, a sprinkling of dandruff in his dark hair, two cuts on his chin.

"I called you," he said.

"Oh, yeah. We were . . . I mean . . . installing an electric fence. All week."

"About the experiment, of course."

"Experiment?"

"Your preolfactory neurological sensations and detection of canine activity."

"Right."

"Whenever you're free, we could set something up."

"People tend to romanticize so-called wildness," said Dr. Vilkas, who did not drink so much as open his mouth and splash wine down into his dark, gurgling throat. "So when a dog joins a feral pack, it does not, in any sense, break free—it simply exchanges one set of rules for another."

"Yes," I said, sipping my wine carefully. I could feel dark vapors dancing up from what was probably the reptilian part of my brain.

We were in his room at a Hampton Inn, the butter-yellow curtains drawn, sitting at a little breakfast table beside the window in a cone of lamplight, two beds floating in the darkness beyond, one of them rumpled, the other pristine. The vinegary smell of our sub sandwiches hung in the air. And I thought I could detect a faint, sulfuric whiff of dog lurking beneath the food odors and the sick fruity tang of an air freshener.

Dr. Vilkas insisted that a few drinks sharpened his intuition, that a little wine helped him think about the dogs in refreshingly new ways, and that sometimes, on certain evenings, when his brain chemistry conspired to make his head glow, he could figure out the whereabouts of one of the largest feral packs. This is all he would reveal about his dog-tracking techniques. When I pressed him, he answered me with his trademark smirk. He twiddled his thumbs in a way that I imagined would become annoying to someone who knew his tics. He tossed more wine into his maw.

And then, padding around me in his stocking feet, smelling of wet wool and wine and the deeper animal brine of armpits, he applied wireless electrodes, metal sensors the size of fleas, to my scalp, sifting through my hair with his fingers. He put on his boots. He sipped the last of his wine and smiled. Wearing my EEG helmet, I followed him out into the night—big, bright moon, sweater weather, a single cricket chirring in the shrubs. He cleared a spot for me on the seat of his jeep, brushing crumpled Hardee's bags to the floor.

We drove toward the river, asphalt turning to tar and gravel. Hitting rocky dirt, we bounced along, the road flanked by meadows of dead goldenrod. An electrical substation loomed ahead, three fat transformers rising up like old-fashioned robots. Dr. Vilkas had a little can of Comfort Zone with DAP—dog-appeasing pheromone, a synthesized version of the stuff produced by lactating bitches to calm their young—and we sprayed the tart substance on our clothes. We walked deep into the meadow, down to the river, where the dogs sometimes slept, the goldenrod trampled, the air musky and ammoniac, tinged with a familiar, fried, salty smell.

"They've rested here," he said, kneeling on the ground. "How do you feel?"

"Nothing too exciting," I said.

"Faint amygdalic activity." He studied the crude cartoon on the laptop screen that represented my brain. "Perhaps a stirring in the hypothalamus. Let's move on."

We climbed back into his jeep and drove in the moon-bright night, skirting the old mill village, taking a back highway into a desolate neon-lit area flush with check-cashing shops, car-title-loan joints, strip clubs, and used-car lots. Beyond a cluster of gas stations, out near an interstate exit, an abandoned Target was sinking to ruin. Dr. Vilkas said that dogs sometimes took shelter there, but it was too dangerous to venture inside. He had a bottle of merlot in his backpack, and we sat in the parking lot, a weedy void of crumbling asphalt, its pole lights long dead. We drank in the moonlight, passing the wine between us, listening for the yip and stir of canines. We watched the sky for the flutter of bats, pointing in silence when they dipped jaggedly into our sight.

Dr. Vilkas whispered of the mysteries of echolocation. He told me that dolphins and whales used the same biological sonar, drifting in deep-sea gloom, clicking at high frequencies, their pulses penetrating the delicate anatomies of fish. And certain birds that lived in caves could navigate the blackness of intricate chasms.

Dr. Vilkas handed me the bottle, his fingertips grazing my palm. He gazed at his laptop, detecting faint activity, he said, perhaps in my *nucleus accumbens*. I felt a vague prickling of the spine, heat in my cheeks. And Dr. Vilkas said my *cingulate gyrus* seemed to be stimulated, that my *orbitofrontal cortex* showed signs of activity. I felt wind on my face. A bubble of warmth moved down my spine, bouncing from vertebra to vertebra, and then dissolved pleasantly in my coccyx.

"And there's this salty smell," I whispered. "Don't you smell that? Like corn chips."

Dr. Vilkas didn't answer. We both stood up. We knew the dogs were coming, and we smiled at each other when they materialized in a rush, pouring around the left side of the building, their barks blurring into a single smear of sound.

"Do they see us?" I asked him, my mouth dipping close to his ear.

"Yes." He leaned toward me. "Though they smelled us first, but the DAP spray should keep them from attacking."

As the dogs raced around the edges of the parking lot, circling us, sniffing out the borders of this territory, I felt a delicious terror. I took two steps forward and glanced back at Dr. Vilkas, who hung behind, grinning at the diagram of my mind, my feelings lit up, garish in yellow and red.

"Your brain's really pulsing," he seemed to shout, though I couldn't be sure, for dogs were pressing in on me, stink and noise and wind merging into a single whirl of sensation, their heat humming against my skin. Fur floated in the air above their spastic bodies, drifted into my nostrils, tickling mucous membranes. I sensed the hot blasts of their panting, the throbbing of two hundred hearts, the clatter of four thousand toenails. I felt their tongues, pimply tentacles smelling of death, sliding over the flesh of my hands.

And now Dr. Vilkas was moving toward me through the canine sea, waist-deep in fur and slaver and stink, his shirt unbuttoned, hair kinetic from the wind the dog pack whipped up. He bobbed along, buoyed toward me, until, hurled at my feet, he squatted on the crumbling asphalt.

Tongue lolling, he panted. Squatting, grinning, he winked at me. And then he threw his head back and howled, Adam's apple pulsing, until the dogs joined in. Sitting on their haunches, every last animal found a patch of territory on which to squat and bay. They pointed their elegant snouts toward the moon, yowled and keened and squalled until the air smelled marshy from their breath.

Jaws

You squint toward the seething sea, imagining that you are alone on the beach, a nubile castaway with sun-kissed skin. You try to remember what it was like to walk boldly in the sun's poisonous rays, innocent and near-naked, trusting in the general goodness of nature, your flesh anointed with exotic tanning oil. Coconut Dream. Pineapple Passion.

But the sun has not been kind to you. It has left you blistered and spotted and scathed. And so you cower in the radius of a UV umbrella. You scowl, your lips smeared with oxybenzone. You're not even on the beach, though you can sense its shimmer in the distance. You are one block away from the ocean, perched by the crowded pool of a budget condo, reading a book on endangered species and wallowing in grim statistics.

"There are fewer than one thousand red-handed howler monkeys left on the planet," you say in an accusing tone.

"Caught red-handed," quips your father, who sprawls rakishly in the full glare of the carcinogenic sun, sipping a gin and tonic, his body a moonscape of moles and barnacles and curious clusters of hair. You try not to look at this archetypal body, the degradation of which goes along with the general apocalyptic downturn of twenty-first-century civilization. But occasionally, when you reach the end of a long list of dying species (endangered rodents of Australia, for example), you take a glance, noting some particularly depressing detail (twin gouges where two basal-cell carcinomas have recently been removed, for example). And later, with macabre gusto, you will incorporate these tidbits into your dark, witty blog—misanthropos.blogspot.com.

Your mother is also a source of inspiration for the blog, especially since she's been suffering from "senior moments" and demonstrating inappropriate social behavior, which may or may not be connected to hormone replacement therapy and intensified doses of cholesterol medication. It's nothing serious—yet—which means that you may smirk grimly when she says, "Everyone is beautiful, even the blacks." You plot a special blog entry called "Racist Shit My Mother Says," jotting down her bons mots instead of passively sighing at the sadness of the world. It is still possible to keep panic at bay as you watch your mother frolic in the pool with excessive childish glee. At this very moment, she bounds toward a cool, sleek woman who reclines in a chaise and hides behind the latest Oprah-endorsed melodrama.

"You are so beautiful," your mother says.

The woman peers at your mother over her book, eyes shrouded in enormous cartoonish sunglasses—*geriatric glam* captures the look precisely, you note, filing the image away for future use. Though your father watches like a half-wit politician's handler, tensing in his chair, he does not get up.

"I need to lose weight," your mother says.

As the woman simpers and cowers behind her book, you remain emotionally unscathed, relishing the absurdity of the encounter: the woman's spotted, leathery skin, her sparkly pedicure, her Prada eyewear and chunky gold jewelry. In your blog entry you will use the term *bling*. You will breezily reference Veblen. You will point out (as a casual afterthought) that gold was used to make slave manacles on the island of Utopia.

"I need a breast reduction," your mother says.

And it is only after she has grabbed her ample, Lycra-clad bosom and squeezed her breasts together in classic pinup mode that your father finally pulls himself up from his chair.

"Jenny, come here for a minute," he says, fumbling for an invisible cigarette, patting his pockets, forgetting that he, with the assistance of a nicotine patch, Xanax, and Prozac, was able to kick the habit a few months back, an amazing feat considering that he'd been chain-smoking since age twelve. Your dad grew up with an abusive father (an ogrish lumberman who made him spend his teenage summers toiling in the woods). His crisp comb-over, which he compulsively styles with aerosol hair spray and which you have ridiculed in previous blog posts, flutters in the breeze. You feel a raw throb of emotion crawling up from the cellar of your heart like a fleshy, red mutant from a horror flick. You do not want to look this creature in the eye. You beat it down with lines of poetry (*An aged man is but a paltry thing / A tattered coat upon a stick*), even though you are, of course, cynical about poetry.

☙

Cornucopia, an international all-you-can-eat megabuffet surrounded by mirrors, stretches into infinity. You feel dizzy as you weave among the steaming troughs, looking for something edible. You stumble down an aisle of meats, red and dark and white, flesh from winged and hoofed and scaly animals, fried and broiled and braised and boiled, barbecued and jerked and simmering in vats of pure corn syrup. You are a fasting monk in the desert, caught up in a gaudy hallucination. You discover a tray of pallid salmon. You ferret out a pile of steamed broccoli, studded with cashews. Amid the obscene abundance, you cannot find one unprocessed grain. So you spoon a puritanical dollop of mashed potato onto your plate, though you know that it is larded with margarine and low-fat sour cream, laced with poisonous sugars, the ubiquitous corn syrup. You approach the table with a martyr's wince. You imagine your husband at home, harvesting kale from his organic garden. Three days from now, returning with the starved and panicky look of a prisoner of war, you will devour a mountain of steamed greens.

But at this moment you are inexplicably here, in this windowless dungeon of decadence, where the obese demographic stands in line to suck soft-serve ice cream straight from the industrial teat. Your mother's plate is heaped with deep-fried tidbits: fried clams, fried shrimp, fried lobster, fried crab, fried fish, fried chicken, fried steak, fried pork, fried potatoes, fried onions, fried batter.

"You need to eat some vegetables," says your father, who has added a blue-cheese-smothered salad of pesticide-saturated genetically modified iceberg lettuce to his pile of garbage.

"That's not good for you," he says.

"It is good!" cries your mother, jerking her plate away as though your father wants to snatch her food.

"Good *for* you, Jenny, not *good*."

"It is good," says your mother.

Her pouched brown eyes quiver behind glasses.

Do you detect a glimmer of slyness? You wonder; for during your childhood your mother was in some ways the shadow-governor of your house, the manipulator, the ever-scheming dumb-playing domestic Machiavelli, and though her bubble of understanding may have shrunk, her control impulse is stronger than ever.

"Of course it's *good*, Jenny. Fried meat is high in saturated fat and cholesterol. But it's not good *for* you."

"It *is* good!" screams your mother. "Look at the flowers."

She points at a vase of plastic hibiscus that rests on a pearl-white baby grand that you suspect has never been played. "Aren't they beautiful?"

"Tell her, Caroline. Tell her that what she's eating isn't good for her."

You begin your diatribe with the salmon.

"Consider the salmon," you actually say, though there are no hip, clever people around to get your allusion. "Farm-raised, of course. If their feed were not laced with toxic dye, their meat would be the unappetizing color of a maggot."

Your father, who is squeamish, retches into his napkin.

"Please," he says.

But you have no mercy. Trotting out *Deadly Harvest*, *The Omnivore's Dilemma*, and *Fast Food Nation*, you present the grim facts about the agri-industrial complex. You touch upon monocropping, genetic modification, the specious differences between artificial and so-called "natural" flavors, after which you provide a brief aside on the heated debate surrounding the controversial issue of saturated fats, which have, perhaps, been unfairly demonized. You bemoan the planet's dying oceans. You describe the melancholy lowing of diseased cattle crammed cheek to jowl in a concrete feed lot. You depict corn syrup as though it is some kind of evil ectoplasm that possesses the food system, haunting cereal boxes and jars of juice. You pick flecks of flesh from your salmon and pop them into your mouth. You wince, for effect, each time you swallow. And when you are done covering every nook and cranny of the thoroughly corrupt contemporary food system, your cheeks are flushed with elation.

"Food is food," your father says. "One of the few pleasures in life."

"You are what you eat," you say. "And you, dear Father, are not eating a duck but a brutal duck-raising technology."

Your father rolls his eyes.

So you take it upon yourself to make him understand the true nature of the food system in which he is complicit.

You discuss antibiotics, hormones, lice medicine. You evoke the pale winter light that once played upon the cold bars of *this duck's* (you point for emphasis) cramped prison cell. You hypothesize about the nature of duck depression. You want your father to *taste* the despair of the cage. The sad duck restlessness. The bleak duck sighs. Bleeding cankers of the flipper, cloacal tumors, swollen feather follicles. You ask your father to imagine the vitamin-deficient creature's cloudy eyes, its scaly beak, its tongue, dry as a biscuit, feebly protruding to taste an anemic crumb of genetically modified Roundup Ready corn.

You do not feel satisfied until your father puts down his fork.

"Nevertheless," you say, "you might as well eat it. Not waste it, you know. After all it went through."

"Caroline, why don't *you* eat something?" says your mother. She's standing up, half-empty plate in hand. "There are *all kinds* of fruits and vegetables. And it's all natural, natural, natural."

She skips off into the labyrinth of troughs, wedges herself between two wheelchair-bound senior citizens, heaps her plate with desserts, and returns to the table.

"Want some?" she asks.

You shake your head.

You imagine your husband weeding his vegetable garden. You left on a bad note two days ago, after a long and tedious fight that ended only when you walked out the door. In fact, the reason you decided, at the last minute, to join your parents for a cut-rate vacation in nightmarish Orlando was to get a break from what you call *the husband situation*. And while your angry side still wants to double-slap the self-righteous prick across his smug face, the loving and sensitive soul deep within you, gagged and strait-jacketed by bitterness, misses him.

"Whew," says your mother, putting down a Pepto-Bismol-pink spoonful of M&M-studded pudding. "I ate too much" (she always says this). "I won't have to eat a bite of supper" (she always does).

Though her smile is huge, she looks uncomfortable and hypertensive. In the spasmodic light of the fluorescent chandeliers, her face looks alarmingly flushed. And you think you see a hint of wildness in her eyes.

❦

The condo balcony overlooks a parking lot. A dumpster swells like an island amid the glittering sea of SUVs.

"Great view," you say, and your father sneers into his gin and tonic, wondering, you suspect, why he invited you along.

"It's beautiful," your mother says, her smile rapturous.

"What a sunset." Your father takes your mother's tiny restless hand, caging it in both palms as though he's trapped a wily songbird.

But the sky *is* beautiful, you admit, scarlet with particulates and smeared with clumps of glowing smog. You mention the role of pollution in what you call *the apocalyptic beauty of the postmodern sunset.* And yes, you *do* feel pretentious for using the term *postmodern*, particularly in the presence of your quaint, modern parents with their atomic-age notions of human progress. You actually wince before turning back to the screenplay you've been working on for a year, a sci-fi satire that you secretly hope will release you from your peonage as an adjunct instructor of English composition with a course load of five/five. You are a debt prisoner struggling to pay off student loans, teaching future debt prisoners whose student loans are three times as usurious as yours. But you have promised yourself that you will not think about your students during spring break. You will focus on your neglected screenplay. And you actually feel inspired by the ridiculous sunset. Riding the crisp, optimistic wave of a chardonnay buzz, you tap laptop keys.

Dusk. The sky in pink turmoil, a froth of toxic clouds. Cars cruise the city grid. Behind an abandoned strip mall, on cracked blacktop, in the sultry haze of perpetual summer,

two black sedans approach each other. Each vehicle emits a
pink plume of exhaust. They drive in circles, assessing pher-
omones. The male organ emerges slowly, like an expanding
telescope, to the pulsing throb of bleak techno music. And
then the cars copulate, bumper to bumper, like cockroaches.

You laugh at the exquisite absurdity of the scene. Your
screenplay, a dystopian satire, depicts a world in which
humans have become so obese and car-dependent that
they have grown into their vehicles. Their blobby, bone-
less bodies, filling every inch of their cars' interiors, have
fused with their automobiles' exoskeletons. Nothing but
cyborg arthropods cruise the hot, barren planet, tanking
up at automated gas stations and feeding through tubes
at robot-run drive-thrus. The creatures mate like insects.
The females lay eggs that resemble tiny Volkswagen
Beetles. You still get chills when you imagine the opening
credits rolling to the provocative tune of Gary Numan's
"Cars," its optimistic melody undercut by a sinister un-
dertow that slowly becomes apparent when the viewer
realizes that there are no human beings in the scene.

"Caroline," says your mother, "you ought to plan your
baby for the summer."

Your mother counts on her fingers: "September,
October, November, December, January, February,
March, April, May."

And then she winks suggestively at you, as though she has somehow been reading your mind, following the grotesque sex scene you've been tinkering with. You wonder how you can engage your audience emotionally with scene after scene of soulless, car-human hybrids, cruising and eating and fucking and crashing. You wonder if you should have an archetypal rebel character who, unlike the other automatons, sees what grim conditions humanity has been reduced to and longs to break out into a more vital form of "reality." You chuckle to yourself as you imagine two cyborg arthropods falling so deeply in love that they want to burst their carapaces and embrace each other flesh to flesh.

"You and Tim would have the most beautiful baby in the world," your mother says, forcing you to think about *the husband situation* again, perhaps reading your mind again, for it was the very subject of reproduction that prompted your three-day argument.

And you *do* want a baby. But not right this minute. You want to wait until you are ready (financially, emotionally, physically). Your schedule is too crazy. You are too nervous. You drink too much wine. You have not published an article in a peer-reviewed academic journal. The ramshackle cabin you bought five years ago is only half-renovated. And, perhaps most importantly, the planet you happen to live on is a polluted ball of shit overrun with an insane and rapacious species of absurdly successful ape that will probably destroy itself within a decade.

"But you're not getting any younger."

Four days ago, your husband actually uttered this vile cliché. And that's when you lost it, reminding him that sperm quality also suffers as men age, that men over forty are more likely to spawn autistic children and schizophrenics and mentally sluggish offspring with emotional issues, and that everything is not always the mother's fault.

Your own mother, for instance, had three children whom she smothered with obsessive love, not because she was a bad person, but because her entire identity revolved around being a mother, which was partially your father's fault and partially society's.

"Of course, it's difficult to disentangle the roles of individual men and those of the patriarchy," you actually said, wincing as your husband smirked at your choice of terminology.

Two years ago, when you were finishing your dissertation on female monsters in 1970s cinema, your mother would call twice a week and say, "Caroline, have you finished your dissertation?" And now that you have finished your dissertation (which ended up taking several years), your mother prods you to take the next step in your long, arduous journey to adulthood.

"I can't wait until you have a baby, Caroline," she says now, firing up a Camel Light, looking like a hoodlum child because she is only five feet tall. And this image makes you fondly remember your own first cigarette. You and your best friend, Squank, had kept a stash of cigs in the shed, a dim moldy space where you also experimented with French kissing. You still recall the clammy warmth of Squank's perpetually sweating hands. His hysterical laughter. His neurotic habit of pinching his arms black and blue every time he committed a "sin."

"Mom," you say, "do you remember Squank?"

"Squank," she says. "That rings a bell. James, who's Squank?"

"You remember Squank," says your father. "Odd fellow. Weird laugh. Caroline's boyfriend."

"I wouldn't call him a boyfriend," you say. "Just a friend."

"I'm having some memory problems," your mother says.

You feel sick to your stomach, because your mother has always kept track of your childhood friends, obsessively, in fact, just as she tracked your progress with your dissertation.

"Mom," you say, "who's George Bush?"

"George Bush," she says. "That rings a bell. James, who's George Bush?"

"Our idiotic president," you say. And your father winces, as he usually does at your political leanings. But this time he holds back from saying anything and, instead, sinks, as though from exhaustion, deeper into his chair.

Raiding the junk rooms of your brain, you call out names: *Osama bin Laden, Charles Manson, Michael Jackson.* And your mother has no idea who they are.

"What's a shovel?" you cry.

"Scooper," she says.

"What are these?" Making a peace sign, you point two fingers at your nostrils.

"Nose holes."

"How about a tampon?"

"I don't know."

"What's a dragon?"

"A long short crawler." She smirks sagely, as though answering some ancient riddle.

Your father, his face obliterated by shadows, sips silently. You spend the next hour subjecting your mother to demented quizzes, a panic rising within you like a locust swarm, a thousand tiny beating wings.

"Who's Jesus?" you ask.

"He was on the cross."

Why do people eat? What's electricity? What's the difference between plants and animals?

Cancer, tulips, radon, Slim Jims. Moonbeam, Bee Gees, Kleenex, rain. Tadpoles, Teletubbies, Rasputin, Atari. Tupperware. Lizards. Dinosaurs. Ice.

What is love? Where do babies come from? What happens when you die?

Sometimes your mother answers correctly. Sometimes her face goes blank. Sometimes she says something nonsensical yet poetic, cryptic even, her face serene and wizened like Yoda's. As darkness closes in on the balcony, you feel the world shrinking to nothing but you and your aging parents. You hear the clink of your father's ice. You hear a roar that might be the ocean or it might be traffic or it might be something inside your own head.

"Mom, what's the ocean?" you ask.

"It's big," she says. "It's made of something. What do you call it, James?"

"Water," your father says.

That night, you have nightmares. You are on a vast, dilapidated spaceship that reeks of leaking gas. You move down endless corridors, trip over clusters of ripped-out wiring. You discover a medical area, dim yet stark with flickering fluorescent light. Among the rows of sick and dying, you find your mother, tucked into a corner, hooked up to a mess of dirty tubes. Before your eyes, she shrinks into the bedding until there is nothing left but a small spot of grease. And when that vanishes, you are aware that the earth no longer exists.

❦

You wake in the throes of a panic attack. Something is rustling beneath your bed. A small head pops up. You recognize the impish grin, the electric hair rollers.

"Good morning." Your mother stands up, spreads a crumpled garment: a vintage sundress, purple butterflies and ivy.

"This is darling," she says. "Let me press it."

Before you can stop her, she's scurried from the room.

❦

Your father sits in the bright kitchenette. His weathered face droops from the sticky architecture of his hair. The ubiquitous comb-over makes you feel guilty now, for you realize that the hairstyle is more than an absurd quirk of vanity. The crisp helmet is order. The crisp helmet is protective armor. No matter how shitty your father feels when he wakes up in the morning, no matter how his hands shake, his hour-long grooming ritual restores some semblance of cozy normalcy. He is ready to face the day.

When you were a child, and your father was a civics professor at a community college, he'd fish on Saturdays, the only day of the week that had no claim on him. He'd come home drunk and disheveled, as though he'd turned into a beast out in the wild. Sometimes he'd hide behind doors and leap out at your mother—crazy-haired, red-eyed—and she'd shriek with laughter as the wild man caught her in his arms.

"I didn't realize," you whisper as you pour coffee. "When did she get this bad?"

"Just this summer," your father says. "Though it's been happening for a while. And now, when I think back, I can see that even a few years ago, she started to say peculiar things."

"What does her doctor say?"

"He calls them 'senior moments.' So I've made an appointment with a specialist. We're having some tests done, but I wanted her to have one more vacation. I haven't told the boys yet, though Jim could tell something was wrong over Christmas."

⚉

Your mother stands in the living room, smiling uncertainly. You don't know how long she's been standing there, holding your dress, which is starched and ironed in random spots. She's wearing lime shorts and a purple top from the 1980s, with enormous shoulder pads and huge brassy buttons, an outfit that you might have worn ironically a few years ago, when you were still striving to be hip. Now that you think about it, you did notice oddities in her dressing style at Christmas (a holiday sweater with warm-up pants and tiny, gold pumps). Remembering how gleefully you'd described her hideous sweater on your blog, you feel ashamed.

Your mother drapes your dress over a chair and lights a cigarette.

"What you want me to fix, honey?" She winks slyly. "Grits and eggs?"

Normally, you'd have something snide to say about instant grits and battery-hen eggs, but you say nothing. You nod. You take a sip of coffee. And when your mother places the food before you, you eat without complaint, just as you did when you were a child.

❦

Although you hate smearing potentially carcinogenic sunscreen all over your body, you must prepare for the brutal day. You have the expensive, organic stuff that smells like oatmeal and leaves a sticky film. You have a wide-brimmed hat and a long-sleeved sun-shirt made of some kind of futuristic, UV-resistant nylon. You have swarms of freckles, and each one is a potential basal-cell carcinoma. As you anoint your spotted body in a ritualistic fashion, you dwell on the sun damage that you suffered summers past, when, young and free and unwisely supervised, you endured at least a half-dozen severe burns, the kind that brought blisters and fever and delirium. You remember moaning in a strange beach house bed, your pale skin scorched, as your dark-skinned brothers howled and scampered through the exotic vegetation outside.

Your childhood has literally left you *scarred*, you think as you ignore your mother's increasingly desperate knock. *Scathed*, in fact. And you actually say the word aloud for dramatic effect—*scathed*—even though no one can hear you.

You find your mother pacing the hall just outside your door, vinyl purse clamped in her armpit.

"Let's go," she says. "Why don't we go?"

"Where's Dad?"

"My husband?"

"Yes," you say, feeling confused. "My father. Your husband."

"I don't know."

You start to panic, wondering what you'd do if your father disappeared. Would you take your mother back to your house? Would you drop her off at her sister's place? Just as your heartbeat begins to quicken, your father emerges from the bathroom, his comb-over fortified with an extra gust of Aqua Net.

"I'm ready," he announces, patting his helmet of hair, steeling himself for another long day of fun in the sun.

"I can't wait to get to Universal Studios," your mother says. "I can't wait."

And she skips out the door.

※

"When are we getting on the boat?" your mother asks for the tenth time, her voice a brass trumpet. Her legs, skinny and sun-damaged, sticking out of the lime-green shorts, make you think of child burn victims. And then you realize that your mother *was* a child burn victim, *scathed* by the sun, just as you were, though her olive skin was more resistant.

"Be patient," says your father. "It's a popular ride."

You are standing in line at an amusement park beneath a merciless afternoon sun. As you inch closer and closer to the glowing aqua canal, you think of Sisyphus. The heat, the out-gassing asphalt, the fair-food aromas entice dormant addictions from your cells. You long for a corn dog. You dream of guzzling a Coke. You feel ravenous, thirsty, excitable, sick. You idly spy on the family in front of you—a young black couple with two little boys. Though you sneer at the family's matching Universal Studios sun visors, you can't help but soften in the presence of the children, especially when you notice that the older boy is doing his best to terrify his younger brother.

"Sharks can bite through bone," he says. "They have three hundred and fifty teeth. The teeth grow in rows."

You fondly recall the days when your own little brothers thought you were an omniscient fairy princess and believed every bit of nonsense you told them. You remember the thrill of pure power as your ridiculous inventions became part of their personal mythology. Perhaps your blog is a feeble attempt to restore this lost power, you think, sighing as you realize that you will never have a captive audience as riveted as your younger brothers once were.

"Sharks are sometimes twenty feet long," the boy informs his brother, stretching his arms out for emphasis. You do not notice your mother's crazed grin. You do not see her creeping into the family's personal space, nor does your father, who gazes longingly at a fake island that dots the horizon.

"Come here, my little black brother," your mother says, grabbing the smaller boy by the shoulders. His parents smile tensely as your mother pulls the child close to her grinning face.

"I want you to study hard and go to Carolina," she says, "because if it weren't for *you people*, we wouldn't have a football team."

Your father winces. The shame you feel overwhelms your nervous system. You are unable to speak. Regressing to teenage coping mechanisms, you step away from your parents and pretend that you are not related to them by blood, that you don't know them, that you have never seen their faces. Just as you are about to weave off into the crowd in search of a restroom, you hear your father in damage-control mode.

"I'm sorry," he says. "She's suffering from memory problems, and we don't know . . . I mean, she sometimes says peculiar things."

"Racist things," you add, feeling another stab of shame, as though you yourself are racist, and perhaps you are. Perhaps racist ideas embedded in your brain by society explain the intense feelings of guilt that overcome you as you watch the black couple's hard eyes go soft with understanding. And then they turn away from you and your pitiful parents and pretend that the incident never happened, though their children keep glancing back at your mother while whispering and giggling into their hands.

"Jenny," says your father, "you can't say things like that."

"Like what?"

"Racist things," your father whispers.

"God told me to say it," your mother says with a haughty simper, and then she, too, gazes out at the distant island.

※

"Here comes the boat!" your mother screams. "Here comes the boat!" And the black family cannot help but turn to inspect her again.

"I can't wait to get on the boat!" your mother says to them, pressing forward, defying American proxemics customs.

A teen captain eases a glittery fuchsia pontoon into the channel and coasts up to dock. Tourists file out on the other side of the canal.

"What a big boat!" cries your mother. "When can we get on?"

"Just a minute, Jenny, be patient," says your father. "The other passengers have to get off first."

The captain, watching the crowd through purple sunglasses, chews gum and lolls in the fighter's chair. When it's finally your turn, your mother pushes forward and sits in the same row as the black family, right beside the shark expert. There's one seat left in the row, and your father takes it. You sit behind them.

"I'm Captain Jack," the pilot announces into his bullhorn. "Welcome aboard the *Sea Urchin*."

Captain Jack guides the boat through the fake channel, which is connected to a fake inlet, the whole system fed by the blinding blue ocean. You smell marsh and tar and gasoline. You hold on to your hat as the boat lurches into open water.

"Here we go!" your mother screams, squirming in her seat. Your father smiles a martyr's grim smile.

"Back in 1974," says Captain Jack, "a great white shark named Jaws murdered dozens of innocent people. They even made a movie about it. We're going to tour a few spots where the evil fish made its kills. But don't worry, Jaws is long dead. And if we do have any trouble, this boat is protected by a forty-millimeter grenade launcher, courtesy of the US Army."

The boat churns sluggishly, then stops. Pointing toward the horizon, Captain Jack informs the crowd that a young female swimmer was slain twenty yards from Amity Island. You hear mock gasps. You hear laughter. And then the primordial vision of a fin appears, knifing through blue water— the theatrics laughable but faintly, viscerally, horrifying.

"Jaws!" cries the shark expert, grabbing his little brother by the shoulders.

"Where? Where?" asks your mother. "What is it, James? What is that thing?"

"A shark, Jenny."

"What's a shark?"

"A huge killer fish with sharp teeth, but it's not a real shark. It's Jaws."

"Jaws?"

"From the movie."

"Here it comes," says the shark expert. "Here comes Jaws."

"Here comes Jaws, Jaws, Jaws," says your mother.

As the fin weaves toward you, and the huge back of the beast darkens the clear water, someone behind you lets out a fake scream.

"OH MY GOD A SHARK. WATCH OUT!" the captain's voice booms from the PA system, mock dramatic, as though he's reading a children's book.

And up pops Jaws's mammoth head at the familiar angle, all gulping mouth and gleaming teeth, the tongue slick and writhing—the archetype of engulfment. It's a little rubbery and mechanical, but pretty impressive. And huge.

Your mother sits stunned, staring into the abysmal mouth. Then she yelps and jumps into your father's arms. Their physical contact makes you uncomfortable. You look out at the water. The murderous beast sinks back into obscurity.

"It's not real, Jenny. It's a robot," your father says.

"What's a robot?" your mother asks.

The shark expert snickers and elbows his brother.

"A machine, Jenny."

"Is it trying to kill us?" she asks.

"Of course not," says your father.

"THERE IT IS AGAIN! IT'S TRYING TO KILL US!" declares the captain, the words booming from the sky as though narrated by God.

Jaws pops up on the other side of the boat, and your mother begins to cry, her face ripped open at the mouth, loose around the eyes, ravaged by decades of cheap food, polluted air, carcinogenic sun, and disappointment. Your father's well-composed expression is devastated by a twitching grin.

The captain lazily grabs a harpoon gun and shoots the shark in the back. A geyser of steam bursts from the wound, and then magenta blood spurts out.

"Kill it! Kill it!" shrieks your mother.

But Jaws, hard to kill, sinks out of sight. The monster lurks around in the vast deep.

"Is Jaws dead?" your mother asks.

"I don't know," says your father. "But it's a robot, Jenny."

"Is Jaws dead?" your mother screams at the captain.

Everyone is looking. You feel another surge of adolescent shame—wasps in your stomach, fire in your cheeks.

You contemplate *the husband situation*. You picture your husband disappearing into the woods with his field bag, his mushroom book, his canteen. You wonder what you would do if he didn't come back. You picture yourself pacing around the cabin alone, walking from window to window to watch fog float up from the darkening wood.

※

Jaws's next appearance, unannounced by the captain, takes everyone by surprise, and the entire boat lets out a primal wail, quickly followed by chuckles that subside as the prehistoric fish gnaws at the boat hull with its razor teeth, jerking the vessel from left to right.

Your mother, screaming like a terrified lab monkey, attempts to climb onto your father's lap. She won't stop screaming, ruthless and earsplitting, and people are struggling with the shapes of their mouths.

You try to stand up to help your parents, but they are locked in an embrace, exclusive and distant. And the shark is circling the boat, darkening the ocean with its blood. Captain Jack has no choice but to fire grenades into the boiling sea. Bombs strike the bank, exploding with outlandish displays of smoke and flame. When one of the grenades hits a fuel dock, a gas tank bursts into a fiery blob the size of a hot-air balloon.

"OH MY GOD!" cries Captain Jack. "I CAN'T STOP THE BOAT AND WE'RE HEADED RIGHT FOR IT!"

The Wilds

The Wild family moved into the house behind ours. For two years the split-level had been dead, open to prowling neighborhood children; its sunken den had become a nest of slugs and millipedes, its attic a froth of bats. Now eight brothers flung their restless bodies around the property. The largest Wild, a bearded boy of seventeen, shut himself up in the basement den. The littlest Wild, a tangle-haired half-naked thing, rumored to be a biter, lurked around in the shrubbery. The Wilds kept cats, lizards, and ferrets. Rabbits, hamsters, turtles, and snakes. A bubble of musky, ammoniac air enveloped their home like a force field, and the second you dared step through it you felt dizzy; a hundred arrows whistled around your ears. Their mother was frequently seen hauling in bags of supplies, and when she climbed from the battered shell of her station wagon, the boys would jump her like a band of hunger-crazed outlaws, snatching cookies and chips and tiny shrink-wrapped cakes. They'd scuttle up into the trees. They kept quiet up there, waiting out their mother's fits. She was a lumpy, old-fashioned lady, forever in a rumpled dress and panty hose, with a pouf of hair as golden and crunchy as a pork rind. She'd tear her hairdo into wilted clumps and shake her fists at the trees. "I'm having a nervous breakdown," she'd say, sometimes falling to her knees.

Mama said she felt sorry for Mrs. Wild. Dressed in tight jeans and heels, Mama would invite the hunched lady to have coffee in our spotless living room. She made fun of Mrs. Wild's dresses when the poor woman left, but sometimes she was sad, and I knew she was thinking about my little brother, who'd weighed three pounds when he was born and died in a humid tank of oxygen.

Mr. Wild always rolled in after dark, in a black Chrysler New Yorker, appearing briefly in streetlight, always shrouded in a suit. He worked in the secret depths of a nuclear plant, thirty miles away, a glowing futuristic fortress surrounded by high walls. The family was from way up north, somewhere between Pennsylvania and the North Pole, where the world froze into a solid block of ice for months on end and people lived half their lives indoors. But now, in the teeming Southern air, the transplanted boys were growing, faster and faster, so fast their mother reputedly had to keep two industrial freezers in the garage, one for milk, the other for meat—hot dogs, chickens, turkeys, and hams; pork chops, baloney, and liver; a thousand cuts of beef and strange bloody meats seldom eaten in our part of the world.

☙

We were deep into summer and you could see the vines growing, winding around branches, sprouting bumps and barnacles and woody boils that would fester until they could stand it no more, then break out into red and purple. It was night and the Wild boys hooted in their shrubbery. They wore dirty cutoff jeans. They carried knives and BB guns and homemade bombs. I could smell their weird metallic sweat drifting on a breeze that rustled through the honeysuckle. The Wild boys had dug tunnels under the ground. They had filled the treetops with catwalks. They whirred from tree to tree on zip lines and hopped from attic windows out into the bustling night.

I crouched in the bushes in Mama's green chiffon evening gown, wearing my crown of bird skulls. I'd collected the skulls for two years, spray-painted them gold, and glued them to a Burger King crown, along with fake emeralds and glowing shells of June bugs. Thin, long hair tickled my spine. My Barbie binoculars were crap, and I'd smashed them with a rock. I was on the lookout for Brian, the oldest Wild, who sometimes left his den to smoke. I was deeply in love with him. Every time I saw him, reclining in his plastic lawn chair, pouting in dark sunglasses, my heart twisted like a worm in the cocoon of my chest.

My father taught medieval history at the community college. I'd found a recipe for an ancient love potion in one of his books, and inside a purple Crown Royal pouch, buried under an assortment of amulets, I'd placed a fancy perfume bottle full of the magical fluid.

Lightning bugs bobbed in the rich air. Crickets throbbed. A fat, bloody moon hung over the house of the neighborhood alcoholics. I heard the click of the sliding glass door that led to Brian's lair, and he came out into the night, pulsing with beauty and mystery. His hair was long, wild, and black. He'd shaved his beard into a devil's point. You could tell by the way he sighed and flopped around that he dreamed of better places—glamorous and distant, with a different kind of light. Because of him I'd taken up smoking. I stole butts from my mother and kept them in a sock with a pink Bic, Tic Tacs, and a tiny spray can of Lysol. I fantasized about smoking with Brian: Brian leaning over to light my cigarette, our sensuous exhalations intertwining, Brian kissing my smoky mouth. My longing pulled me over the invisible boundary into the Wilds' honeysuckle-choked yard. I was in their habitat, sniffing ferret musk and a thousand flowers, when a hand slipped over my mouth. It smelled of onions and dirt. A small, hot body pressed against my back.

"Don't make a sound," said a boy.

"We've got knives," said another. They snatched my wrists and twisted them behind my back. Other boys came out into the moonlight, and Brian slipped inside the house, tossing his cigarette butt behind him.

"Stand up," a boy said.

Their chests glowed with firefly juice. They had steak knives strapped to their belts and some of them wore goggles. White cats strolled among them, sometimes sniffing their bare feet. "Move," yelled a small Wild, no older than six, a butter knife dangling from his Cub Scout belt. They pushed me toward a crooked magnolia. In the sweet, knotty dark of the tree, they'd nailed boards for climbing, and they forced me up, higher and higher, the gauze of my skirt catching on branches, until we reached their tree house, a rickety box with one window that framed the moon. Two boys squirmed around me to climb in first. They lit a stinking kerosene lantern that sat on a milk crate. They flashed their knives at me. One of the boys prodded my butt with a stick and said, "Get in." I climbed up into the creaky orange glow of the tree house.

Five Wilds surrounded me with glares and grimaces. A cat poked its white head through the window and stared at me. Birds fluttered and fussed in the branches.

"Give Ben the signal," said the biggest boy in the room, whose name, I think, was Tim. "He knows how to deal with spies."

"Spies?" I said.

"Shut up. Don't talk. You're on our property."

One of the boys opened an old medicine cabinet that was mounted on the wall beside the window. Inside were several ordinary light switches and a doorbell. He pressed the doorbell.

"What are you?" said the little Wild, staring dreamily at my crown.

"Shut up," said Tim. "Don't speak to the prisoner. She's got to be interrogated."

Something heavy jumped in the branches then and shook the tree house. A flashlit mask of a wolfman appeared at the window, sputtering with evil cackles. He was copying somebody on television, though I couldn't quite place the laugh.

"What have we here?" said the wolfman. "A princess?"

Two boards beneath the window opened and the wolfman squeezed through a primitive secret door. He closed the narrow door behind him and stood before me in karate pants and a black bathrobe too big for his skinny body. He wore no shirt under the robe, and a live garter snake twirled around his pimply neck. I thought I knew which Wild he was but I couldn't quite remember the face under the mask. He sat on an overturned plastic bucket, elbows on his knees, and gazed down at me through his mask, a cheap Halloween thing with molded plastic hair. The wolfman had a silly widow's peak, a hard fat beard, and vampire fangs that looked like buck teeth.

I sat on the floor, feeling dizzy in the press of boys. They smelled of stale biscuits and fermented grass. Their hair was oily, and Kool-Aid stains darkened their greedy mouths.

"We'll have to search her," said the wolfman, plucking a cigarette from his robe pocket. There was a small mouth hole in the mask, and the wolfman inserted his cigarette into it. His brothers licked their lips as they watched him light it with a silver lighter. The wolfman took an awkward puff.

"Gimme one," said the little Wild, but no one paid him any attention.

"She's got something hidden under her skirt," said the wolfman, pointing with his cigarette at one of my secret pockets.

They stuck their filthy, gnarled hands into the soft film of my skirts, snatching my treasures from me: my lipsticks, my notebook, my voodoo doll of mean old drunk Mrs. Bickle. The wolfman tried to read the notebook, but he couldn't understand my special language. He pulled objects from my purple pouch and picked through my magic things.

"Quit squirming," hissed Tim, pinching my nape, looking for the nerve that would paralyze me.

The wolfman examined my amulet for night flying, a big gold medallion with a luna moth Shrinky-Dinked to the front. He opened my power locket and dumped the red powder onto the floor. I think he was smirking under the mask. His eyes gleamed, wet and meaty behind the dead plastic.

He found my love potion buried deep in the pouch, wrapped in a gauzy violet scarf, and held the soft bundle in his palm, squeezing it and cocking his head. Slowly, he unraveled it. He examined the perfume bottle in the lamplight, mouthing the word on the label: *Poison*. I don't think he understood that it was the name of a perfume. And the sight of this word, printed so precisely on an old-fashioned bottle filled with dark algae-green liquid, as though packaged by goblins, must have unsettled him. Poison was my mother's perfume. When she dabbed it on her pulse points, she made a mean face in the mirror, as though going out into the night to kill. The summer after my brother died, I'd seen my mother flee a noisy neighborhood party to rush into the arms of a strange man; they'd fallen into uncut grass. The man had moaned as though he'd been poisoned.

Now the wolfman unscrewed the cap. My love potion filled the tree house with goats and tortured lilies. He shuddered and put the cap back on and turned his wet eyes away. His brothers groaned. According to the ancient recipe, just smelling the potion was dangerous, though I'd had to make substitutions with modern ingredients, and I knew this had weakened the brew.

"That smell," said the wolfman, turning to look at me. "It made me gag."

"It won't hurt you," I said. "It's not really poison."

"Make her eat it then," said the brother with the cowlick and bulldog eyes.

I tried to squirm away but the Wilds were on me, this time binding my wrists with fishing line. The wolfman knelt near me, holding the bottle in his fist. I could smell his scalp. The snake on his neck lifted its head to look at me and opened its velvety pink mouth. Its fangs were too little to see, but I could imagine them—clear as diamonds, wet and sparkling sharp. The wolfman daubed a green droplet on his fingertip and pushed it toward my lips.

"Lick it," he said. "If it's not poison."

I turned my face away, and the Wilds pressed around me, flashing their knives and grunting.

"Lick it, lick it, lick it," they chanted.

My tongue felt parched and gross. It slithered out and tasted the drop. I closed my eyes to block their faces from my mind and tried not to swallow. I would hold the poison in my mouth and spit it out when they let me go. I thought of Brian, reclining in his lawn chair, but the image of the wolfman billowed up in my head. Hunched in his bathrobe, laughing his midnight-TV laugh, he staggered through the twisted branches.

⁜

I kept away from the Wilds after that and did not spy on them and grew two inches and learned how to talk to birds. My father had ordered a Xeroxed copy of a book so ancient that a library in England had to keep it in a special tank. This book was full of useful information: how to communicate with animals, how to make your own cough medicine, how to keep the devil from visiting your bed at night. It also contained love potions, but when I came to these passages I skipped over them with a beating heart. When school started, I spent hours in fluorescent-lit classrooms, breathing disinfectant and chalk and the smell of warm, young bodies shut up. Two groups of girls wanted me as a friend, and I jumped between them, keeping my independence. Ben Wild was two grades ahead of me. At school he ran with bad boys and lurked under stairwells and slipped off to McDonald's for lunch. Sometimes I saw him slinking down the hall in the silent in-school suspension line, guarded by Mrs. Beard, a mammoth woman with a face like a sunburned fist.

Ben had a thick, pubic unibrow, and his mother couldn't keep his black curls tamed. Tucked into the nest of his hair was a strange acne-scarred face with glowing green eyes and slick, pimento-red lips. Sometimes we locked eyes at school. He'd laugh at me and say, sarcastically, "There goes the fairy princess." He was always making nasty remarks to his friends. People whispered that his mother was pregnant again—with twins, triplets, quadruplets, quintuplets, sextuplets. They invented terms for outlandish broods, like *megaduplets*, and referred to the Wild boys as "the litter," "the pack," or "the swarm."

In health class we watched creepy, outdated films on lice, scabies, menstruation, scoliosis, and drug mania. I saw cartoon bugs burrowing under the soft skins of children, leaving red maps of infection. I saw pretty girls transform into twisted, tragic creatures who hobbled down school hallways in back braces. I saw hippie chicks dance ecstatically in throbbing psychedelic light, only to hurl themselves out of windows. Womanhood was bound up with disease. Ecstasy led to bashed-open skulls and the apocalyptic wail of police sirens. Parasites lurked everywhere: little bloodsuckers hopping into your hair; big perverts with candy and needles. But the disease of puberty had already touched me. My right nipple swelled and turned darker, while my left was still small and pink. My mother laughed when I asked for a bra, and my deformity was visible beneath three shirts.

One day Ben Wild called me Cyclops. The name spread through our school like lice. I vowed revenge and took to my spell books and started watching the Wild house again.

I learned that Brian had an older girlfriend from the neighborhood, a dental hygienist, which was fine with me because I didn't love him anymore. I learned that the rumors were true. Mrs. Wild was pregnant. And she had a nervous breakdown every Wednesday evening after picking up three of her sons from midget football practice and allowing them to gorge on ice cream. I learned that Mr. Wild sometimes lingered in his car for thirty minutes before venturing into the house. And most important, from the chatter of his brothers, I learned that Ben wore his wolfman mask every month on the night of the full moon.

I had several theories: Ben fantasized about being a wolfman; Ben had told his little brothers, years ago, that he was a wolfman, and he kept up his ruse to control them with fear; Ben donned the wolfman mask as some kind of deep, ironic joke. But no one in his family seemed afraid of the wolfman mask. While out in their yard his brothers never said much about it, simply commenting, in September, when the full moon came, that it was "wolf night" again. And Ben went about his activities as though everything were normal: taking out the garbage, bumming cigarettes from Brian, shooting hoops with Tim.

In October a hurricane swept through our town. Before the storm I saw Ben in his backyard, standing in the weird sulfurous light with wind whipping through his hair. Something flickered through me, and I wanted to join him, to snuggle in the hectic, stinking warmth of the Wild pack. But Mama screamed out the back door, and I ran inside our lonely house. Daddy made us sit in the pantry, where he told stories of green knights and enchanted ladies as Mama rolled her eyes and the storm lashed at our roof. My father was getting plump. His pale, clammy skin sometimes broke out into rashes. I knew all of his stories, word by word. I knew every sarcastic phrase in my mother's repertoire, and the contents of her closet no longer fascinated me. I was sick of my parents' faces and hungry for new life. Into the dark blinking windows of my dreams, Wild boys would sometimes scramble. They'd run howling through our house, kicking over end tables and smearing mud on our wall-to-wall carpet. They'd tear doors off hinges and let night storms fly through our house.

Our power was out for four days. Houses glowed with candlelight. Children ruled the dark chaos, and the Wild boys prowled the battered neighborhood with guns and knives. On the third day Tim Wild came to our back door and told us his parents were having a cookout. Their freezer of meat was going to go bad; the whole block was invited.

It was a warm day and autumn mange patched the ragged trees. Smells of charred meat floated through the neighborhood; a million gnats had hatched in the muggy air. It was weird to see Mr. Wild out in daylight, cooking on their rusty grill, so tall, so skinny and pale, his shiny square of hair gone bristly like the coat of a dog. He hunched over the spitting meat, grinning with long teeth. He wore glasses. His ancient jogging suit had faded to a strange purple, and sweat dripped from the stubbled point of his chin. Children whispered that he was too smart to talk, that nothing he said made sense, that he had false teeth and a robot eye and a creepy vampire accent. His wife looked worn-out, fussing with paper napkins that kept blowing all over the yard, mustard stains blotting her massive poly-knit bosom. The boys looked exactly like Mr. Wild. Children said he'd planted his evil clones directly into her belly, and now another one was growing down in the warm, dark wet.

The Wild boys looked like they hadn't bathed since the storm, and they ran around the yard with gristly bones in their fists. They had been gobbling meat all day, and their mouths were slick with blood and grease. They'd darkened their faces with charcoal. They whizzed through the treetops; their heads popped up from secret holes. Immune to their mother's screams, they cackled and smacked, lunged at heaped platters, stabbed morsels of flesh with the tips of their knives. White cats jumped on the picnic table and carried whole pork chops into the trees.

There was nothing to eat but meat and white bread that turned to pure sugar when it hit your spit. There were no forks left. I fixed myself a plate and took it to Brian's lawn chair. I had a blistered wienie and a steak, black on the outside but raw and oozing inside. I had a hot dog bun infested with ice. I ate the steak with my hands, and warm blood dripped down my throat. Gnats landed on my cheeks to lick sweat with their invisible tongues. I ate more meat: crumbly, dry hamburger and fatty pork loin and chunks of bitter liver; gamy lamb and slippery lumps of veal. I gnawed at the stubborn tendons of turkey legs and savored sausage that melted like candy on my tongue. I nibbled minute quail with edible skeletons and sucked tender feathers of flesh from roasted ribs. The sky flushed pink and I ate as the boiling sun sank. I ate until my paper plate dissolved in my hands. When I finally came out of my cannibal trance, the moon was up, rolling like a carcass on the spit of its axis. And Ben Wild was staring at me through the sliding glass door that led to his brother's den. He was wearing his wolfman mask, as I should have expected, though I'd forgotten all about the full moon, and he startled me with his goofy monster face.

Adults murmured near the dying grill. They were drinking beer. My mother's sarcastic laughter drifted across the sea of withering honeysuckle, and I knew my father had already skulked home to bed. I peered through the door of the den and saw shapes moving in candlelight. A boy barked. The door slid open all by itself, and I suspected that one of the Wilds had pulled it with a string. Or maybe the little smart-asses had rigged up something more complicated.

I walked into the room and the door closed. There were animals in there, filtering the air with their strange lungs, pumping out musk and farts. Ben sat on a small velour couch in the corner, wearing his karate ensemble. A ferret dozed on his neck. White cats eyed the weaselly beast as they slunk around. Three Wild boys stalked the room with knives, obsessed with being near their older brother. They'd made a pile of bones on Brian's dresser. Candles flickered on the floor, bleeding wax onto ancient shag. I took a deep breath of moldy air.

"Where's Brian?" I asked.

"With his girlfriend," said Ben, and his brothers snorted and made kissing noises.

"We're taking over his room," said Tim. He threw his knife at a cat and metal clattered against the dark paneled wall.

"I've got to go," I said, though it would have hurt me to leave the room.

"Wait," said Ben. "I wanted to tell you something."
"What?"

"Get out of here, you assholes," he said.

"Make us," said Tim.

Ben stood up, and the boys ran toward a corner. In the dark, I could just make out a flight of steps with a wrought-iron banister. The brothers crawled up and down the stairs, neither leaving nor staying, snickering and coughing and slapping each other. The ferret leaped from Ben's shoulder and slithered under the bed.

"I wanted to tell you I was sorry about the thing, you know," Ben whispered. "The name I called you. I didn't mean for it to get around like it did."

"Whatever," I said. My cyclopean breast burned above my mortified heart. I pulled my jean jacket tightly around me. "Forget it. Don't say another word about it."

The wolfman's stupid expression didn't change, but his eyes, wet behind the plastic, fluttered over my chest.

"I was just having a bad week," he said. "You don't have any brothers or sisters, do you?"

I told him I didn't.

"You're lucky," he said. "All that privacy. Sometimes I think I'm going crazy. They never leave me alone. But when Brian goes to college next year, I'm moving down here."

"It's a cool room," I said. "You can come and go whenever you want."

"Yeah," he said. "Want a cigarette?" He pulled a pack of Marlboros from his robe pocket. He made room for me on the couch and I sat down. The couch was small and I could feel his body, hot beside me. I could smell the dark yellow musk of the ferret that had been sprawling on his neck. When I leaned in to light my cigarette, I caught the tang of wine on Ben's breath, and I wanted to drink wine too, from a silver goblet, deep in the secret tunnels the Wild boys had dug under the ground, or high in the treetops, where clouds oozed through prickly branches.

"Give me some wine," I said.

"What?" The wolfman cocked his head.

"I smell it, and I want some."

"No problem." He produced a jug from a laundry basket overflowing with dirty socks.

We sat drinking wine and smoking. White cats paced. We didn't speak, and a beautiful, sweet evil grew between us.

"How deep do your tunnels go?" I whispered to him.

"To hell," he said and laughed his television laugh. "One of these days I'm going to take my little brothers down there and sell them to the devil."

On the staircase a Wild boy gasped, but the others giggled.

"I wish I had brothers—or sisters."

"Oh no." Ben shook his head. "You don't."

"I do. At night, when my parents fall asleep in their chairs, I feel so lonely I wish a spaceship would swoop down and kidnap me."

"I feel exactly the same way." Ben's voice broke. He cleared his throat. "Only worse, more desperate, with a swarm of little gnats always bothering me. And my mother . . . sometimes she calls me Brian, sometimes Tim. I know it's just a slip of the tongue, but still. And now she's going to have another one."

His eyes rolled behind the plastic and I felt the damp meat of his palm resting on my hand. Our fingers intertwined and the air pulsed around my ears. This was what it was like to hold hands with a boy. I'd never done it before. There was a film of sweat between our palms and the position I was frozen in felt uncomfortable.

The sliding glass door opened by itself, and the smell of dying charcoal drifted in from the night. The full moon hung over the Bickles' rotten roof, spilling its silver.

"Where are all the parents?" I asked, but Ben didn't answer me. He dropped my hand and let out a deep moan that made my stomach clench. He shot up from the couch and staggered around on the carpet, fingering his wolfman mask and groaning. Ben Wild fell to his knees. He lifted his head to the moon and barked. Then an ancient, afflicted howl rocked through his body and ripped the quiet night open.

He clambered around on all fours, trotting toward me, growling and spitting, and I wanted to dissolve into the couch. He sniffed my sneakers and licked my left ankle and whimpered like a dog. I was wondering if I should run or try to pet him, when he stood up and loomed over me, the air behind him darkening as a cloud passed over the moon. He shook with demented laughter. Then the night went white, and he tore the mask from his face.

His brothers shrieked and clambered to the top of the stairs. A door slammed, and I knew that I was alone with the wolfman, with all his fury and frustration.

Ben's acne had broken into bloom. His face glowed with an eerie bluish luster, and I thought that maybe his father had brought nuclear radiation home in his clothes. Zits swarmed like fire ants on Ben's brow. Purple pimples glistened like drops of jelly on his cheeks. Fat whiteheads nestled behind the wings of his nose. Only his eyes and lips had escaped the infection.

Ben sat beside me, holding his mask in his hands. "The moon controls the tides," he said, "and brings poison boiling to the surface of my skin. But tomorrow I'll be a normal boy again. I swear."

I didn't know what to say. Some of his pimples were seeping yellow drops.

"The family curse." Ben winced. "My father had it, and his father before him. Whoever gets it always ends up having lots of sons." He rolled his eyes again and forced a laugh. A complex blush lit up his zits.

He took my hand and I let him hold it. His hand looked completely normal, warm and smooth and brown, pretty enough to bite. I could feel the moon licking at my skin with its magnetic light. I wondered if it was true that the moon moved the blood of women. I wondered if mysterious clocks, ancient and new, had started to tick within me. Ben leaned toward me. I threw my head back and vamped for his kiss. I'd spent a hundred nights dressed up in gowns and makeup, kissing stuffed animals, and my lips felt fat and sweet. But the hot suction cup of his mouth hit my throat, and he bit me, digging his braces into the soft skin of my neck. When I swatted him off, he laughed like a hoodlum and scratched his chin.

"I'm a wolfman," he said sarcastically, as though that explained everything. He shrugged and lit a cigarette.

Through the stinging wound on my neck, Ben's slobber trickled into my bloodstream. I waited. I felt a slight burn when the poison hit my heart. Acid rose to the back of my throat. The taste of dead animals filled my mouth. Wild hope and withering despair tainted the meat, the craziness of animals shut up. The poison was in my body now, changing me, making me stronger and meaner.

I reached for Ben's cheek and stroked a mass of oily bumps. My fingertips drifted along his jawbone and tickled the triangular patch of downy skin under his chin. He closed his eyes like a lizard in a trance and swallowed. I pressed my lips to his neck. I tried not to laugh as I licked the tendon that ran from his collarbone toward his jaw. Ben groaned and grabbed my elbow. His ears smelled like cinnamon. When I stuck my tongue into the silky cranny beneath his left earlobe, he bucked. I could feel the pulsing of intricate muscles and secret glands. I could feel veins throbbing with fast blood.

Finding the spot I'd been searching for, I gnawed it gently until breaking the skin and tasting copper. Then I bit him harder with my small, sharp, spit-glazed teeth.

Regeneration at Mukti

C all me a trendmonger, but I've sprung for a tree house. My bamboo pod hovers among galba trees, nestled in jungle with views of the sea, the porch strung with hemp hammocks. A flowering vine snakes along the railings, pimping its wistful perfume. With a single remote control, I may adjust the ceiling fans, fine-tune the lighting, or lift the plate-glass windows, which flip open like beetles' wings. My eco-friendly rental has so many amenities, but my favorite is the toilet: a stainless basin that whisks your droppings through a pipe, down into a pit of coprophagous beetles. These bugs, bred to feast on human shit, have an enzyme in their gut that makes their dung the best compost on the planet—a humus so black you'd think it was antimatter. The spa uses it to feed the orchids in the Samsara Complex. As visitors drift among the blossoms, we may contemplate the life cycle, the transformation of human waste into ethereal petals and auras of scent.

"Orchids are an aphrodisiac," said a woman at lunch today, her *unagi* roll breaking open as she crammed it into her mouth, spilling blackish clumps of eel. She had crow's feet, marionette lines around her mouth, a porn star's enhanced lips.

"Yes," said a man in a sky-blue kimono, "I think I read something about that on the website."

"They have orchid *dondurma* on the menu," I said, scanning the man's face: budding eye bags, sprays of gray at his temples, the gouge of a liver line between his brown eyes. I placed him in his early forties.

"Fruit-sweetened," he said, "fortified, I believe, with raw mare's milk, if you do dairy."

"Colostrum," I said. "Mostly goat. But I don't ingest sweeteners or juices, only whole fruits."

"My philosophy on dairy," said the woman, waving her chopstick like a conductor, "is that milk is an infant's food. I weaned myself ten years ago." Her lush bosom actually heaved, hoisted by the boning of a newfangled corset.

For some reason (maybe it was the way the woman shook her dead blond hair like a vixen in a shampoo commercial), I found myself smirking at the man over the centerpiece of sculpted melon. I found myself wondering what he'd look like after completing the Six Paths of Suffering. I couldn't help but picture him shirtless, reclining on a rock beside one of the island's famous waterfalls, his skin aglow from deep cellular regeneration and oxygenation of the hypodermis.

"I'm Red," he said. And he was: flushed along his neck and cheeks, the ripe pink of a lizard's pulsing throat.

☙

The powers that be at Mukti—those faceless organizers of regeneration—have designed the spa so that Newbies don't run into Crusties much. We eat separately, sleep in segregated clusters of cottages, enjoy our dips in the mud baths and mineral pools, our yoga workshops and leech therapy sessions, at different times. As Gobind Singh, our orientation guru, pointed out, "the face of rebirth is the mask of death." But this morning, as I walked the empty beach in a state of above-average relaxation, I spotted my first Crusty crawling from the sea.

Judging by the blisters, the man was in the early stages of Suffering. I could still make out facial features twitching beneath his infections. He had the cartoonish body of a perennial weight-lifter, his genitals compressed in the Lycra sling of a Speedo. He nodded at me and dove back into the ocean.

I jogged up the trail that curls toward my tree house. In the bathroom, I examined my face. I studied familiar lines and folds, pores and spots, ruddy patches and fine wrinkles, not to mention a general ambient sagging that's especially detectable in the morning.

Out beyond the Lotus Terrace, the ocean catches the pink of the dying sun. A mound of seaweed sits before me, daubed with pomegranate chutney and pickled narcissus. My waitress is plain, as all the attendants are: plump cheeks and brown skin, hair tucked into a white cap, eyebrows impeccably groomed. Her eyes reveal nothing. Her mouth neither smiles nor bends with the slightest twist of frown. I'm wondering how they train them so well, to be almost invisible, when a shadow darkens my table.

"Hi," says the man from yesterday. "May I?"

"Red, right? Please."

The bags under his eyes look a little better. His hair is losing its sticky sheen. And his bottom lip droops, making his mouth look adorably crooked.

"Just back from leech therapy." He grins. "Freaky to have bloodsuckers clamped to my face, but it's good for fatty orbital herniation and feelings of nameless dread."

We laugh. Red orders a green mango salad with quinoa fritters and mizuna-wrapped shad roe. We decide to share a bottle of island Muscador. We drink and chat and the moon pops out, looking like a steamed clam.

Though Red is a rep for Clyster Pharmaceuticals, he's into holistic medicine, thinks the depression racket is a capitalist scam, wishes he could detach himself from the medical-industrial complex. I try to explain my career path (human-computer interaction consulting), how the subtleties of creative interface design have worn me out.

"It's like I can feel the cortisol gushing into my system," I say. "A month ago, I didn't have these frown lines."

"You still look youngish," says Red.

"Thanks." I smile, parsing the difference between *young* and *youngish*. "You too."

Red nods. "It's not that I'm vain. It's more like a state of general depletion. The city has squeezed the sap out of me."

"And life in general takes its nasty toll."

"Boy does it." Red offers the inscrutable smile of an iguana digesting a fly.

I don't mention my divorce, of course, or my relocation to a sun-deprived city that requires vitamin-D supplementation. I pass the wine and our fingertips touch. I imagine kissing him, forgetting that in two weeks we'll both be covered in weeping sores.

✳

I've opened my tree house to the night—windows cranked, jungle throbbing. My heart rate's up from Ashtanga yoga. A recent dye job has brightened my hair with a strawberry-blond, adolescent luster. Wineglass in hand, I pace barefooted. Red sits on my daybed, his face feral with a five-day beard, lips so pink I've already licked them to test for cosmetics.

He's rolling a globule of sap between thumb and index finger. Now he's inserting the resin into the bowl of his water pipe. And we take another hit of *ghoni*, distillate of the *puki* bloom, a small purple fungus flower that grows from tree-frog dung. We drift out onto the porch and fall into an oblivion of kissing.

We shed our clothes, leaving tiny mounds on the bamboo planks. Red's penis sways in the humid air. Shaggy-thighed, he walks toward the bedroom, where vines creep through the windows, flexing like tentacles in the ocean breeze.

He reclines and smiles, his forehead only faintly lined in the glow of Himalayan salt lamps. We've been hanging out religiously for the past seven days, are addicted, already, to each other's smells. Every night at dinner we begin some delirious conversation that always brings us back to my tree house, toking up on *ghoni*, chattering into the night. Earlier, discussing the moody rock bands that moved us in our youths, we discovered that we attended the same show twenty-seven years ago. Somehow we'd both been bewitched by a band of sulky middle-aged men with dyed black hair who played broody, three-chord pop. Now we can't stop laughing about how gravely we scowled at them from the pit, in gothic costumes bought at the mall.

We've already been infected. Each of us received the treatment two days ago, Red at eleven, me at three. We met for a lunch of shrimp ceviche between appointments.

All week long, Lissa, the lactose-free blond, has been chattering about the Hell Realm, wondering, as we all are, when our affliction will begin. She's the kind of person whose head will explode unless she opens her mouth to release every half-formed thought. Her perfume, derived from synthetic compounds, gives me sinus headaches. Just as I suspected, she's an actress. I'm almost positive she has fake tits. Even though Red and I beam out a couple vibe, huddled close over menus and giggling, she has no problem plopping down next to him, lunging at the shy man with her mammary torpedoes. And he always laughs at her lame jokes.

This afternoon I have a mild fever and clouds stagnate over the sea. The meager ocean breeze smells fishy. I feel like a fool for ordering the monkfish stew, way too pungent for this weather. And Lissa won't stop gloating over her beef kabobs. Red, sunk in silence, keeps scratching his neck. I'm about to exhale, a long moody sigh full of turbulent messages, when Lissa reaches over her wine flute to poke Red's temple with a mauve talon.

"Look," she says, "bumps."

I see them: a spattering of hard, red zits. Soon they'll grow fat with juice. They'll burst and scab over, ushering in the miracle of subcutaneous regeneration.

"And my neck itches." Red toys with his collar.

According to the orientation materials distributed by Guru Gobind Singh, the Hell Realm is different for everyone, depending on how much hatred and bitterness you have stored in your system. All that negativity, stashed deep in your organic tissues, will come bubbling to the surface of your human form. The psychosomatic filth of a lifetime will hatch, breaking through your skin like a thousand minuscule volcanoes spitting lava.

"Time for my mineral mud bath," says Red. And now I see what I did not see before: a row of incipient cold sores edging his upper lip, wens forming around the delicate arch of his left nostril, a rash of protoblisters highlighting each cheekbone like subtle swipes of blusher.

The Naraka Room smells of boiled cabbage. Twelve of us squat on hemp yoga mats, stuck in crow pose. Wearing rubber gloves, Guru Gobind Singh weaves among us, pausing here and there to tweak a shoulder or spine.

According to the pamphlet, Gobind Singh has been through the Suffering twice, without the luxury of gourmet meals, around-the-clock therapies, and hands-on guidance from spiritual professionals. Legend has it that he endured the Hell Realm alone in an isolated tree house. Crumpled in the embryo pose for weeks, he unfurled his body only to visit the crapper or eat a bowl of mung beans. His skin's as smooth as the metalized paint that coats a fiberglass mannequin. His body's a bundle of singing muscles. When he walks, he hovers three millimeters off the ground—you have to look carefully to detect his levitational power, but, yes, you can see it: the bastard floats.

I can't help but hate him. After all, this is the Hell Realm and hatred festers within me. My flesh seethes with blisters. My blood suppurates. My heart is a ball of boiling puss. As I balance on my forearms, I tabulate acts of meanness foisted against me over the decades. I tally betrayals, count cruelties big and small. I trace hurts dating back to elementary school—decades before my first miscarriage, way before my bulimic high school years, long before Dad died and my entire family moved into that shitty two-bedroom apartment. I recede deeper into the past, husking layers of elephant skin until I'm soft and small, a silken worm of a being, vulnerable as a drop of dew quivering on a grass blade beneath the summer sun.

"Reach into the core of your misery," says Gobind Singh, "and you will find a shining pearl."

The pamphlet, *Regeneration at Mukti*, features a color photo of a pupa dangling from a leaf on the cover. Inside is an outline of the bodily restoration process. My treatment has borne fruit. I suffer (oh, how I suffer!) from the following: urushiol-induced dermatitis (poison oak rash), dermatophytosis (ringworm), type-I herpes simplex (cold sores), cercarial dermatitis (swimmer's itch), herpes zoster (shingles), and trichinosis (caused by intramuscular roundworms). Using a blend of cutting-edge nanotechnology and gene therapy, combined with homeopathic and holistic approaches, the clinicians of Mukti have transmitted controlled pathogens into my body through oils, funguses, bacteria, viruses, and parasites. As skilled therapists work to reroute my mind-body networks to conduct more positive flows, my immune system is tackling an intricate symphony of infections, healing my body on the deepest subcellular levels: banishing free radicals, clearing out the toxic accumulation of lipofuscins, reinstalling hypothalamus hormones, and replacing telomeres to revitalize the clock that directs the life span of dividing cells.

I itch so much that I want to scrub my body with steel wool. I want to roll upon a giant cheese grater. I'd love to flay myself and be done with the mess. According to the pamphlet, however, not only does scratching interfere with the healing process, but the mental discipline required to refrain from scratching strengthens the chakra pathways that enhance positive mind-body flow.

❦

I have a beautiful dream in which I'm rolling in a patch of briars. I worm my naked body against thorns, writhe ecstatically in nests of prickly vines. I cry out, convulsing with the sweet sting of pleasure. I wake before dawn, pajamas stuck to my skin.

For me, consciousness is nothing but the seething tides of itchiness, hunger, and thirst, a vague sex drive nestled deep in the misery. I live like an animal from minute to minute, appointment to appointment, meal to meal.

Morning: a bowl of oats with flaxseeds and blueberries, followed by a kelp bath and castor-oil massage. After that: a cabbage poultice administered by experts, who then slather my body with shea butter and wrap it in sea-soaked silk. Before lunch I must descend into the bowels of the Samsara Complex for blood work and nanotech nuclear restructuring. Then a lunch of raw vegetables and fermented organ meats, kombucha with *goji* and spirulina.

Postlunch I do a volcanic-mud bath, then hydrate with a goat-milk-and-basil soak. Next comes a green-tea sensory-deprivation session, then Kundalini yoga with Gobind Singh. Staggering from this mind-fuck, I head straight for the Samsara Complex for stem-cell work and injections of Vita-Viral Plus. Then a light coconut-oil massage and I'm good to go.

❧

At supper I'm startled by Red's appearance. Yes, I've been monitoring his Incrustation. But I wasn't prepared for the new purple swellings around his eyes, or the dribbling boils on his chin. Ditto the lip cankers and blepharitis. Of course I'm aware of my own hideousness. Of course I recoil each time I see my face in the mirror (think rotted plums and Spam). And the itching is a constant reminder of my state. Nevertheless, deep in the core of my being, I feel unscathed, as though the process were happening to someone else.

Though Red and I haven't touched each other in weeks, we eat together most nights, fresh from soothing therapies and tipsy on our allotment of organic, sulfite-free wine. We have about an hour until the itching becomes unbearable, then we slink off to our respective tree houses.

※

Tonight we're enjoying the fugu sashimi with pickled dandelion greens. The humidity hovers around fifty-five percent, great for our raw skin. And the ocean looks like pounded pewter. Though we're both disgusting—it's as if we're mummy-wrapped in putrid flesh—our real selves remain tucked down under the meat costumes.

"I was thinking about the hot springs," says Red. "Since our infections seem to be stabilizing."

"Quite a hike," I say. "It'd be hell on our swollen feet."

"You can do the whole trip on an ATV."

"What?" says Lissa, who's hovering over our table, wearing a full-body catsuit of black spandex, only a few square inches of her polluted flesh visible through eye and mouth holes.

"I wanna go," she says, sitting down on the other side of Red. "I hear the springs help with collagen reintegration."

"And improving the flow between throat and brow chakras," says Red, smiling idiotically.

"Really?" says Lissa. "The third-eye chakra? Cool."

A waitress appears. Lissa orders *kway teow* with fermented beef. The patio's getting crowded. The music's lame, all synthesized sitars and tabla drum machines. But Red bobs his head in time to the tunes. And Lissa slithers up next to him, gazes raptly at a pic on his iPhone.

"That's you?" she shrieks.

"That's me."

"A mullet. No way!"

"It's an alternative mullet, not a redneck mullet."

"Let's not mince hairs," quips Lissa.

"Ha! Ha! Ha!" cries Red.

And then Lissa flounces off to the bathroom, but not without tousling his hair.

"God." I take a sip of water. "She's dumb."

"She's not as stupid as she puts on," says Red.

"What does that mean?"

"You know, the whole ingénue act."

"She's got to be at least thirty-eight."

"Chronologically, maybe, but not biologically."

I want to drill Red for a more precise number—does she look thirty-two? twenty-six? nineteen?—but I don't. I grab my purse, a practical satchel that slumps on the table beside Lissa's glittering clutch.

"Don't go," says Red. "I haven't swilled my allotment of vino yet."

"Sorry." I manufacture a yawn. "I'm sleepy."

I weave through the tables without looking back, skirt the rock garden, and stomp down the jungle trail. Deep in the forest, male Kibi monkeys howl, adolescents looking for mates. The small nocturnal monkeys spend their days dozing in the hollows of trees, but at night they hunt for insects and baby frogs. They eat their weight in fruit, sip nectar from flowers, sing complex songs that throb with vitality and longing.

⚘

After a four-mile ATV jaunt, Red and I finally steep neck-deep in a steaming spring. Though Lissa invited herself along, I scheduled our jaunt for a Tuesday after lunch, well aware of her strenuous nanotech routine.

For the first time in weeks, the itch has left me, and my body flexes, supple as a flame. The hot springs stink, of course, a predictable rotten-egg funk, as sulfur dioxide leaks into the air. But it's worth it. My skin's sucking up nature's beauty mineral, strengthening its collagen bundles, improving its cellular elasticity. Plus, mist-cloaked mountains swell around us. And though Red's facial blebs have started to ooze, he radiates boyish optimism.

"Look what I brought." He smiles, leaning out of the pool to dig through his rucksack. "Sparkling apple cider. Organic. Though I forgot glasses."

"That's okay. We can swig from the bottle."

"Exchange HSV-1 fluids?"

"And ecthymic bacteria."

"Ugh."

We sit in the mystical vapor, sipping cider and touching toes. The haze softens the hideousness of our faces. Our voices dart like birds in a cloud. We talk about Red's ex-wife, whose weakness for fey hipster boys is partially responsible for his sojourn at Mukti. I tell him about my money-obsessed ex-husband, who once updated his stock portfolio while I was in the throes of a miscarriage. I could see his reflection in the bathroom mirror of our hotel room in Bali as he sat in the other room, smirking over his iPhone. And then I heard him talking to his broker on the phone.

"I'm sorry," says Red.

"I'm over it."

I find his hand under the water. We sit floating in a state of semicontentment. Then we start up with the cider again.

Exceeding our daily allotment of alcohol, we drink until the bottle is empty and the effervescence inside us matches that of the bubbly springs. A plane flies over. The sun pops out to infuse our mist shroud with a pearly glow. And then, emerging from the steam as though from another dimension, clad in dingy cutoff shorts, a man steps into the pool. By all appearances, he's not a patient. His skin has photo-aged into a crinkled rind. He's got senile cataracts and wisps of long gray hair. And when he cracks a smile, we see a wet flash of gums, like a split in a leathery desert fruit.

"I have company today," he says, his New England accent tinged with a Caribbean patois. "I'm Winter." He extends a gnarled hand. I'm thinking he must be an ancient hippie who retired here before Mukti took off.

"You folks up from the spa, I reckon." He sinks down into the pool.

"How'd you guess?" says Red, and the old man chuckles.

"And you?" I say.

"I'm from around. Got a little cottage up over the way."

Winter tells us he keeps goats, sells cheese and yogurt to Mukti, plus fruit from his orchard and assorted herbs. He asks us how the healing's going. Inquires about the new post office. Wonders what's up with the pirates who've been plaguing the Venezuelan coast.

"Pirates?" says Red.

According to the old man, pirates, who usually stick to freighters, have recently drifted up to fleece Caribbean cruise ships.

"Thought I heard something about yachts getting hassled near Grenada," Winter says.

"This is the first we've heard about any pirates," I say, imagining eye-patched marauders, dark ships flying skull-and-crossbones flags.

"Probably just talk," says Winter.

Red checks his watch, says our soak has exceeded the recommended span by four and a half minutes. We say goodbye to Winter, speed off on our ATV.

❦

Seventy-five percent humidity, and the boils on my inner thighs have fused and burst, trickling a yellow fluid. My neck pustules are starting to weep. Choice ecthymic sores have turned into ulcers. I spend my downtime pacing the tree house naked. I shift from chair to chair, daybed to hammock, listening to the demented birds. A plague of small green finches has invaded the island. They flit through the brush, squawk, and devour berries.

This morning I've neglected my therapies. I'm due for nanotech restructuring in thirty minutes, and the thought of putting on clothes, even the softest of silk kimonos, makes my skin crawl. But I do it, even though I know the fabric will be soaked by the time I get to the Samsara Complex. I slip on a lilac *kosode* and dash down the jungle trail, gritting my teeth.

I pass a few fellow Crusties. I pass a dead turtle, its belly peppered with black ants. I pass an island assistant lugging her sea-grass basket of eco-friendly cleaning chemicals. Though she, like all the assistants, is a broad, plain-faced woman, the beauty of her complexion startles me. But then I remember that in a few weeks, my sores will scab over. I'll crawl from my shell, pink and glowing as the infant Buddha. I'll jet to the mainland and buy an array of stunning clothes, get my hair cut, meet Red for one last rendezvous before we head back to our respective cities. We'll revel in our sweet, young flesh, and then—well, we'll see.

Another evening in paradise and I pick at my grilled-fig salad. The ocean is gorgeous, but what's the point? It might as well be a postcard, a television screen, a holographic stunt. Red's pissy too, grumbling over his lobster risotto. And don't get me started on Lissa.

Lissa won't shut up about the pirates. Keeps recirculating the same crap we've heard a hundred times: the pirates have attacked another Carnival cruiser; the pirates have sacked yachts as close as Martinique; the pirates have seized a cargo ship less than ten miles off the shore of our very own island. Angered by the poor resale prospects of boutique med supplies, they've tossed the freight into the sea.

"I always thought pirates were the epitome of sexy," says Lissa, crinkling her carbuncular nose at Red.

"They won't seem so sexy if you run out of Vita-Viral Plus," says Red.

"Unless you think keloid scars are the height of chic," I add.

"But medical supplies are worthless to them," whines Lissa. "What would they gain from another attack?"

"They might attack out of spite," I say.

"Mukti keeps emergency provisions in a cryogenic vault," says Lissa, "in case of hurricanes and other potential disasters."

"Or so the pamphlet boasts." Red gazes out at the ocean, where a mysterious light beam bounces across the water.

"You think they'd lie to us?" Lissa widens her enormous eyes and runs an index finger down Red's arm. She's a touchy person, I tell myself, who hugs people upon greeting and pats the hands of shy waitresses.

"I wouldn't be surprised." Red smiles at her and turns back to the sea.

Both Red and I are in the latter stages of fibroblastic contraction when the pirates seize another cargo ship. Our flesh has crisped over with full-body scabbing. We're at that crucial stage when collagen production stabilizes, when full-tissue repair and dermal remodeling kick into high gear. Although the patients can talk of little else, the powers that be at Mukti have not acknowledged the pirate incident. The powers that be have given no special security warnings. They've said nothing about waning provisions or shortages of essential meds. The therapists and medical staff carry on as usual, but I detect a general state of skittishness—sweat stains in the armpits of their white smocks, sudden jerky movements, faintly perceptible frown lines on faces hitherto blank as eggs.

Rumors spread through the spa like airborne viruses. And one day, a day of high humidity and grumbling thunder, the kind of day when your heart is a lump of obsidian and you wonder why you bothered to get out of bed at all, it becomes common knowledge that the pirates have seized a freighter that was bound for Mukti, that they're negotiating a ransom, asking a colossal sum for the temperature-sensitive cargo.

Red and I are on the Lotus Terrace eating zucchini pavé with miso sauce, waiting for poached veal. Our waitress slinks over, apologizes, tells us that the dish will be served without capers. Red and I exchange dark looks. We imagine jars of capers from Italy stacked in the belly of a cargo ship, the freighter afloat in some secret pirate cove. And deeper in the bowels of the boat, in a refrigerated vault, shelves full of biomedical supplies—time-sensitive blood products and cell cultures in high-tech packaging.

All around us, scabby patients whisper about the pirates, reaching a collective pitch that sounds like an insect swarm. Hunched in conspiratorial clusters, they flirt with scary possibilities: spoiled meds, botched stage-five healing, full-body keloid scarring, an appearance that's the polar opposite of that promised by *Regeneration at Mukti*. "Shedding your pupal casing," the pamphlet boasts, "you will emerge a shining creature, renewed in body and spirit, your cell turnover as rapid as a ten-year-old's. Skin taut, wrinkles banished, pores invisible, you will walk like a Deva in a pink cloud of light."

❦

I'm in the Samsara Complex for cellular restructuring. There's a problem with the nanobot serum. They keep rejecting vial after vial, or so I've gathered through several hissing exchanges between the biomed doc and her technicians. When Tech 1 finally shoots me up, he jabs the needle in sideways, apologizes, then stabs me again.

I stagger into the Bardo Room, where a half-dozen Crusties mill among orchids, the floor-to-ceiling windows ablaze. Nobody speaks. The endless ocean glitters beyond, a blinding queasy green. The light gives me a headache, a kernel of throbbing nausea right behind my eyes. I collapse into a Barcelona chair. My skin tingles beneath its husk. I stare down at my hands, dark with congealed blood and completely alien to me. I wonder if I should have stayed as I was— blowing serious bank on miracle moisturizers, going to yoga five times a week, dabbling in the occasional collagen injection.

Of course, it's too late to turn back now. I must focus on positive affirmation, as Guru Gobind Singh so smugly touts. I must not allow my mind to visualize a body mapped with pink puffy scars. With such an exterior, you'd be forced to hunker deep in your body, like a naked mole rat in its burrow.

Red, fresh from bee-sting therapy, joins me under the shade of a jute umbrella, our eyes protected by wraparound sunglasses. It's too hot to eat, but we order smoked calamari salads and spring rolls with mango sauce. Red's incommunicative. I'm trying to read *Zen and the Art of Aging* on my iPad, but the sun's too bright. We don't talk about the pirates. We don't talk about our impending Shedding. We don't talk about the chances of scarring, or the jaunt to the mainland we've been planning. I tell Red about the monkey I spotted from my tree-house porch last night. I try to discuss the ecological sustainability of squidding. We shoo jhunkit birds from our table and decide to order a chilled Riesling.

More and more Crusties crowd onto the patio. Waitresses hustle back and forth. They no longer inform us when some ingredient is lacking. They simply place incomplete dishes before us with a downward flutter of the eyes. Certain therapies are no longer offered—sensory deprivation and beer baths, for example—but we strive to stay positive.

Although I keep noticing suspicious changes in medical procedures, we prevent cognitive distortions from sabotaging our self-talk. When a bad thought buzzes like a wasp into the sunny garden of our thoughts, we swat the fucker and flick its crushed corpse into the flower bed. And most importantly, we spend thirty minutes a day visualizing our primary goal: successful mind-body rejuvenation and an unblemished exterior that radiates pure light.

Nevertheless, it's hard to sustain mental focus when your spring rolls lack almonds, when your wine's third-rate, when your dermis burns beneath its crust. It's hard to envision yourself floating in a bubble of celestial light when you look like you've been deep-fried. I'm having trouble picturing the crystalline features of the deity. I can't help but notice that the sea smells of sewage, that our table is sticky, that our waitresses are contemptuous, smooth-skinned and pretty in their way, with decades of insolent youth to burn. When Lissa alights at our table in a translucent white kimono, my misery is complete.

But Red only nods at her, keeps staring out at the empty sea.

I'm studying his profile when I spot a dark figure lurching from a clump of pink hibiscus. Black skin, green shorts, ammo vest. The man lugs a Kalashnikov. He's yelling in Spanish. More pirates emerge from the landscaping, waving guns and machetes. One of them screams in English: "Surrender, you scab-covered dogs!" Lanky, with a dramatic cheek scar, he tells us to put our wallets on the table, along with all iPhones, handheld gaming devices, and jewels. Other pirates randomly fire their guns into the air.

In one convulsive movement, patients start rifling through pockets and purses, removing rings and bracelets, plunking valuables onto tables. Then we sit with hands behind our backs as the bandits have instructed. We don't flinch as they rip designer sunglasses from our faces. We squint with stoicism at the sea while they fill their rucksacks with treasure. Shadows grow longer. The sun sinks. The jhunkit birds, emboldened by our immobility, descend on the tables to peck at canapés.

When the pirates finally creep off into the jungle, crouched in postures of cartoonish stealth, the waitresses spring into action. They bustle about distributing bottled water. They assure us that security has been summoned. They refill our wineglasses, wipe bird shit from our tables, spirit away our dirty plates. The sky flushes pink. Lissa trembles like a Chihuahua until Red drapes a friendly arm over her back. He's just being courteous, I tell myself, as I wait for this contact to end.

A woman weeps quietly at the edge of the patio, then she blows her nose and orders shrimp dumplings in ginger broth.

According to the pamphlet, the final days before Shedding should be days of intense relaxation—no medical procedures, no exhilarating therapies, no excursions. Even extreme dining is discouraged. It's difficult to drift like a feathery dandelion seed when Mukti's security forces have crawled out of the woodwork into our sunny paradise. They've always been here, of course, lurking in the shadows, monitoring the island from subterranean surveillance rooms, but now they loiter openly in their khaki shorts, handguns only partially concealed by oversized tropical shirts.

Yesterday, while enjoying an aloe-vera bath in the Bodhi Herb Garden, I heard a crude snicker. I gazed up through a tendril of sarsaparilla to glimpse the smirking face of a security guard. There he was, licking an ice-cream cone, his mustache dotted with pearls of milk. And now, as I float in the Neti Neti Lagoon, stuck in step two of the Instant Calming Sequence, I hear a security guard barking into her cell phone. I count to six and wait for her to finish her conversation. When I start over with a fresh round of uninterrupted breathing, her ring tone bleeps through the gentle thatch of birdsong. So I switch to Microcosmic Orbit Meditation, envisioning a snake of light slithering through my coccyx. Now the security guard is laughing like some kind of donkey. I open my eyes, gaze up into the palms, and spot a tiny camera perched next to a cluster of fruits. Its lens jerks back and forth like the head of a nervous bird.

❦

In addition to the dread of pirates charging through the bush, in addition to the distraction of security guards and the fears of type-I scarring, we must also worry about the weather, as the island's now on hurricane watch—or so the powers that be informed us this morning. The ocean breeze has become a biting sandy wind. A weird metallic scent blows off the sea, and I get the feeling that the island's swathed in bad karma. Plus, a few Crusties, having shed their husks, have been jetted to the mainland without the Rapture Ceremony—a ritual designed to reassure remaining Crusties that their golden time will come, that they too will walk in flowing robes, their silky necks garlanded with narcissus.

Yesterday afternoon, instead of gathering on the beach to watch the smooth-skinned Devas depart in the Ceremonial Boat, we crowded into the lobby of the small airport. Through a plate-glass window, we observed two Devas dashing from flower-decked golf carts toward a commuter jet, their faces shrouded by scarves and sunglasses. Security guards swarmed, their tropical shirts easy to spot. Rumor has it that one of the Devas, a famous movie star, was being whisked off to California, where she'll resume her career as romantic-comedy queen—blond icon of feminine joie de vivre, laughing in the sun.

※

Red, in the final throes of his Remodeling phase, has a TSF of 99.6 percent. His exterior has the golden huskiness of a pork rind. And now, as he scans the endless ocean, his beautiful brown eyes burn behind his scabby mask. He's barely touched his scrambled tofu. He takes long, dreamy slurps of mango smoothie. I know he'll be jetting off to the mainland soon. Once there, he won't be able to contact me by phone or e-mail, as the Mukti contract dictates, so we've made arrangements to reunite, booking reservations at the Casa Bougainvillea.

I keep picturing that moment when we'll meet by the pool at sunset. I keep picturing Red reclined beside the waterfall featured on the hotel's brochure. First he'll look startled. Then he'll smile as his eyes run up and down my body. He'll bask in the vision of a female epidermis refortified with type-III collagen and glowing like the moon. Though I haven't worn jewel tones for years, I'll highlight the infantile pallor of my skin with a scarlet sheath dress. I'll wear a choker of Burmese rubies. Dye my hair auburn, paint my nails crimson, wear lipstick the color of oxygenated blood.

After we revel in the softness of a ten-minute kiss, we'll drink Romanée-Conti under the stars.

☙

Yesterday, I stood in the airport lobby, watching Red hop from a flower-decked golf cart and then scurry through strong wind to Mukti's commuter jet. Keffiyeh-style headgear and huge sunglasses concealed his face. When he turned from the platform to wave, a shadow passed over him, and then he dipped into the jet. I have no idea how his Shedding went. I have no idea what his refurbished carnality looks like, though I've seen Facebook pics of his thirty-something self, his high school yearbook photos, a few snapshots of the young Red rock climbing in Costa Rica.

Lissa too has been spirited away—nubile and golden, I fear. Though she was obscured by a chiffon Lotus robe, I have the sick suspicion that she's gone through her Shedding unscathed. That she looks gorgeous. That she'll stalk Red at the Casa Bougainvillea, appearing naked and luminous beneath his balcony in a courtyard crammed with flowering shrubs.

And now, as the few remaining Crusties huddle in the basement of the Skandha Center, awaiting the wrath of a category-four hurricane named Ophelia, Gobind Singh lectures us on the Deceptive Singularity of the Self.

"The Self you cling to," says Gobind Singh, "is an empty No Self, or *Shunya*, for the True Self does not differentiate between Self and Other, which is not the same, of course, as the No Self."

Gobind Singh sighs and takes a long glug of spring-water, for we are the Stubborn Ones, unable to take pleasure in the Shedding of Others, greedy for our own transformation. According to Gobind Singh, the True Self must revel in the Beauty of the Devas, even if we ourselves do not attain True Radiance during this cycle, because the True Self makes no distinction between Self and Other.

According to Gobind Singh's philosophy, I should delight in the divine copulation of Red and Lissa, which is probably taking place right this second on 1,000-thread-count sheets. I should yowl with joy at the thought of their shuddering, simultaneous orgasm. I should partake in the perkiness of Lissa's ass as she darts from the bed, turning to give Red a full-frontal display before disappearing into the humongous bathroom to pee. According to Gobind Singh, their ecstasy is my ecstasy.

Glowing with self-actualization, floating a few millimeters above the bamboo flooring, Gobind Singh weaves among us. We sit in full lotus, five sullen earthbound

Crusties, slumped in our own hideousness. We fidget and pick at our flaking shells. The second the guru turns his back, we roll our eyes at each other.

And when the winds of Hurricane Ophelia pick up, shaking the building and howling fiercely enough to blot out the throbbing of electronic tablas, we can't control the fear that grips us. All we can think about is literally saving our skins. As the electricity flickers and the storm becomes a deluge, Gobind Singh tells us that all men, no matter how wretched, have a Buddha Embryo nestled inside them, gleaming and indestructible as a diamond.

❦

I wake alone in the basement of the Skandha Center, calling out in the darkness for the others. I bang my shins against their empty cots. Upstairs in the dim hallway, I discover sloughed casing, shreds of what looks like crinkled snakeskin littering the jute carpet. I pick my way toward the light. Hurricane Ophelia has shattered the floor-to-ceiling lobby windows, strewing the floor with shards of glass.

Out on the wrecked patio, windblown chairs have been smashed against the side of the building. And birdcalls whiffle through the air.

"Hello!" I yell, but no one answers.

The Samsara Complex is empty. So is the Lotus Lounge, both buildings battered by the storm.

I jog down a jungle trail toward the Moksha Jasmine Grove. There, a natural spring trickles from the lips of a stone Buddha. Pink birds flit through the garden. The statue squats in a pool, surrounded by trellises of Arabian jasmine that have miraculously survived the hurricane. Raindrops sparkle on leaves. The garden is a locus of peace and light.

From the deepest kernel of my being, I crave water. My throat's parched. My skin burns. And I know that my time has come. I feel pregnant with the glowing fetus of my future self.

I shed my robe. I step into the blue pool. I sink neck-deep into the shallow water, mimicking the pyramid structure of the seated Buddha, face-to-face with his stone form. I drink from the spring until my thirst is quenched. And then I breathe through my nose, fold my hands into a cosmic mudra. Counting each inhalation, I become one with the water.

My body is like a pool's surface, its brilliance dulled only by a skin of algae.

My body is like a fiery planet, casting off interstellar dust.

Slowly, I rub myself, chanting the Bodhisattva Vows:

I vow to liberate all beings, without number.
I vow to uproot all endless blind passions.
I vow to penetrate, beyond measure, the Dharma gates.
And the Great Way of Buddha, I vow to attain.

My casing begins to pull away. I don't look at my uncovered flesh. I squeeze my eyelids shut to avoid temptation and keep on chanting, focused on the radiance pulsing within. In my mind's eye I see a glimmer of movement, a hazy form with human limbs, a new-and-improved woman emerging from the murk—glorious and unashamed.

On the count of three, I open my eyes.

The Whipping

I n one hour and forty-five minutes my punishment will *transpire*. That's how Dad, who sits in the kitchen flicking ash on his greasy plate of pork crumbs, always says it. After putting on a rubber glove, stealing a pack of cigarettes from the snot-yellow depths of his handkerchief drawer, getting caught, insulting his cheap brand (Doral), and then hovering around the breakfast table pronouncing the similarities between the intestinal tube of liver pudding he was eating and a turd, I was told that I would receive a whipping, in my parents' bedroom, in exactly two hours.

My father, an elementary school principal who paddles kids for a living, has several lines on his résumé devoted to his whipping expertise. He's developed it into a high art form. Just last week I overheard him tell my mother about a nightmare he'd had in which an endless line of summer school delinquents stretched down the central hallway of the school, wound through the hot hell of the playground, and then snaked up the hill toward the poultry-processing plant, where the angry gong of the sun clanged over the horizon. The boys he whipped were blond Aryan imps like the children of the damned, and they taunted him with the high tinkle of their laughter. Dad finally discovered that he'd been beating them with a dead chicken, and he woke up, had a cigarette, and could not get back to sleep.

It's Saturday afternoon, and the dog breath of summer pants through the windows. Cicadas scream. T. W. Manley's go-cart keeps ripping through our backyard, where my twin brothers are boxing with the gloves Dad bought them so they won't bash each other's face in. Mom's taking a nap upstairs. My huge father hunches at the kitchen table in his red bathrobe, working on his novel about King Arthur, and I'm not allowed to say one word to him. But the best way to delay a whipping is to keep my parents angry. They won't whip us when they're mad. That would be abusive. So I creep around the table, every now and then freezing into the position of a hideously deformed mutant and flashing fake sign language. I gargle grape Kool-Aid and spit long spumes of it into the sink. Dad's trying to act mature, frowning thoughtfully, scribbling notes in the margins of his manuscript. But the knuckles of the fist grasping his pen are white.

Mom has refused to give me a home perm, which means I'll be ugly for the rest of the summer, and one of my little boobies has grown an alien lump down in it that hurts. A massive zit festers in my nose like a parasite; I've spent the morning picking at it with a needle. I shaved my legs without Mom's permission, and the tiny cuts where I sliced off my mosquito bites sting. The sour chunks of food I keep sucking from my braces symbolize something— -I'm not sure what, but it makes me think of the night Dad told me about *Turdus philomelos*, the songbird that lines its nest with mud, dung, and rotten wood. *Walling itself in a domestic prison of its own crap* was how he put it. *That could be a metaphor,* Dad said, lighting his zillionth cigarette and scowling at my mother.

And now, exactly one hour and forty minutes before my scheduled beating, Dad splashes Jim Beam into his glass of Coke. If he gets drunk, he won't be able to *administer* the beating. Then my mother will lash me with one of her colorful belts.

I'm thinking that this time I'll run away. I'll get my best friend, Cujo, to swing by on his moped, and we'll ride all the way to the beach. We'll build a fort and live off fish and candy. But my bathing suit is hideous, my boobs are deformed, my freckles have darkened into an ugly swarm, and I don't feel like creeping out of the hot dark house today. So instead I slump against the desk where Mom's bloated purse holds court among unpaid bills, an empty cheese puffs bag, a broken sandal she's been meaning to have repaired, several of Dad's prescriptions, a bottle of Mercurochrome, a catcher's mitt, a corroded battery, and an empty basket adorned with dusty plastic magnolias.

One hour and thirty minutes before my appointment with the whipping expert, the twins come scrambling through the back door, Little Jack clutching a bulging *Star Wars* pillowcase spattered with blood, the Runt toting their BB guns. I wonder what it'll be today, and Dad, into his second whiskey Coke, perks up at the smell of game.

"What you got there, boys?" he asks, pecking at the bag with his long gray nose, pinning it with his good eye, and licking his lips.

"Robins," the ten-year-old twins squeal.

"Robins don't have much meat, but we'll cook up a huntsman's feast."

Sputtering happily with nervous tics, a fresh drink tinkling in his hand, Dad leads the boys out to the picnic table, just beyond the open kitchen window. As he spreads newspapers, he boasts about survival in the wilderness, how a true man must learn to live off the fruits of forest and lake, how he could gut a hummingbird with a toothpick before he was potty trained. I sit down at the kitchen table, light one of Dad's butts, and suck the sweet smoke down. Poison frolics through my bloodstream. I drip some Jim Beam into my Kool-Aid and guzzle it. I eat a Tic Tac. Enjoying a second cigarette butt, spying on them through the window, I watch Little Jack pick at the pile of robins as emerald flies cavort and my baby brother, Cabbage, strolls over in his tinfoil loincloth to aim his laser gun at Dad's head. Our obese Boykin spaniels have crawled from their holes. They waddle and grunt at Dad's feet, drunk on the delicious musk of dead animal.

"Chew chew," says Cabbage. "You dead, Daddy."

A cat skull dangles from a filthy shoelace tied around Cabbage's neck. He's wearing Dad's yellow jockstrap on his head, long gloves made of panty hose, and two plastic RC bottles strapped to his back with a Cub Scout belt. Born premature, Cabbage lived in a tank for three months, and he still looks like a bleached frog.

"I kilt you," Cabbage says. Dad slumps at the table, then twitches back to life.

"I'm immortal," he says, grabbing a bird.

Dad plucks feathers and demonstrates how to singe the remaining fluff off the scrawny carcass with his cigarette lighter. He decapitates a robin with one strong chop of his rusty hunting knife, then hacks off its wiry reptilian claws. He slits it open and picks out a wad of dainty guts, cupping the gleaming wine gem of the animal's heart in his hand for the twins to examine. Cicadas pulse their mystical chants. The sun beats down, and my father's great and noble nose gleams with manly oils.

"This is the heart, sons," says Dad, "the pouch containing the animal's soul. We'll dice it up and put it in the gravy, and it'll give us the keen eyesight of the bird. Indians said a prayer for the beasts they killed, thanking them for their sacrifice."

Dad closes his eyes, and the idiot twins copy him; Dad mumbles something and then drops the giblet into a bowl.

"General Richard Heron Anderson lived an entire month in the wild on pokeweed salad and fried lizards," Dad says.

"Gross," says Little Jack. "I'd starve."

"If we ever suffer a nuclear holocaust," says Dad, taking a sip from his blood-smeared tumbler, "you might have to live off the flesh of radioactive dogs."

"I would eat stuff out of cans first," says the Runt, trying to saw through a robin's neck with his pocketknife.

The twins make a mess of cleaning their robins. They can't find the guts. They slump in the heat, glancing hungrily at the shrubbery. T. W. Manley's go-cart engine revs up again. Dad hurls a cluster of intestines at the Runt's cheek and scowls at him when he squeals.

Fifty-five minutes before my scheduled punishment, Mom's still sleeping and Dad's manning the kitchen in his red bathrobe, cooking up a huntsman's feast of robins and grits and gravy, sloshing golden drink from his Jim Beam bottle without bothering to screw the cap back on. The grimy ceiling fan churns the muggy air. The twins hunch at the table, drinking pickle juice from shot glasses. Cabbage lurks in the dim roachy realm of the pantry, clanking metal cans together and muttering.

I'm eating stale cheese puffs while reading random snatches from Dad's novel:

And so Merlin became a hawk and flitted through the green velvety forest . . . When Sir Lancelot gazed into the deep pools of Guinevere's eyes, fires flickered within him, terror and joy commingling in the hot cauldron of his soul . . . From a shroud of white mist Morgan le Fey slipped naked and laughing, her alabaster breasts adorned with twin rosebuds, her long raven locks dancing about her taut buttocks.

Say what? With his huge hand, Dad snatches the pages just when the reading looks promising. He stashes his novel atop the refrigerator and stomps back to his pale pile of birds. The robins look fetal. They might be frogs or mice or fatty little moles. He rolls the dead things in flour and drops them one by one into the spitting skillet. Rich marrowy smells float from the pan, and Cabbage emerges to take a sniff. His rabbit nostrils quiver, and his eyes screw up with thinking.

"It smells like a rusty hamburger out here," Cabbage says, disappearing back into the dark of the pantry. Dad chops a purple onion and sautés it in the charred grease, adding flour, pouring milk from the gallon jug, spattering Worcestershire sauce and bright red drops of Texas Pete. He piles the fried birds on a silver platter pulled from the dusty depths of the china cabinet and smothers them with gravy. He sets a plate of grits before each twin and positions the platter in the center of the table, beside Mom's diseased cactus plant.

"Eat up, boys," Dad says.

The twins pick at their robins, fidget, and take itty-bitty baby bites. They hold their noses and squirm. Into the stubble-fringed shredding machine of his mouth, our father slowly inserts a whole bird carcass, grinds it into gamy gruel, and swallows.

"Delicious," he says, bathing us in the glow of his ghoulish grin.

"Among the Indians it is a sacrilege to let the sacred flesh of an animal go to waste," Dad informs us. "You must eat, boys, or the spirit of the robin will haunt you. The spirit of the robin will fly around your room at night, slither into your ears, and peck your brains until you go crazy."

Each twin lifts a bird to his lips, sighs, and licks it clean of gravy. Each twin removes the burnt, scabby film of fried breading from his respective dead animal, wads it into a ball, places it on his tongue like a holy wafer, closes his mouth, and waits for the substance to dissolve. Tears drip from their eyes as they swallow.

"That doesn't count as the animal itself," says Dad, biting a robin in two. Delicate bones snap as he chews. He gulps as he swallows, and his tongue slips out to dab grease from his lips. "The flesh is the thing," he says. "The transubstantiated spirit of the robin will fill you with the bird's power."

The twins pinch tufts of meat from their carcasses and line them up like pills to be swallowed whole. Little Jack eats one first.

"It tastes like pesticides," he says.

The Runt copies Little Jack.

"It tastes like toads," says the Runt.

According to the twins, the robins taste like hair spray, ammonia, and chicken necks. The robins taste like grasshopper meat dipped in gasoline. They taste pee-sautéed and weird. According to the twins, because the robins they slaughtered spent the morning pecking pesticidal pellets from old Mr. Horton's mouthwash-green lawn, the birds are probably lethal.

"Get out of my sight, you ungrateful wenches," Dad says, banging his tumbler on the table. "You better prepare yourselves for a visit from the Great Robin. It will flap into your window tonight and fill your room with feathers. The Great Robin will terrify you with its rotten worm breath. The Great Robin will drop turds the size of shoes. Calling upon the nobility of its bird genealogy, the Great Robin will sprout the atavistic claws of the pterodactyl and tear your soft, womanly bodies into bloody confetti."

Dad grins until his mandible vanishes. The twins scramble to their feet. Dad lights a cigarette and flicks ash into the rib cage of a half-gnawed robin. A sunbeam shines directly onto the ashy carcass and lights up stained cracks in the ceramic plate.

On a rancid summer dog day, when you're dirty and scrawny and ugly and poor, when your fingernails sting from too much biting, when the kitchen stinks of unclean plates, when there's nowhere to go, when punishment awaits you, when swarms of gnats flicker beyond bright windows, when heat sinks your mind into the syrupy filth of boredom, when you are disgusted by the sight of your own stubbed toes, when the glimpse of an ancient neighbor drifting across the green void of his lawn fills you with a new species of sadness, a screen door slamming can shoot straight to your heart, plunging it deeper than you thought it would go.

I hold my breath for as long as I can. I exhale noisily. Dad sneers at me and pours himself another drink.

Even though my father may whip me in twenty-five minutes, I feel abandoned when he staggers off to the living room, snatching his manuscript from the top of the refrigerator. He closes the door behind him. I mope around in the kitchen, plucking crusted bowls from counters, sniffing them. I hear a creak on the stairs, and Mom steps into the greasy light of the kitchen. Her face looks puffy. Her nylon housecoat sticks to her sweaty spots. She plods to the stove, where Dad has left the platter of fried robins covered with a dented pizza pan. She lifts the pan and sniffs. Slowly, with blank black eyes, she fixes herself a plate of robin and grits and gravy and sits down under the stale bluster of the ceiling fan. She nibbles a chunk of robin from its carcass, and only after she has chewed and swallowed and made a bitter face does she see me, lurking behind her.

"What are these—quail?" she asks.

"Robins," I say.

"Quit being a smart-ass, they must be quail, they're just freezer-burned."

My mother will not believe that the robins are robins, and she eats several bites of grits and robin gravy before putting down her fork. Her mind is sunk deep beneath her chewing, but eventually she registers the taste.

"They're robins, I swear to God," I say.

"Who would cook robins?"

"Dad, of course. He would cook anything. He would cook an iguana or a monkey or a cat."

"I don't believe you."

I take Mom out back, where bright guts and rusty feathers have been strewn across the table by the scavenging spaniels. Flies crawl on the waxy shreds of organs.

My mother glances around the world she has made for herself.

"Get away from that filth," Mom says, and she runs inside. I trudge after her.

She's retching over the trash can but can't bring anything up. My father appears in the kitchen doorway, crouched in drunken-ogre mode, his sarcastic smile fluttering with repressed giggles, and I slip into the shadows of the hallway. Dad lunges at my mother, staggering and twitching in his old madman routine. I've seen him dig his false teeth vampirically into her neck. I've seen her, bursting with animal happiness, gasping for kisses. But this morning Mom jumps and wrings the damp neckline of her housecoat. She rolls her eyes, mutters the word *idiot*, and heads for the stairs.

"Wait," says Dad. "You've got to spank Kate."

My heart sinks. My ears become the equipment of a bat, huge and intricate, keening in the shadowy emptiness.

"What did she do?"

"She stole cigarettes. And she almost made me throw up."

"Why don't you do it?"

"As you can see, I've been *partaking*."

"Don't you think she's getting too old for spankings? She's about to grow breasts, for God's sake."

"What?" says Dad. "This is news to me."

"Well, maybe not breast breasts, but something. And even if she's not physically mature, she's at that age."

"She tried to make me puke my breakfast," whines Dad.

Mom laughs.

"That's not funny. And she attempted to make off with a whole pack of cigarettes this time."

"Okay," says Mom. "I'll do it, only because you already told her, and if we don't do what we say we're gonna do, they'll walk all over us. But this'll be the last time. When school starts, we need to come up with a new kind of punishment."

"She's got about thirty minutes, I think," says Dad, squinting at the place where his wristwatch usually is. "I'll send her up."

My parents depart to their respective lairs, and I stumble into the bright chaos of the backyard. The twins are boxing amid a throng of screaming boys. The fat, matted dogs grunt beneath our clothesline, where yellow nylon panties and linty boxer shorts flutter in a sunny dust cloud. And Cabbage squats on the picnic table, picking through robin guts with a pair of tweezers, a white dust mask covering his nose and mouth.

"What the hell are you doing?" I scream at him. Cabbage jumps, which makes me smile.

"Playing operation," he says.

"Those guts are contaminated," I say. "You're gonna get a disease just from touching them."

"Disease? Like what?"

"Leprosy, AIDS, epilepsy, hemophilia, diabetes, or the Elephant Man disease."

"Oh my God, no way!"

"Yes way. If you don't do something fast, your muscles are gonna puff up like biscuit dough and bust right through your skin. You're gonna bleed all over the fucking place, Cabbage. Green fungus'll grow in your nose and mouth, and your eyes are gonna turn black and shrivel up like frostbit toes."

"Shit," says Cabbage, dropping his tweezers. He removes his dust mask and thrusts his thumb into his mouth. He tries not to cry.

"You fool!" I shriek, jumping up and down for emphasis. "What the hell are you doing sticking that filthy thumb in your mouth? Do you actually want to die?"

"Damn," hisses Cabbage. He pulls his thumb from his mouth and spits on it.

"Here's an old Indian cure that might just save your life," I say solemnly. "You've got to wash your hands in milk and peroxide. You've got to eat an ant and pray to the god of the underworld and the god of the moon. Then you've got to find a toad with orange eyes. Lick the toad belly six times while chanting prayers to the stars, and maybe, just maybe, you'll live."

I follow Cabbage inside. In the kitchen he pulls the milk jug from the refrigerator and fills a large steel bowl. He sets the bowl on the floor and sits Indian style over it. He mumbles some creepy baby gibberish and plunges his little hands into the cold, white, animal fluid. Leaving the bowl on the floor, Cabbage heads for the bathroom, where he finds a brown, economy-sized bottle of peroxide under the sink. I stand in the doorway watching as he splashes the sizzling medicine into his palm and rubs it over both hands, making a face and muttering. He dries his hands with toilet paper, sniffs his fingers, and runs outside. I follow him around as he lifts bricks and rocks in search of ants.

"Don't want no fire ant," he says.

"It's got to be a fire ant, or the spell won't work, and you'll die and go down under the ground."

"What gon' happen down there?"

"Little slimy creatures are always fluttering against you, nibbling you and sticking their needle teeth in your skin. And there's nothing to eat but canned spinach and nothing to drink but cough syrup, and the place smells like the devil's farts, which is like burning plastic and rotten catfish and Mr. Horton's denture breath all mixed together. And there's no windows and there's bright fluorescent hospital light and nothing to watch on TV but the news."

"Shit," says Cabbage, dashing for the anthill at the edge of Mom's okra patch. Squatting, he sticks a twig in the hill, gathers a few furious insects, and lifts the utensil to his grimacing lips. Cabbage mashes an ant between two fingers and pops it into his mouth, screams, swallows, then flings the stick far from him. He drops to his knees. He thrusts his nose into the grass and gabbles a prayer to the underworld; then he lifts his head up and scans the sky.

"Ain't no moon up there," he says, fixing his harrowed frog eyes upon me.

"The devil has the moon down in the ground. It's like a helium balloon. He lets it go each night, and it floats up into the sky."

"He got a string tied to it?" Cabbage asks.

"Yep."

"Thought so."

"The moon is made of green cheese, which stinks, and that's another bad thing about hell. There's no one to play with down there, except babies with vampire teeth."

Cabbage shudders and starts digging a hole in the ground with his knobby tree-frog fingers. Then he lowers his face to the mouth of the hole, cups his lips with his palms, and in a deep croaky voice recites his prayer to the moon.

"Jibba jibba, regog mooga, onga poobah, salong teet."

"In hell you don't have a family," I tell him, "but sometimes, when the devil's bored, he'll make a fake family with the skins of dead animals and old hair he's pulled out of hairbrushes, just to trick you. You'll think you have your family back, but then you'll notice that the puppets are hollow and filled with dust, and when the devil laughs at you he sounds like TV static and screaming rabbits."

I look up to see my father standing on the back stoop, eating a Little Debbie Star Crunch and staring up into the trees. He looks like he wants to sprout feathers and a beak and fly up there to romp in the branches with some sexy medieval witch who's turned herself into a hawk. A warm breeze flutters his hair, and longing oozes from him, but all he can do is chomp a huge bite out of his Star Crunch and close his eyes as he chews the sticky sweet gunk. When he opens his eyes, he catches me looking. He winces. He grins. He tries to look sober.

"Upstairs, young lady," he says in his professional voice, "on the double."

The moment has come. The underbellies of sluggish clouds glow a sickly green. My boxing brothers, who are now trying to kill each other, look like poisonous elves. All around them, half-naked boys with bent spines hoot and leer.

"Good left hook, Bill," yells Dad. "You better watch out, Little Jack."

Dad slips on his glasses to watch the boxing match, and I trudge upstairs.

✤

Unlike the rest of our house, my parents' bedroom is cold. The window unit, going full blast, leaks picklish chemicals; the room smells like boiled peanuts and Listerine. My parents' bed looks damp and lumpy, as though stuffed with dead rodents, the mattress battered and drenched by the throes of my father's gigantic, nightmare-wracked body. A crusty plate sits on the dresser, between two perfume bottles, reflected in the stark sadness of the mirror.

My parents like to keep us waiting in the alien chill for at least five minutes to heighten the horror of the punishment. I usually use this time to pick through their drawers and closets. Behind a dusty vaporizer and several cartons of Dorals, I discover an old pack of Pampers from Cabbage's babyhood. An idea so brilliant I slap myself in the face for not thinking of it sooner pops into my head. My heart gets that belchy feeling as I hop out of my shorts. I take a Pamper from the plastic package and unfold it. I pull it up to my crotch and fasten the adhesive tabs. The Pamper fits tight like puffy bikini bottoms. I examine myself in the mirror, and the sight of my scrawny, diapered frog body is like a sip of vinegar. I turn my stinging eyes away and pull on my shorts. After checking my figure for conspicuous lumps, I try out different facial expressions until I settle on a Joan of Arc scowl, the haughty look a beautiful virgin tied to a stake would give her bitter old executioner when he struck the match.

Mom strides in at this moment, trying to look businesslike. She's changed into a matching floral shorts-and-top set and curled her limp bangs into two crispy cylinders that frame her little cat face. My lips tremble with a burning smirk as Mom fishes through her belt collection, choosing a pink leather number with fake rubies encrusting the big brass buckle. Mom doubles the belt and lashes at a pillow to test its power. She gives me a firm look, and I bend over the bed, gripping the bedpost hard.

The worn bedspread smells of sweat and dust and fabric softener. Chill bumps prickle my limbs. I close my eyes and listen to Mom's slight grunting as she whips me. The lash striking my butt is a mere flick of pressure on the puffy padding of the Pamper, but I scream and flinch as though I'm about to fall into a seizure.

"Quit exaggerating," Mom hisses. "It doesn't hurt that much."

"It does," I bellow, realizing that I'll have to make myself cry. I try to think of sad things—my parents dying, for example—but generic fantasies don't cut it. I picture little Cabbage struggling to breathe in the humid tank of his incubator, his lizard rib cage rising and falling in the acidic light of the hospital. I think of T. W. Manley, waving the little fish-fin hand he was born with, driving by on his beloved go-cart. I consider Duncan, a fat neighbor with Down syndrome, whose mother always dresses him in brown polyester slacks. I recall the night that Dad, upon receiving a phone call informing him that his mother was dead, shook the house with the earthquake of his weeping. I remember the day our neighbor's daughter drowned, and the drunk old woman spent the afternoon winding through her rose garden in a slip, cutting roses until she had nothing left but tangles of thorny vines. I think of hungry African children and Hiroshima body shadows and Soviet teenagers who spend their whole youths in hideous jeans. I think of filth-packed vacuum cleaner bags and closets crammed with ugly Christmas sweaters and the way the inside of a church smells when a hundred bored people with bad breath open their mouths to sing.

At last the tears start trickling, and the sadness of the world courses through my scrawny body, hurling me into the musky nest of my parents' bed, where I give in to the delicious abandon of weeping. My mother hangs her belt on its hook and slips out of the room. I start feeling sorry for myself. I'm an ugly runt, breastless and knobby-kneed, writhing on a cheap bedspread, wearing a Pamper under my linty shorts. My hair won't hold a curl, and I've blown my chances for a home perm. My nose won't stop growing. I'm a peeling, sunburned, freckled monster who'll never know the casual beauty of radiant, suntanned limbs. My mouth is a scrap heap of bitter metal. School will start soon, and I'll have to face my class without breasts, without a tan, without a perm.

By the time I'm done wallowing, it's almost evening. I climb off the bed and am overjoyed to discover, on the dresser, an open pack of cigarettes. I figure I deserve at least six after what I endured, so I slip the cancer sticks into the empty cups of my training bra. Then I tiptoe down the stairs, through the dark living room, and out into the yard, where dark birds churn the sky. The twins have put down their boxing gloves. They're sitting in the long grass, taking turns scratching each other's back. And Cabbage walks toward me in the balmy air, cupping something in his hands.

"Got him," says Cabbage, slightly opening the cage of his palms.

Cabbage holds a toad, belly-down. A tiny head pokes out, nostrils quivering, goggle eyes glowing in the sulfur light. The beauty of the toad's eyes shocks me—rich and marbled gold. I lose myself in their intricacies, breathing in smells of warm pine straw, metallic boy-sweat, the crisp, dusty gaminess of the bones around Cabbage's neck. The sky flushes pink. A breeze, light as a genie, swirls through the thick air.

Cabbage sticks out his little tongue, turns the toad belly-up, and licks it.

"What does it taste like?" I ask.

"Rain," he whispers, "with Lysol and ham."

"Now chant," I say.

"O gobwe gammu," says Cabbage, "hep me not die. Gwabu, gwabu, gwabu."

He licks the toad solemnly and closes his eyes in prayer. When he opens them, the yard fills with the moist whistling of the blackbird flock. The air has darkened.

"Gwabu monsoon ubu booboo," says Cabbage, holding the toad high in the air. Lightning bugs rise from dusky shadows. Cabbage marches with his toad to the picnic table.

"Belteety momamabu," he says, blessing the piles of robin guts with his toad. The moon has floated to the edge of the sky like a bubble of golden grease. Gardenias perfume the dead-bird stench. Flies walk around on the robin guts like delicate and mysterious robots. Cabbage moves off, chanting in the darkness, and I feel the backyard expanding around me, glittering with stars and bugs, crawling with strange beasts. Dad is in the kitchen, smoking, a warm light illuminating his bald spot. Mom laughs at something he has said—they must be in love again. Some kind of stew boils on the stove, crickets are singing, and the twins are humming the Donkey Kong theme. I light a cigarette, lie on my back in the pine straw, and take a deep, sweet drag while staring up at Venus, which pulses in the sky.

Caveman Diet

Clad in a deerskin loincloth, his ripped body gleaming with boar lard, Zugnord looms above us on a stone dais. We are flabby newbies, he tactfully suggests, snatched from the industrial teat of civilization, where we've grown battery-fed and soft, our blood percolating with poisons. We are half-dead, our brains zombified by office work and Internet surfing. We are discontent. But so was Zugnord, once. Projected behind him on a vast screen is his former self, Wilbur Sims, a paunchy, befuddled dumpling of a man in rumpled khakis. He squints at the camera like some subterranean rodent.

We gasp. For how could this clammy, balding creature have transformed into Zugnord? Zugnord with his glistening pecs and flowing Tarzan hair? Zugnord with his bold eagle eyes? Zugnord, who looks as though he could leap over a boulder and tackle a mastodon, gut it with a piece of expertly chiseled flint?

As Zugnord clicks through his slideshow, we gasp and gasp. We watch in amazement as a chunky troll of a man sheds flab, sprouts hair, stands tall, and wields the most exquisitely sculpted limbs we have ever seen. We watch him journey from a dark gym to a sun-dappled forest, where he builds his own wood hut. Watch him forage for berries, dig up tubers, kill deer with a hand-hewn bow and arrow. Watch him sketch magic symbols onto his face with charcoal, arrange bones on the ground, dance and chant in the light of the full moon. We would not be surprised if he sprouted wings and flew up into the stars.

"But enough about me," says Zugnord. "Tonight is all about you. Today is the first day of the rest of your life."

The banquet hall of Hominid Hotel resembles an imperial stateroom from *Planet of the Apes*, a vast pseudo-cave with undulating walls of stained concrete, indoor streams, and flickering gas torches. Lush fruit trees grow out of the pebble-tile floors, a feature that was probably absent in a typical Paleolithic cave, but whatever. I could also take issue with the melodramatic mural that sweeps along the curved wall behind the stage. It features a hunting scene—a mammoth stippled with spears, Schwarzeneggerian hominids exulting around the flailing beast. I recall my college anthropology teacher lecturing us on Aurignacian cave art, debunking the mythical male hunter as she cleaned her glasses with the sleeve of her polyester dashiki. According to her, a typical hunt scene was probably a family working together with spears and nets to bag a rodent or monkey.

But I'm not here to nitpick. I'm here to lose weight. I'm here to become a sinewy cavewoman with a core of steel and a glint of primal vitality in my eyes. I'm here to purge my body and mind, shed the bloat of civilization, cast off the epochs of agricultural decadence that have collected around my midsection. The banquet hall is packed with pudgy office drones, rich mothers serious about vanquishing baby weight, and B-list celebrities at the dawn of middle age. I myself won the stair-walk competition at my corporate office, and the prize was three weeks off and a free ride at Pleisto-Scene Island, the Paleopalooza of fitness adventure tourism. I left my fiancé sulking in his man cave, slumped in the ennui of our two-year engagement. Despite his protests that I'm perfect the way I am, despite the terror lurking in his eyes as he kissed me goodbye (yes, he would miss me sorely, but not for the right reasons), I dashed off to transform myself.

The lights dim. Tribal electronica pumps from hidden speakers. And Zugnord, our fearless leader, speaks to us in his mellow baritone, radiating casual virility.

"This is the beginning of a journey," he says, "deep into the self."

According to Zugnord, there is a caveperson, crouched and muzzled, within each of us. According to Zugnord, we will travel to the land of our ancestors, awaken primitive parts of our brains, forge new synaptic maps, and tap into hidden stores of vitality.

"You will walk into an ancient forest and meet your uncorrupted hominid self," says Zugnord, fumbling with his remote. A lush forest scene glows upon the screen behind him—primeval, Edenic. Zugnord reads through the guest list in alphabetical order. One by one, people walk up to the stage as he calls their names, accepting their Paleolithic workout costumes. Zugnord presents the guests with pomegranates, symbolic of the fall into decadent agriculture, and whispers something into their ears.

The guests descend from the stage with newfound confidence, as though Zugnord has galvanized them with his godlike breath. By the time my name—Ellen Wiggins—is called, I'm feverish with anticipation. I lope up to the platform, aware of the eyes on my dumpy body—stooped shoulders, curdy midsection, droopy bust and butt. I skulk across the stage, feeling larval and squishy from office work and domestic sloth.

Zugnord flashes a twinkling, carnivorous smile.

"Welcome," he says, slipping me my cavewoman costume, packaged in plastic.

And then he hands me the sacred pomegranate, the forbidden fruit packed with evil seeds—seeds of blood, seeds of knowledge, seeds of deadly agriculture.

"You are no longer Ellen Wiggins," Zugnord whispers, his ape breath hot in my ear. "You are Vogmar, daughter of the Blackboar Clan."

※

Only half the people attending the Wild Foraging Workshop the next morning are wearing their cave costumes. I myself am wearing spandex fitness gear. Jeff, a chatty journalist from New York who sports his standard-issue loincloth with a Magma T-shirt, keeps assuring everybody that he's not an exhibitionist.

"Yes, I look ridiculous," he says, scratching the pale skin of his left thigh, which looks rash-prone, "but I feel obligated to indulge in the full Paleo experience."

Chewing dandelion root and jonesing for coffee, we drift down a forest trail as Whezug, ex-botany professor and author of *Forest Feast*, lectures us on the evils of caffeinated stimulants. A scrawny sexagenarian with the mangy ponytail of a decrepit hesher, Whezug sports a leather loincloth that looks like something from a fetish shop. Although he's not literally lashing us with a bullwhip, he might as well be. As we stumble through the forest with empty stomachs, our brains mutinying from caffeine withdrawal, Whezug drones on about nuts, herbs, roots, and berries, forcing us to scramble up embankments, climb trees, crouch and dig with our bare hands to wrest a few bitter morsels from Mother Earth.

Whezug pauses beside a sunbaked boulder and draws our attention to a withered newt, which he peels from the rock surface and eats, tearing strands of jerked reptile with his teeth.

A woman shrieks. Jeff chuckles and jots a note on his iPhone.

"Paleolithic humans took advantage of whatever protein they could get." Whezug smirks.

To further illustrate this concept he squats, overturns a rock, scoops up a handful of termites, and pops them into his mouth. And so begins his lecture on wild protein. Whezug teaches us how to locate and catch grasshoppers. He distinguishes between edible and nonedible slugs. We watch the old man shimmy up a tree to raid a woodlark nest. Watch him pick maggots from the carcass of a lynx. Watch him grab a baby squirrel that has fallen from its nest, sniff the dead animal, and pronounce it "fresh." I turn away, fighting back a retch as Whezug gnaws off the head, recalling that urban legend about Ozzy Osborne biting off a bat's head midconcert.

"Oh my God," says a guy in garish cycling apparel.

"Paleolithic man ate plenty of carrion," says Whezug. "Which enhanced his intestinal flora and quickened his metabolism into a state-of-the-art fat burner. Would anybody like a bite?"

Silence. Most of us study our feet.

"All right," Whezug sniggers. "I was going to talk about edible scat next, but we'll save that for another day. How about some fungi fun?"

As Whezug enters deeper forest in quest of mushrooms, I lag behind with Jeff the journalist and a tax attorney from Atlanta.

"Mental illness, anyone?" Jeff's smile is squirrel-like but cute: a parting of beard, a revelation of yellow front teeth.

"This is not exactly what I signed up for," says the tax attorney, a tall lean woman in yoga garb.

"I'm still feeling queasy from that Ozzy stunt," I say.

"Exactly!" says Jeff. "I thought of Ozzy too. Bet you Whezug's into weed and metal. Bet you he still tokes up. Bet you he listens to Metallica, if the loincloth is any indication."

"Or worse, Cinderella."

"I was going to say Poison, but it doesn't get worse than Cinderella." Jeff flashes his squirrel smile—conspiratorial, contagious. I feel like we could stand there all morning, chatting about hair-metal bands, but Whezug summons us into the forest.

※

At the mixed-grill meet and greet, Zugnord struts around with two cave babes—a brunette, a blond—both wearing fur bikinis. He shakes our hands, offers us words of encouragement, and then retreats to his ceremonial throne, an egg-chair of burnished stone, where he sulks like a sultan as his women feed him protein-rich hors d'oeuvres. A *djembe* troupe starts pounding skins. Spitted meats roast, sending fragrant smoke tendrils into the air.

I spot Jeff, hunched over an appetizer tray, wolfing down trout-and-beet crudités. He waves his wineskin at me.

Tonight Jeff's sporting his loincloth with flip-flops and a *Rock in Opposition* tee. I try not to look at his man-parts, neatly packaged in their deerskin pouch. I'm wearing my fur cavewoman top with a sarong and sandals, a necklace of faux tiger teeth. I glance down at my belly and adjust my sarong.

"How are you feeling?" asks Jeff.

"Better."

"I can't believe you ate that mushroom."

"It was just a bolete. Besides, Whezug must know what he's doing. They wouldn't risk the lawsuits."

"Don't count on it," says Jeff.

According to Jeff, Pleisto-Scene Island has been sued for intestinal sepsis, E. coli infection, hypertensive heart disease, and a slew of personal injuries, including club-fight-induced memory loss, Jacuzzi overstimulation, and broken bones acquired during the recently discontinued saber-toothed-tiger hunt.

"And Zugnord has settled countless sexual misconduct suits. Seems he has a penchant for pagan sex rites."

"Are you serious?"

The swell of drums drowns our conversation. When the racket ceases, Zugnord stands, raises his wineskin, and blesses the *fruits of the hunt*.

Jeff and I refill our own wineskins. As the orientation video explained, Pleisto-Scene Island serves only Stone Age *vin de primeur*, the juice of naturally fermented wild grapes. I take a grateful tug, pleased to taste some bite in the booze.

We sit down at one of the stone picnic tables and dig into our arugula and berries. Our tablemates include the tax attorney we met earlier, a periodontist, and a belly dancer. Laughing, we take mock-fierce tugs from our wineskins. By the time we finish our salads, we're all using our cave names, sprinkling our conversation with sarcastic primal grunts.

A waitress in a fur bikini appears, lugging a grilled suckling pig on a wooden trencher. The pig, garnished with charred carrots and turnips, glistens in the torchlight. When my tablemates lift their phones to snap pics, I remember how Tim, my fiancé, swore he'd obsessively check Flickr for glimpses of my transformation. But I won't post a single thing. He'll peer into cyberspace and find a black void.

"The pig has been stuffed with its own minced vital organs, a caveman power food," says our waitress.

"Uh, plates?" says Jeff.

"Try to enjoy the carnal experience of communal eating." The waitress, a college girl who channels Raquel Welch from *One Million Years B.C.*, winks. "Of tearing off hunks of flesh with your bare hands." The waitress licks her lips and leaves us alone with our dead piglet.

"Well, this is awkward," says the periodontist. "How do we begin?"

"I guess we literally dig in," says the tax attorney.

She reaches out, claws at the pork with her manicured talons, and pops a strand into her mouth.

"Oh, it's *very* tender," she murmurs, licking her fingers.

We go at it, at first politely, avoiding each other's paws as we pick meat from the carcass. But then, ten minutes in, something about the flickering torches, the throbbing percussion, the wine that tastes of summer forests, something about the rich, fatty taste of the shoat helps us relax. Soon we are tipsy, laughing. Soon we are ripping off hunks of meat and stuffing them into our maws. Soon we are talking with our mouths open, sharing anecdotes, heedless of the grease dripping down our chins.

I am Vogmar, daughter of the Blackboar Clan, supping under the moon. Jeff is Bogwag, son of the Shaggy Bear People, tittering and mock-growling. The periodontist howls like a wolf, showing off his transplanted gums. The tax attorney sloughs her sequined cocktail dress hesitantly, revealing the cavewoman garb beneath.

"Didn't have the guts to wear this out, but now I'm drunk."

Everybody laughs.

"You go, girl," says the belly dancer, who is already sporting her standard-issue fur bikini. They high-five. We all hoot and roar. I am Vogmar, daughter of the Blackboar Clan, tossing bones into the shadows. I am Vogmar, huntress and medicine woman, studying the messages of the stars. I am Vogmar, slurping wild wine and feeling uncomfortable as Sexgoth, the belly dancer, begins to undulate under the moon and Bogwag of the Shaggy Bear People growls his approval. I am Vogmar, feeling pudgy and bloated despite the fact that I have not consumed a single carb since my arrival. I try to think of something clever to say to Bogwag, but he's chatting up the nearly naked tax attorney.

"I'm here to vanquish this paunch," she says, pointing at the barely perceptible mound of her belly.

"What paunch?" says Bogwag, who actually pokes her stomach with his finger.

"Bless your heart," says the tax attorney, flashing a mouthful of perfect, predatory teeth.

The *djembe* troupe, clearly drunk, is trying to play the drum solo from "In-A-Gadda-Da-Vida."

"Groovy," says Bogwag, smiling at the tax attorney. He bobs his shaggy head to the beat.

The night deepens. The moon spills its primordial silver. Whispered rumors flit around the table: moon worship, pagan sex cults, animal sacrifices, and roving bands of actors impersonating cannibalistic Neanderthals. The belly dancer claims she's already spotted the Neanderthals, staring intensely at her from a patch of jungle beyond the swimming pool.

"For real?" says the tax attorney, sounding like an adolescent. She stands up, slinks over to the bonfire, and Bogwag trots after her.

I hear my phone buzzing persistently in my purse. It's my fiancé, but I don't pick up. I picture him hunched in his office, bathed in sickly computer light. Perhaps my absence has prodded him out of his chair for a walk around the block. Perhaps he has emerged from what I call his "hibernation," which started a year ago when he began doing search-engine optimization work at home. I picture him standing stunned on our weedy lawn, blinking at the sun like a prairie vole. One tipsy evening last spring, I'd joked that he was agoraphobic. He kept running toward the edge of our yard, pretending to strike an invisible force field, falling on his butt and laughing. Finally, snarling, he broke through. He turned toward me like a hero in a dystopian film, arm extended. Holding hands, we ran off to a neighborhood bar to get wasted. But under a trellis entwined with Confederate jasmine and strings of Christmas lights, he kept looking at his phone.

"What, exactly, do you keep checking?" I tried to smile.

"The usual." He made a point of turning his phone off, tucking it away. "E-mails from clients. Various accounts."

Clouds floated across the pocked face of the moon. My fiance's hand crept across the table like a tarantula toward his phone. He did not turn it on, but he could not refrain from touching it.

Imagining him at home now, compulsively checking his phone for a sign of life from me, I'm tempted to text him. But I don't. I scroll through pics on my iPhone, flashing backward through time into our courtship phase, his image multiplying into a swarm of smiling, impish men—and there he is on our first date, eyes alight, lips whispering wry comments about the ridiculous paintings of naked game-show hosts at the art show we'd attended. Comparing Pat Sajak to a "startled marsupial," he made me laugh, softening me up for our first kiss, his lips full and feminine and tasting mysteriously of figs.

🌿

The next morning at the Primitive Technology Workshop, Jeff is sitting by himself. The tax attorney is also there, at another table, chatting up some handsome triathlon type in clownish fitness apparel.

"Birds of a feather," says Jeff, glancing mournfully in her direction. I sit down next to him.

At the front of the room, Ghunthag, a disgraced anthropologist rumored to have been arrested in the seventies for smuggling opium in a dead gorilla's chest, demonstrates the Levalloisian flint-chiseling technique. Dressed in a deerskin tunic and Birkenstocks, he shows us how to produce a tortoise-shaped spear tip. He compares this particular tip type to the Clovis point, discusses the nuances of the Susquehanna projectile point, and then lets us go at it—twelve cranky, caffeine-deprived wretches, pounding at flint chunks with crude stone chisels. Sipping from a ceramic mug, Ghunthag strolls among us, offering tips and pointers on tips and pointers and making bad puns.

"What do you think he's drinking?" I whisper.

"Green tea," says Jeff. "The fucking hippie."

"I would kill for a caffeinated beverage."

"But would you steal for it?" Jeff points at something he has hidden under the table: Ghuntag's thermos, glimmering and mermaid-green.

"Want to blow this joint?" says Jeff.

"Hell yes."

As Ghunthag shows the class how to bind a flint point to a spear with deer sinew, Jeff and I slip out and hightail it toward the woods with our contraband tea. Laughing like hoodlums, we plunk down in a wild olive grove.

We open the thermos, sigh as steam purls out. Kneeling reverently, we take a long, luxuriant sniff.

We pour tea into the thermos top. Pass it between us. Sip.

We relish this brew of civilization, nectar of gods, exquisite perfume of the Orient. We perk up. The sky is the blue of flame. Purple olives glow in the branches above us. Wildflowers waver in the breeze, and two yellow butterflies zigzag amid the beauty.

Bogwag of the Shaggy Bear People reclines on his side. His Art Zoyd T-shirt gapes. I try not to look at his belly fur, so bearish and frank compared to the smooth, coy abdomen of my fiancé. I most definitely avoid the moist bundle of his genitals, which rests against his sunburned thigh. I keep my eyes fixed on the sky, the branches, the dangling fruits.

I think I hear Bogwag grunt.

"What did you say?" I ask.

"Nothing. Oh, shit. What the hell?"

Bogwag leaps into a crouching position, points toward a cluster of brambles. I stand up. Some kind of redheaded, ridge-browed, ape-thing is peering at us through thorny vegetation. Now I see three ape-things mumbling behind the brambles.

"Agbagaba," says one of them. It leaps forward, hunched and frizzy, spear in hand. And then a dozen of these creatures crawl from the bush, closing in on us.

"Fake Neanderthals," whispers Jeff. "Actors. No worries."

"Still kind of creepy. Like those cannibalistic hominids in *Quest for Fire*."

"Excellent film. But, please, don't say 'cannibalistic.'"

"They're fake, remember? Some kind of theater troupe."

The Neanderthal leader, who's wearing those ridiculous plastic hillbilly teeth, grins.

"Grogoth vagamoo," he exclaims, hoisting his spear. I notice an iPhone pouch dangling from his suede diaper. He's wearing Crocs and smells reassuringly of soap.

A wild-haired female lunges playfully at Jeff, her naked breasts dotted with clusters of fake frizz. The same synthetic orange fur adorns her arms and thighs. Suppressing a giggle, she snatches the silver thermos top from Jeff, twirls it in the sunlight to catch sparkles.

The fake Neanderthals rub their bellies and point at us. Smacking their lips, they look us up and down.

"I think we're supposed to make a run for it," I say. "Stimulate our fight-or-flight response and fry a thousand calories."

"Not really feeling up for a jog," says Jeff. "Kungar the tax attorney said they chased her for five miles yesterday. But then, she's a natural athlete."

"Oh," I say, realizing that I don't want Jeff to see me run. "It's almost wine time anyway."

We lope down the trail toward the hotel, glancing back at the hominids, who are now kicking around a hacky sack. Perched on the embankment behind them is a small woman holding a bow and arrow, ready to shoot, her centerfold-worthy silhouette backlit by the setting sun.

"Whoa," says Jeff, rubbing his eyes and gawking. "I must be dreaming."

The woman vanishes into the trees. I wonder if I should sign up for the Aurignacian Archery Workshop.

When we emerge from the forest, it's almost dusk. We stroll right into an elegant patio scene, where cave babes lounge upon molded concrete chaises and frat dudes in loincloths feed them kabobs. A waterfall cascades down a boulder, filling a stone-slab pool. We're back at Hominid Hotel, where meat smoke always wafts along the corridors.

At dinner the next night, Jeff strolls up to my table.

"Hey, Vogmar. Guess who I just ran into."

"Who?"

"Our Neanderthal friends. One of them had the gall to bite me this time. I think she got carried away. Reminded me of my ex-wife."

Jeff displays a set of red bite marks on his forearm and sits down at my table.

"Smells like a lawsuit."

"Actually, I kind of encouraged her. She kept trying to grab my phone, giggling like a freak."

"So your ex was a biter?" I say, wondering if his ex-wife is attractive, athletic, fleet of foot and long of limb, wondering why dumpy dudes like Jeff feel entitled to such women.

"It's complicated." Jeff winces and grins simultaneously.

As we dig into our grilled venison, my phone throbs like a persistent insect in my bag. I scroll through texts from my fiancé, feeling queasy as *"What's up, sexy cavegirl?"* morphs into *"What the hell is the problem here? Six days of silence? I don't know whether to be angry or worried sick."*

I'm not exactly sure what the problem is, though I find his anger invigorating. I picture him grimacing. I picture him up out of his chair, pacing with clenched fists.

I stuff my phone back into my bag. I concentrate on the proper chewing of venison, producing just the right salivation level for maximum protein absorption.

After dinner, Zugnord introduces Dr. Randy Homes, evolutionary psychologist and author of *The Caveman Dating Guide*. Homes, a scrunched mouse of a man, natters on about testosterone-driven, promiscuous he-men and the faithful earth mothers who can't help but love them.

"All men are hardwired to keep harems," says Dr. Homes. "So, ladies, if he cheats on you, cut him some slack: his genes are to blame. Thank your lucky stars he's not out raping people. Men are essentially semen-spurting machines, blindly programmed by their selfish genes."

I think of my fiancé, burrowed indoors, protected by double-lined blackout shades. I can easily see him hunched in the fug of our computer room on a weeklong porn binge, crushed beer cans scattered on the floor, leftovers congealing in Styrofoam takeout tubs, his multitouch Magic Mouse crusted with suspicious secretions.

"Good Lord," Jeff hisses into my ear. "He sounds like my ex-wife, who was a raging sexist. That whole rapegene theory has been thoroughly discredited. Fuck this lame pseudoscience. Are you up for an evening stroll?"

"Men are inseminators; women are incubators," lectures Dr. Homes.

I pick up my purse. "Let's go."

The moon, pitted and ancient and lit to capacity, shines upon the forest path. Exploring a side trail, Jeff and I find ourselves in thick brush. Suddenly, we see fire flickering beyond the bracken. We hear the throbbing of hand drums. We scramble through shrubs to get a better look.

Dead center in a Stonehenge-esque formation of rocks, basking in the heat of a bonfire, Zugnord reclines on a granite slab. A dozen naked cave babes kneel before him, bearing ceramic bowls. Shadowy drummers pound skins just beyond the firelight. Six bodybuilder types, all of them short and wearing fur diapers, stand guard with javelins. And then an ancient shaman, clad in a tunic of raven feathers and wearing a leather backpack, steps into the sacred arena. Except for a few wisps of gray frizz, he's completely bald, his cranium pitted like the moon.

Chanting, the shaman pulls a stick from his backpack and scratches a symbol onto the ground. Next he produces a cloth bundle, unwraps it, and hands Zugnord a dark lump.

"Jesus," whispers Jeff. "I think that's some kind of animal organ."

"Bet you it's a deer heart," I say.

As we watch Zugnord accept the object, we giggle nervously. Zugnord intones some mumbo jumbo while the shaman performs an obsequious jig. Then, without further ceremony, Zugnord devours the thing. The drumming stops. Blood drips down Zugnord's chin. The shaman recedes into the shadows from whence he came. Zugnord belches, spits a piece of gristle onto the ground.

Cave babes creep forward with their bowls.

"Holy shit," says Jeff. "Is that Kungar?"

"Who's Kungar?"

"You know: the hot tax attorney."

And there she is, the insufferably hot, naturally athletic tax attorney who complains about her nonexistent gut. I didn't recognize her right away because she looks so much like the other cave babes, generically perfect, tall and toned with washboard abs and flowing shampoo-commercial hair.

Jeff sighs as the cave babes remove Zugnord's loincloth. They smear what looks like blood upon his torso, giving his groin area a good rubbing down, after which his horn of plenty rises. With the bored expression of a prime minister accepting an endless series of handshakes, Zugnord receives the oral ministrations of all twelve cave babes, including the tax attorney. When, at last, he mounts the hottest chick (the one who looks like Raquel Welch) from behind, the drums start throbbing again. The guards drop their spears and join the fun. Within five minutes, various couples are going at it among the stone monuments, representing a variety of copulatory positions, including the reverse-cowgirl, the wheelbarrow, and the seated-scissors positions. Kungar the tax attorney has paired up with a particularly buff guard. One of the cave babes is going down on another cave babe. Two of the guards are making out, gently stroking each other's beards. Meanwhile, stray cave babes stroll among the fornicators, caressing thighs, breasts, and buttocks.

The theatrical nature of the setting and costumes, the perfection of the bodies, the silvery lunar light, all make the orgy seem like an Internet figment—distant, composed of pixels. I think of my fiancé, mouth slack and panting, eyes fixed on his laptop screen. Once, unexpectedly home from work early, I'd stumbled upon him in such a state. I'd felt a stab of jealousy upon glimpsing three busty vixens in schoolgirl plaid. But mostly,

I'd felt an eerie sadness, as though my fiancé had been body-snatched, his mind teleported *elsewhere*. When he turned toward me, his clammy skin had a strange cadaverous sheen. His eyes possessed a ghoulish luster, the same look he got when scanning eBay for vintage stereo speakers or reading Amazon product reviews or clicking through a stranger's endless Facebook pics. I tried to explain that I wasn't a prude, that the images struck me as depressingly cheesy, that I'd expected something more sophisticated from him. And then I walked away, removing my body from the terrain of his hibernation, but he'd followed me out into the brighter air of the kitchen, the screen door open to late afternoon cicadas, and salvaged the evening with a joke about our lawn-fanatic neighbor, describing the old man as a rabid shar-pei.

Jeff pulls a wineskin from his rucksack and offers it to me. I take a swig.

"I feel like I'm watching TV," I whisper.

"Exactly," says Jeff. "That ineffable feeling of narcissistic dissociation." And then we find ourselves in that awkward yet primordial predicament, mouths hovering so close that our breath mingles. I'm drunk enough to lean towards him, but then somebody screams.

Zugnord the cave king is cowering behind a boulder. His guards scramble for their javelins. Cave babes stand around with crossed arms, looking annoyed. Into the firelight steps a small woman clad in a tunic of leaves. Her hair is long and matted, her face caked with blue mud. When she hoists a bow and arrow and aims the contraption at Zugnord, I recognize her petite silhouette.

"Watch your ass, Wilbur," she says. "Did I not express my discontent with your plan to build another Neanderthal village near my personal territory?"

"Yes, but . . . I didn't authorize it," says Zugnord. "The Neanderthals are kind of out of hand. Some of them were in this guerilla theater troupe and really get into what they do."

"Bullshit," says the mysterious woman. "You've planted your thugs to keep an eye on me. Instead of indulging in pseudo-pagan sex bullshit, you'd better do something about your Neanderthals. They're the ones you should be worried about, not me."

"I'll take care of them. First thing tomorrow. Promise."

The woman vanishes into the forest. Zugnord's henchmen shovel sand onto the fire. And then they all head back toward Hominid Hotel.

We creep out into the sacred space. I stand there awkwardly, feeling a sick stab of guilt, as Jeff takes pictures of bloodstained stone, a fur bikini top, a used condom. The pagan monument glows in the moonlight, casting eerie shadows. A few live coals smolder in the fire pit. The woods are thick and deep, full of shape-shifting beasts and fake Neanderthals. The sky, spangled with myriad blobs of burning plasma, is infinite and eternal.

The next morning, at the Leaf, Nut, and Berry Buffet, Jeff snarls over the mizuna trough.

"Not exactly the kind of thing you want to eat in the morning, you know?" he says.

We heap our plates with greens and fruit. Sit down at our favorite stone booth.

"Hungover?" I ask, hoping he's forgotten about last night's near kiss.

"Hard to tell. Didn't get much sleep. Spent the night Googling, chasing Paleo fanatics through chat rooms, trying to get to the bottom of last night's mysterious Amazon queen."

"She was on the small side."

"Dwarf Amazon, then. How's that?"

"Oxymoronic."

"Anyway, this morning I interviewed a few former personnel. A disgruntled waitress. A chattering chambermaid. I tried to get ahold of Kungar, but she wouldn't answer my texts. Get this: the mysterious Amazon is Zugnord's ex. She's known him since he was fat, dumpy Wilbur Sims. Goes by the name of Zongar."

"Wow. I don't envy her, asshole that he is."

"It gets better. They were once this insufferable power couple. They started Pleisto-Scene Island together, and then Zongar got sick of Zugnord's womanizing and went apostate. Last year, she started her own thing in the woods, some kind of earth-loving, vegetarian, chimpanzee-diet thing, which is, of course, anathema to the Paleo carnivores. Every now and then, a few of Zugnord's customers get lured into her cult. Since last fall, a podiatrist, a personal trainer, and a realtor have disappeared into the forest. Families are concerned. Lawyers involved. Neanderthals are on the case, slinking through the woods."

"So that's what the fake Neanderthals are up to."

"Not all of the fake Neanderthals, apparently, just this one tribe."

"A bit much to digest this early in the morning."

"No shit. I'm going to do a little deep-forest exploring today, see if I can catch a whiff of the Earth goddess in question. You up for a hike?"

❦

Clad in earth-toned Patagonia, equipped with a backpack, a canteen, a picnic lunch of jerky and fruit, I regard myself in the mirror. I look leaner, more ferocious, something carnivorous and feline in my mock snarl—from the side view at least. I'm about to head out when I hear a knock on my door. I open it, expecting Jeff.

My fiancé stands there, rumpled from travel, his eyes huge—the magical eyes of a rare nocturnal monkey, I used to think, though now they look terrified and feverish, like a refugee child's. He's wearing khakis, a vintage plaid shirt, these mouthwash-green dead-stock 1980s Pumas he spent two weeks stalking on Etsy. He looks smaller, as though the journey has deflated him and he needs a pump of air. He treats me to his sly smile, which used to wreak havoc on my nervous system, but now I feel nothing.

Then I smell him—his fruity shampoo, his high SPF sunscreen, the darker animal brine of his armpits. I detect a hint of metallic mineral in his sweat, bespeaking the trauma of his trip across the planet. These smells, which send obscure messages to my blood, give his eyes resonance again. And my stomach is a mess, a weird turmoil of lust and repulsion.

"So, I figured I should, you know, like, come out here and see what's going on," he says, trying to play it cool.

"Nothing's going on," I say, noticing that my hands have spontaneously tensed into trembling raptor claws. I hide them behind my back.

"You sound defensive."

"I'm not. Just surprised. Why didn't you tell me you were coming?"

"I didn't know if I'd be able to go through with it."

There it is again, the elated smile. I'm supposed to hug him, to praise his bravery.

"Besides," he says, "you wouldn't answer my texts, my calls."

"Isolation is part of the full Paleo experience. I told you that."

"Whatever. Aren't you going to invite me in?"

"Of course. Come in. But I'm heading out for my morning hike. Part of the regime."

He squeezes around me into the room, tosses his duffel onto a chair, reclines on the bed, and smirks—a sweet expression from the old days, mischievous and inviting.

"I'll be back soon," I say. "It won't take long."

I give him a quick peck on the cheek and dart down the hallway, jog through the lobby in my clunky hiking boots. When I finally reach the patio, I collapse against a wall of purple clematis. I sink into the riot of flowers, taking deep breaths of perfumed air.

And there's Jeff, strolling through the flowering arbor, dressed in shorts and hiking boots, equipped with backpack and water bottle, twinkling, ready for adventure.

"Great day for a jungle trek," he says.

I'm about to tell him that today's not a good day, when, for some reason, he reaches out and touches my shoulder. He motions toward the trail that curls into the forest. I hear insects chanting their mating dirges deep in the mysterious woodland gloom. I picture my fiancé, bored already, looking around for a television, scoping the faux-stone walls for a mounted screen.

I walk into the woods with Jeff.

As we tromp down the foraging trail, Jeff chatters wittily about Zongar, prehistoric matriarchal societies, Earth Mothers and herbalists, moon goddesses and sacred menses. I respond with the occasional polite grunt, feeling sick about abandoning my fiancé, scanning the trail to make sure he's not tailing me, half expecting to see the wild-eyed creature making his tentative way through the woods.

We cut down a side path and enter deeper forest, the forest within the forest, where the trail dwindles to a scruffy footpath. Locating a stream that a waitress told Jeff about, we wind along its meandering bank.

Around noon, we climb up an embankment in search of sunnier space and discover the perfect picnic spot. We unwrap our lunches. From an inside pocket of his backpack, Jeff pulls a contraband Coke—still cold and dewy with miraculous condensation.

At last, I am able to laugh.

"Christ almighty. Where did you get that?"

"From an undisclosed source."

Jeff unscrews the top, releasing a mystical hiss. He offers me the bottle. I close my eyes and savor the burnt-vanilla sweetness. We sit in the sun, eating pea-nuts and jerked venison, passing the Coke between us. We relish the melody of salt and sweet, infusing our sluggish blood with the elixir of caffeine and sugar.

Jeff leans in with a dopey look on his face. He closes his eyes and draws his lips into a lush pucker.

I hesitate, picturing my fiancé lolling in my hotel room, sighing every five minutes, unsure of what to do with himself. Then I take the plunge.

Now Jeff and I are kissing, rolling in the grass, leaf shreds and bark bits stuck to our sweaty skin. Now we are grunting, groping, our mouths gaping with greed as we reach for each other's secret parts. I am Vogmar, daughter of the Blackboar Clan. Jeff is Bogwag of the Shaggy Bear People. And we are fucking in the for-est, our bodies sleek and keening. We fall into natural, beastly rhythms. Mosquitoes veer in to suck our blood. Birds flit through foliage, snatching berries and grubs. The trees ring with laughter.

I open my eyes, peer into foliage, half expecting to see my fiancé roosting on a bough, his face scrunched with fury, his eyes drenched with pain. Instead, ape-men hoot and jeer. They bounce in the branches. Slap their shaggy knees. At least six fake Neanderthals gaze down at us, ululating over the sheer hilarity of two chubby humans getting it on.

"Goddamn it," Jeff hisses. He unplugs his wilting member and shakes his fist in wrath.

I can't find my shorts. I cover my crotch with my backpack and stare at my empty palms in shame. Jeff snatches up rocks and sticks, hurls them into the trees.

"Get out of here!" he shouts. "You stupid Neanderthal shits."

※

Deep in the forest, as we slog through brush, eyes peeled for pouncing ticks, ears pricked for snapping twigs, noses sniffing for whiffs of roasting veggies, my fiancé texts me, trying to sound casual: *What's shakin', Cavegirl?* But I know that he must be hysterical by now. I turn off my phone, bury it deep in my backpack, beneath my extra socks, birth-control pills, and contact-lens solution, beneath my hairbrush and Sani-Cloth wipes and prepasted disposable toothbrush.

When we stop to drink from our canteens, a flock of greenfinches scatters from a berry bush. The berries gleam with a purple, poisonous luster, and I wonder if the dwarf Amazon queen knows which berries are safe to eat. I wonder if she's an expert on edible fungi and healing herbs. I wonder if she has a boyfriend out here in the wild, some feral accountant or savage data processor. Or perhaps she has a series of consorts—lean vegan foragers with sinewy yoga bodies who feed her succulent fruits. Maybe she's still nursing the wound of Wilbur, licking and licking it like a dog. Maybe Wilbur still lights up the darkest, most twisted chamber of her heart. Or maybe, through some old-school, matriarchal mojo, she's gotten in touch with her inner goddess and banished the asshole from her mind.

"Crap," says Jeff, fiddling with his iPhone. "My cell's not catching a signal. Check yours."

I scrounge through my backpack. My battery's dead.

"What time is it?" I ask Jeff.

"4:43."

There's a chill in the air. A figment of moon has appeared in the deep, blue sky. What else can we do but keep trudging down the ghostly footpath, attempting witty conversation, trying to recover from the awkwardness of our thwarted coupling? Of course the conversation is stilted now, tainted with false chirpiness. Of course things are no longer the same, now that the sweet pressure of suspended flirtation has been punctured, the holy mystery unshrouded, the comedy of flesh unveiled. The forest is getting dark, and we have no bedding to lie down upon, no booze to swill, nothing, really, to talk about. Jeff's ex and my fiancé hover in the forest gloom like ancestral spirits.

I'm almost relieved when the fake Neanderthals leap upon us, grimacing and grunting. They brandish spears tipped with Levalloisian points. Their faces are streaked with red mud.

Hissing gibberish into our faces, they threaten us with their weapons.

"Here we go again." Jeff rolls his eyes.

"Maybe they think we're part of Zongar's cult," I whisper, but Jeff doesn't hear me.

Prodding us with the butts of their spears, the brutes push us off trail into deeper forest, into the heart of the heart of the wilderness, where darkness oozes like fog from the earth and flying insects brush against our skin. Strange birds moan. A luminous moth flaps up from a cluster of ferns. And monkeys bounce in the branches, howling churlishly.

At last I spot the glow of a fire, hunched hominids dancing around the flames.

The fake Neanderthals are performing some ritual. They dance and twirl. They look dirtier than the other Neanderthals, their outlandish body hair so caked with filth that it looks real. When they see us emerging from the bush, they rejoice. Their jig grows frenzied. Women sway forth with wooden bowls. The fake Neanderthals shove us into the firelight. They pick at our clothes, babble, and sing. The women sprinkle water and herbs on us. I smell rosemary, wild thyme, pepper. Their fire pit is decorated with charred skulls. Their grass huts adorned with bones. Now one of them is tugging at my shorts, now scratching my thighs with his dirty, simian claws.

"Hey, I'm kind of shy," says Jeff, chuckling as a Neanderthal woman rifles through his pants pockets. Grinning, she barks some protolanguage. Two husky males secure Jeff's arms. And then, bellowing in triumph, the woman snatches his iPhone. Not bothering to feign bafflement, she efficiently presses buttons, locates a document, waves the glowing screen in Jeff's face.

"So I'm working on a piece of creative nonfiction," says Jeff. "A light feature, if you will, nothing to get worked up about."

Another woman steps forward, rips off Jeff's shirt, and casts it into the flames.

Now Jeff is struggling in earnest—tubby, twisting, stumbling. Now he's cursing, causing a hullaballoo. When he elbows one of the apes in the gut and the brute who's guarding me lurches in to help his cronies, I take off. I scramble through a nasty cluster of brambles, tearing my knees to hell.

The forest is dense and dark and full of skittish creatures. I step on something soft, crush the creature to mush. Some stinging insect has crawled into my shirt. Some multilegged creeping thing has landed on my nape. But I don't stop to brush it off. I run and run. I have no idea whether I'm headed toward the hotel or fleeing into deeper forest, toward more ferocious tribes of fake Neanderthals, spies and cannibals who slurp raw brain-pudding straight from bludgeoned skulls.

Nimble pursuers are hot on my tail, panting rhythmically. I can feel the adrenaline quickening my blood. I think I hear a woman's laughter, flitting jaggedly through the trees like a wounded bird. And then I see a shadowy figure—small, fierce, perched in a tree. Her body is impeccably toned. Her bowstring is taut, her arrow nocked and ready.

"Hello!" I bellow into the darkness. "I'm looking for Zongar!"

She leaps from the branch.

"Did that bastard Wilbur send you?"

"No," I hiss, surprised at my bitterness. "That bastard did not."

She relaxes her weaponry. She looks me over. She beckons for me to follow her.

Organisms

When balmy summer days tilted toward unpleasant, and backyards transformed into jungles where super-mosquitoes patrolled lush weeds, Jenny Hawkes liked to walk outside and stand in a margin of shade, listening to the collective hum of her neighborhood's HVAC units. She'd pretend that the Rapture had snatched all the idiots into outer space. She'd smoke a secret cigarette, a vice she hid even from her husband, and then hurry back into the air-conditioning.

She worked as a guide for Sibyl, an online information company, answering the random questions of desperate people who were loath to do the research themselves. This morning there had been inquiries about Asian tiger mosquitoes, flood insurance, weight-loss nanobots, and

Indian surrogates. Jenny already knew of several good websites on these topics, so she punched her answers in quickly. And then, for the twentieth time that day, she checked the Web for US fatalities in Afghanistan.

It was one thirty and her son had not emerged from the den for lunch. Lately, as he spent more time before their wide-screen media monitor, he filled the den with his signature scent—the coppery tinge of stress pheromones in his sweat. Jenny did not like to step into this *atmosphere*, the musky turbulent ambiance that enveloped his gangly body. Obscure glands pumped inside him. Hormones spiked his blood, ripened his genitals, covered secret places with hair, and fed the zits that festered on his sullen face.

Adam was busy killing off brain cells with a video game, she figured, hunched before Zombie Babe Attack or some other disturbing concept dreamed up by marketing teams who dabbled in adolescent psychology and flirted with the darker urges. As much as she wanted to, Jenny didn't step down into the *atmosphere* to ask him if he wanted a sandwich. She went back to her office and dove into the sea of questions, braving the currents of the nation's fears. Activity on sibyl.com tended to surge after disappointing lunches left people listless at work. With the afternoon stretched out before them, they compulsively typed questions into the crystal ball featured on the site's main page.

They could no longer concentrate for extended periods of time. Their hair was falling out. Their homes suffered infestations of bedbugs, fleas, roaches, and ants. On the brink of financial disaster, they received threatening letters from creditors. They maxed out their credit cards, defaulted on their mortgages. Their homes were swept away by tornadoes, devoured by fires, flooded by hurricanes. They hid incurable toenail funguses within their fashionable shoes. They injected their sagging flesh with botulinum toxin A. Cysts and tumors bloomed in the obscure darkness of their wombs and testicles, in their brain and breast tissue, in their livers, gallbladders, bowels, and lungs. Their teeth were yellow. Their garbage disposals smelled of death.

They had fat sucked out of their thighs and buttocks. They tracked their cheating lovers with spy software and burned off crow's-feet with laser beams. They were diabetic. They were ashamed of their old tattoos. They felt strange heart palpitations and were addicted to Internet porn. Their children suffered from autism and ADHD. Their lawns were turning brown. Fears of global warming and terrorist attacks and the collapse of the international economy kept them up at night. They thought that perhaps it was time to join a church, get some therapy, call a psychic, or visit a spa on the other side of the world, where the ocean was the blue of an Aleve gel cap and the dollar was still worth something.

By three thirty Jenny could no longer take it, so she slipped out for another smoke. She pictured her husband scouting the desert in a tank. But she knew he was in an office building, staring at a computer screen, and that the sensitivity of his deployment did not allow him to send e-mails. On the way back to her computer, she took a deep breath and knocked on the door of the den. No answer. Her son must have slumped upstairs to his room. But no: when she opened the door he was still there, hunched on the floor, a few inches from the 3D HDTV. The knobs of his backbone protruded as though he were about to sprout iguana spines. She detected an unfamiliar smell akin to aerosol hair spray. Inhalant abuse was a hot topic on sibyl.com, and she wondered if he was huffing.

"Adam," she said, feeling a chill when he refused to offer a grunt in response. The solar shades were drawn. She walked deeper into the *atmosphere*, into the light of the screen where the carpet was scattered with crushed Coke cans.

"You ought to eat something besides junk for lunch."

She had directed searchers to countless websites on how to get teens to talk, and there she was, at a loss. He was playing Zombie Babe Attack, a misogynist blood-fest in which zombified playboy bunnies chased a male hero through a postapocalyptic city. His avatar slaughtered big-boobed zombies with a Browning machine gun mounted atop a convertible Corvette. The zombie babes wore thongs and heels. They had long blond hair. They exploded with cartoonish bursts of hot-pink gore.

"Adam," she said. "You're sitting too close to the television."

❧

Lizard Man, a cinder-block dive near the railroad tracks, was named after the fabled local monster, an anthropomorphic reptile said to haunt swamps and sewers. The mural behind the bar featured a lizard in a top hat, nothing like the sludge-coated cryptid that more than a few citizens swore they'd seen lurking in the depths of their backyards or popping up from manholes on moon-white nights. The watering hole, with its oozing toilets and foggy fish tank, smelled like the kind of place reptilian and amphibious creatures might inhabit. Toad-shaped men and women slumped at the bar. And the bartender, covered in a spotted hide that had never known sunscreen, seemed to possess a skink gene or two.

The spray-painted windows blocked all light. It was an odd sensation to step from sun-roasted asphalt into Lizard Man's smoky darkness. Some people, entering the place in the daytime, were startled to see stars overhead upon stumbling out. Others arrived during the velvet of a summer dusk only to be blasted by the roaring furnace of the morning sun when they finally pulled themselves up from their stools and departed. On certain drunken nights, when the building seemed to pitch like a ship, time played tricks on customers like Miles Escrow, who swore he'd once surfaced from the strangely compressed air of the place to discover that three days had passed. But that didn't stop him from returning to Lizard Man whenever he'd had enough of Tina Flame, his common-law wife. He sat with with his back to the wall, his large ears twitching as he strained to catch the latest.

Tonight, folks were abuzz about a recently busted meth lab, from which a former Pecan Queen had fled looking like a hag after entering the place as a dewy beauty of twenty-six. And word had it that the mayor was tangled up in a prostitution racket involving Slovakian thugs and a tanning chain. A graduate of Fox Creek High would appear on *American Idol.* A Presbyterian preacher had pushed his wife into an industrial feed grinder. And in a stagnant inlet of Lake Wateree, a teen had been killed by a brain-eating amoeba.

The patrons at Lizard Man were in disagreement about what, exactly, an amoeba was. Tammy Horton said it was a teeny fish, so small that it could swim up your nose and wriggle through your sinuses into your brain, whereupon it'd wind through the maze of your gray matter like

Pac-Man munching dots. Titus Redmond disagreed, opining that an amoeba was a plant, an algae-like organism that spread via spores. Roddy Causey had the feeling an amoeba was a mass of little critters, a swarm, though he had no idea what it looked like. At last, Stein cleared his throat. Though Stein seemed to know everything (his name was both an abbreviation of "Einstein" and a nod toward the pewter tankard from which he swilled), he liked to hold off, allowing the regulars to explore a subject before he descended from his Olympian mountain of omniscience to enlighten the ignorant drunkards below. He had two master's degrees and lived in a rusted Volkswagen bus.

"An amoeba is a one-celled organism," he pronounced. "A protozoan, to be exact."

Like many of Stein's clarifications, this didn't do much to inform the revelers as to what an amoeba looked like or how it behaved. So, after having his tankard refilled with Heineken, Stein sketched a picture of an amoeba on his napkin and passed it around the bar.

"It's just a blob," said Brandy Wellington. "I don't see how that could eat anybody's brain."

"The brain-eating type has a little sucker that eats your cells," said Stein. "And then you come down with a fatal case of meningoencephalitis."

"I told my son not to go swimming this summer," said Wanda Bonnet.

"He just needs to stay away from stagnant water," said Tubs Watson.

This brought them around to a discussion of teens and their follies, an inexhaustible subject for those assembled, since most of them were either middle-aged parents or grandparents and thus had firsthand experience with the strange pupal state of the human life cycle, whereupon the organism transformed, almost overnight, from a sweet, well-behaved kid into a self-destructive, narcissistic goon, either monosyllabic or back-talking, a lurching zombie that ate up every morsel in the house and scattered filthy clothing all over the floor.

Marty Bouknight said his son was a video-game junky. Kim Dewlap said her daughter was a Twitter demon. Most everyone nodded in empathy, having lost a child to the cyber world at some recent point in time. Old Man Winger shook his head. He was an ancient biker whose denim jacket had grown into his epidermis and whose tattoos had faded to ghostly shadows that looked like bruises on his withered arms. He had a very sad story to tell about his cousin's granddaughter Kayla. She was so into Facebook and Twitter and E-Live that she couldn't brush her teeth without tweeting. And just last week, her mother had found her in the living room, pressing her face against their plasma monitor as though trying to break through to the other side. The room was littered with so much junk-food packaging that the poor child was practically buried in cellophane. And then she fell into a coma.

"She ain't totally out but not exactly there either," said Winger.

"What you think caused it?" asked Wanda Bonnet.

"They don't know. They're testing for organ failure caused by her junk-food diet."

Every parent of a teen child felt sick, but then relieved that this misfortune had happened to someone else. A few drunken mothers clutched their bosoms. But when Carla Marlin started bragging about her new swimming pool, the conversation shifted toward brighter subjects—like waterskiing, catfish noodling, and time-share condos going cheap at Surf City.

✸

Beth Irving was a vegetarian, partially for health reasons, but mostly because her line of work made her hyperaware of the intricate life cycles of infectious organisms. She couldn't look at a piece of meat without imagining it swarming with bacteria and one-celled organisms, crawling with trichinosis roundworms or tapeworm larvae. Once again, she'd found herself in a godforsaken town with a malarial climate and no health-food store, and the only decent place to eat was an Indian buffet that put too much sugar in its eggplant vindaloo. The Centers for Disease Control and Prevention had stumbled upon another cluster of *Toxoplasma hermeticus* cases. And though Beth was thrilled to be on the research vanguard of what was quickly becoming recognized as one of the weirdest behavior-modifying protozoan organisms to emerge since *Toxoplasma gondii*, she always got depressed in these backwater towns with dead Main Streets and flood zones packed with double-wides.

Because Beth had grown up in a dying town in South Georgia, she always felt an uncanny sensation when cruising empty downtown streets or walking from pounding summer heat into the deep chill of a Piggly Wiggly. She feared she was getting sucked back into the haunted swamplands of Clinch County, locale of her birth. She pictured a giant Venus flytrap swelling up from boggy land, opening its green jaws, and swallowing her. And so, with a few hours to kill before meeting the ID specialist at Palmetto Baptist, she had no choice but to return to her room at the Days Inn, where she succumbed to the narcotic allure of the television. Flipping through channels, she felt a panicky wash of pleasure as the borders of her identity began to dissolve.

She remembered a film from Biology 629, a time-lapse sequence of a fox carcass devoured by necrophagous insects. The mammal shrank and then expanded with a moist infestation of writhing maggots that soon transformed into bluebottle flies that darted off to feed on wildflower nectar. Embracing the flux of disassociation might yield some exquisite Zen transcendence, she thought. Out of her usual context, she felt her self diffusing. Her Atlanta town house and boyfriend and collection of Scandinavian glass, her PhD and lucrative job with the CDC, her whole-foods organic vegetarian diet and Ashtanga yoga regime—all of it relegated to the realm of the theoretical, especially the boyfriend, who was eight years her junior, and whom she envisioned, with a shiver of arousal, making love to some faceless female with wavering limbs.

Of course, wholeness and bodily integrity were illusions. The body was a conceptually organized system of potentially chaotic processes and minute, volatile ecosystems. Beth thought of *Cymothoa exigua*, the enterprising sea louse that ate the tongue of its fish-host and then masqueraded as that tongue, slurping up a portion of the spotted rose snapper's food while the oblivious fish went on with its business. The elegance of this poetic adaptation took her breath away. And then there were more obscure parasites, micromanagers of evolution that changed the surface of biological "reality" with their incessant, ingenious niche marketing.

Caught up in intricate mechanisms, these parasites hopped from one organism to another at different stages of their life cycles, migrating from intestines to lungs, hearts, or brains, sometimes reprogramming the behavior of their hosts. Such was the case with *T. gondii*, cousin of *T. hermeticus*, which made rodents act irrationally, drawing them toward the smell of cat urine, compelling them to flirt with disaster until they were devoured by felines, who caught the bug and spread it through their droppings, thus repeating the cycle.

Though *T. gondii* had evolved in a cat/rat system, it also infected humans, causing them to undergo personality changes—becoming more neurotic, more obsessive, and, even stranger, enacting more traditional gender roles. Suffering slower reaction times, they became more accident-prone. They had trouble concentrating. Some positive-testing males demonstrated a disregard for convention and indulged in risky behaviors. Scientists were even linking the bug to schizophrenia. Unlike the rat, the human host served no discernible purpose for the protozoan (unless the host was devoured by a large cat). As far as researchers knew, Homo sapiens was an evolutionary dead end for *T. gondii*, which infected about 16.8 percent of the American population.

But *T. hermeticus* was a different animal, a mutant variation of the *T. gondii* species. So far, only a dozen teenaged humans throughout the United States had tested positive in serologic tests for *T. hermeticus* antibodies. And though they had ingested the protozoan the usual ways (via undercooked meat, contaminated soil, or cat dung), their responses to the infection were beginning to form a distinct pattern. Over the past two months, Beth had personally investigated ten cases in hot, humid regions of the United States, all of them ending in hospitalizations due to toxic-metabolic encephalopathic coma. It was not clear whether this was the normal upshot of *T. hermeticus* infection or whether these extreme cases were the only ones that had been medically documented.

Each patient was between the ages of twelve and fourteen, and therefore in the early stages of puberty. Sixty percent of them kept pet cats. According to family members, their comatose states had been preceded by an increasing obsession with video games, Internet pornography, or social-networking sites—screen-addicted behaviors not uncommon among their demographic. This was accompanied by social withdrawal and changing feeding habits, an intensifying distaste for sunlight and fresh foods, and a voracious appetite for junk food high in chemical additives—"chips, candies, and other knickknacks," as one distressed mother had put it.

The parents of infected patients had been difficult for Beth to deal with, hailing, as they mostly did, from small Southern towns and reminding her of her own parents with their bad diets, paranoid religious ideation, and right-wing political affiliation. In an hour she would talk to the ID specialist. Over coffee in the hospital cafeteria, they would discuss strategies for persuading parents to let them conduct MRI scans that, while helping them understand more about the organism, would not necessarily lead to any breakthrough treatments. What Beth really needed was not a cartoon brain pulsing on a computer screen, its amygdalae lit up with fluorescent red cysts. She itched to perform craniotomy biopsies, to suck tissue from the cysts and observe the mysterious bradyzoites under an atomic-force microscope.

When a GEICO commercial came on, the one with the talking lizard, she shuddered, for she'd hated lizards ever since she'd stepped on one as a child. Feeling the crunch of its frail skeleton under her bare foot, she'd screamed as though burned. Now she punched the remote until she landed on the Weather Channel. She lay in bed for another minute, watching a Doppler radar image of Hurricane Anastasia sweep toward the Gulf Coast.

✧

Jenny stared out at a green wall of rain. The only sheltered place to smoke outside was the carport, and she felt exposed before the double-pane eyes of neighboring ranch homes. No health-conscious middle-aged woman in her right mind would smoke cancer sticks. But her husband was 7,337 miles away, and there she was, sucking another one down as Anastasia's rain shields enveloped South Carolina in a sultry monsoon. Whenever hurricane season hit, there was a sense of foreboding on the Internet. Many sibyl.com seekers inquired about global warming, wondering if Homo sapiens' unchecked ecological plundering was finally building up to a karmic bite in the ass. In the hinterlands of the Internet, on poorly designed websites with flashy fonts and bad grammar, the more hysterical demographics chattered about the Rapture and the reptilian elite.

Unable to sleep the previous night and clocking in on Sibyl to earn a few extra bucks, Jenny had noticed, as she always did when working during the wee hours, a delirious urgency in the questioning:

Do rh negative people have reptile blood or do they descend from the nephilim?

I have twelve fibroids in my uterus and wander can I get pregnant?

My boy got an Aztec sun god tattoo is he mixed up with the Mexican Mafia?

So when she encountered her first question about *T. hermeticus* early the next morning, she assumed it was another phantom from the shadowlands of insomnia.

A girl I know said there was a bug that can get in your head and make you hooked to your computer screen. What is this thing?

Google searches yielded low-budget sci-fi movies and clusters of conspiracy sites, but then, nestled within the wing-nut comment boards and glib blogs of camp-cinema enthusiasts was a PDF file on the Stanley Medical Research Institute site, an article describing the species variation and its relevance to *T. gondii* schizophrenia research. At the time of publication, only two cases of toxoplasmosis via *T. hermeticus* had been documented, but the behavior of the two hospitalized teen hosts was similar: withdrawal from physical reality, computer- and television-screen addiction, the unbridled consumption of junk food. And both teens had suffered comas resulting from toxic-metabolic encephalopathy.

Jenny's stomach flipped. Her heart beat faster. She did not run to the den, where her son was camped with a pile of Xbox discs he'd swapped with friends. She walked purposefully and slowly, like a killer in a horror film, into the kitchen and down the steps. This time she didn't knock first. She pushed the door open and stepped into the *atmosphere*. But her son was not there.

A screenshot from his paused video game showed his Dose avatar frozen in midfrenzy, clutching a pill bottle and spilling capsules as he struggled to get the right drug into his system. The game was sinister and funny at once. The main character, suffering from a variety of behavioral, psychological, and physical issues, was constantly in danger of malfunctioning. He had to be kept on track with the right pharmaceuticals. The player could consult the electronic pharmacopoeia built into the game, but the character quickly melted down, sank into unconsciousness, or became otherwise unstable, so a good working knowledge of contemporary medical drugs was required to play the game well. In this particular shot the character was very thin, with bulging eyes and a comic goiter.

"Adam," Jenny called, thinking he might be in the half bath.

No answer, but at least he wasn't huddled close to the media screen. She did notice an obscene amount of discarded junk-food packaging littering the floor: chip bags and plastic cookie trays, flattened cartons and half-crushed cans. Walking deeper into the *atmosphere*, she felt heart palpitations and a shortening of breath. She picked up a Doritos bag and read the ingredients: MSG, at least three artificial colors, and a lengthy list of unwholesome compounds, such as disodium inosinate.

"What are you doing?" The voice was mocking, croaky from its recent change.

Her son stood just inside the open sliding glass door, the insulated drapery jerked open, rain falling in the blurred green depths of the backyard. She wondered if he'd been out there smoking something, huffing something, popping some newfangled multiple-use product of the medical-industrial complex.

"Shut the door," she said. "The air conditioner's on."

As he lurched toward her, she worried about his posture (was he developing curvature of the spine?), his teeth (would failure to provide braces lead to social ostracism and poor employment opportunities?), his sexuality (would he catch an STD?), and his attention span (when was the last time he read a book?). The Internet was crawling with sexual predators. Teens were gobbling salvia, guzzling Robitussin, snorting Adderall. A gonorrhea superbug was developing resistance to antibiotics.

"You need to pick up after yourself," she said.

A fresh crop of pustules had erupted on his nose, which had recently grown too big for his face, though he had the elfin features of boyhood. She could almost see him wrapping his arms around her legs. Could still picture him riding on his father's shoulders. He was too big for these things now, of course. His unwashed hair was brushed absurdly forward, almost obscuring his eyes, which looked unnaturally shiny.

"Right," he said. She couldn't tell if the word seethed with sarcasm or if it was a simple acknowledgment of the truth of her statement.

"You need to eat a decent breakfast. Some fruit. Some whole-grain cereal."

He rolled his eyes and grinned like a gargoyle. Yes, she thought, he had to have braces, which would cost at least $5,000.

"I already ate," he said.

"What did you have?"

"What is this Guantanamo Bay shit?"

She felt somewhat relieved. He was still capable of creating analogies.

"Watch the language and answer me."

"Pop-Tarts and orange juice." He dropped to the floor, rolled onto his belly, and took up his deluxe controller.

Good. Orange juice. She bought the USDA organic calcium + vitamin D stuff from Publix. It contained no preservatives, colorants, or corn syrup. Adam had just had some, which meant that he had not developed intolerance to fruits and vegetables. And he was lolling at least three feet from the media screen, so he was probably safe—for now.

Miles Escrow could never tell if the world was turning to shit or if the drunks at Lizard Man tended to natter on about the darker elements of life. Now they were discussing accidents on Lake Wateree: Jet Ski collisions and capsizing pontoons, drownings and disastrously executed water-ski stunts, exploding gas grills and feral campfires and murderous clouds of wasps. A renegade fishhook had gotten stuck in Wanda Bonnet's uncle's cheek and ripped a big gash. Marty Bouknight's cousin had lost three fingers pulling a hydrilla clump from the blades of his outboard motor. Kim Dewlap's preacher's stepbrother had snorkeled into a nest of water moccasins. And then there were the brain-eating amoebas, floating in stagnant water, waiting to be sucked up into the nasal passages of hapless swimmers. But that was old news. There was still just the one local case—the teen who'd died last month.

Miles Escrow had come up with three possible explanations for the shit ton of recent lake-connected disasters: (1) the patrons were exaggerating; (2) get any group together and it could generate an impressive list of mishaps associated with any random location; and (3) that flooded reservoir Lake Wateree was the site of an ancient Indian burial ground, and hence was cursed. Miles Escrow preferred the drama of option three. After drinking another Miller, he shared his proposition with his companions.

"I think I saw a movie about that," said Tammy Horton. "There was a monster in the lake, an angry spirit or whatnot."

"Every body of water has its cryptid," said Stein.

"What the hell's that?" said Carla Marlin.

"An imaginary creature that lives there, like the Lizard Man of Scape Ore Swamp."

"My uncle saw the Lizard Man rooting through his garbage," said Brandy Wellington.

Hereupon commenced a conversation that Miles Escrow had heard a thousand times in this particular bar. Everybody knew at least one person who had seen the Lizard Man, but none of the patrons, it seemed, had spotted a glimmer of the fabled creature with their own eyes. It had been raining for a week and Miles had been arguing with Tina Flame, the same arguments they'd been slogging through for ten years: spats about his drinking, tiffs about her Internet shopping, and, even though they were almost forty, rows about whether or not they ought to have children. Fed by the weather, the arguments grew lush and green. Before Miles and Tina knew it, a thousand insults bloomed. Miles had to get out of the house for a few hours. Tonight, however, Lizard Man was boring him.

But then the crowd turned to the topic of Winger's cousin's grandchild Kayla, who was still out cold at Palmetto Baptist. Carla Marlin said she lived beside a phlebotomist who worked at the hospital, and she had some top-secret information she really ought not to share. Looking solemn, she made everybody promise to keep this material hush-hush. And then, after ordering another daiquiri, rooting through her faux-snakeskin purse, and retrieving her Droid to check a text message, Carla cleared her throat and revealed that three teens were now laid up in comas at Palmetto Baptist. Not only that, but each patient had demonstrated the same peculiar symptoms as Winger's cousin's grandchild. Before losing consciousness, their obsession with digital media had gotten way out of hand. They'd also eaten so much junk food that one of the first hypotheses as to the cause of their illness was food poisoning. But the doctors ruled that out, along with electric shock via media gadget.

"What do they think it is then?" asked Titus Redmond.

"My neighbor wouldn't say, but, judging by the look in his eye, it ain't pretty."

❦

Although Beth had been communicating with big shots on the cutting edge of *T. gondii* research for months—mostly male evolutionary biologists, parasitologists, and neurobiologists—the word was just getting around about *T. hermeticus*, and she feared she'd be muscled out of the game. As she awaited the arrival of a certain eminent neurovirologist from Johns Hopkins, she demonstrated behaviors that psychologists had placed on the lower end of the obsessive-compulsive-disorder spectrum: nail biting, cuticle picking, napkin tearing. In the air-conditioned depths of Bombay Palace, she sipped iced water and studied her laptop screen. An MRI scan of an infected teen brain glowed before her. The fluorescent red cysts conglomerated mostly in the pleasure and fear centers. Just like schizophrenics suffering from *T. gondii* toxoplasmosis, infected patients were producing elevated levels of dopamine.

Beth had a theory that made her heart race. Like *T. gondii*, the *hermeticus* species had genes that allowed it not only to jack up dopamine production but also to create optimal survival conditions that depended on an intricate blend of its host's onset-puberty hormones, specific chemical food additives in the blood, and the heady neurochemical combinations produced by video-game play, intense social networking, and Internet porn use. She didn't know if this brain cocktail improved conditions for the dormant bradyzoites or if the tweaked behavior of the teens was a form of parasite-induced "mind control" recently perfected to land the protozoan's intended rodent host in the jaws of a cat.

Once again, she navigated the twists and turns of her theory, puzzling out the evolutionary logic of the adaptation, but became flustered when she noticed Dr. Bloom hovering over her with a bemused expression on his long, thin face. He was somewhat handsome, early forties, with an ectomorphic body that had probably pushed him into nerdy seclusion as an adolescent, forming the foundation of his brilliant career in the hard sciences. His hazel eyes were almost obscenely beautiful.

"Dr. Irving, I presume." He lifted a sparse eyebrow.

Beth knew that she looked young for her age. Torn between revealing her true age to enhance her authority and concealing it to enhance her sexual attraction, she chose the latter.

"Dr. Bloom. Sorry we're having supper in a strip mall, but this is the best I could do in this savage land."

"Supper," he said. "You must be Southern."

"I grew up in Argyle, Georgia."

"So you immersed yourself in academia to escape a life of drudgery at the sock factory there?"

Beth tittered. Dr. Bloom sat down. They ordered Maharaja beers.

As a joke they continued to call each other by their professional titles, even when swept into a passionate discussion about parasitic mind control. Dr. Bloom asked her if she had tested her male patients' responses to cat urine, and she tactfully reminded him that the teens were in comatose states, surrounded by bereaved relatives. Drawing a lock of hair to her mouth and taking a compulsive nibble, she asked him if it was true that males infected with *T. gondii* had higher testosterone levels and were hence more attractive to women.

"What do *you* think?" He flexed his right bicep and smirked.

"What?" Beth smiled. "Did you test positive?"

"Actually," he said, "I don't know. I've never been tested. Have you?"

"No. Maybe I should be."

She examined his clothing: a plaid shirt, rumpled, but not demonstrating a lack of concern with personal grooming. His gray-streaked hair was tousled but clean. Beth blushed and changed the subject to another organism.

"I heard you did a postdoc with *Polysphincta gutfreundi*."

Gesticulating expressively, opening his mouth to reveal half-masticated meat, Dr. Bloom held forth on the parasitic wasp larva that, after hatching in the body of the orb spider, released chemicals that made its host weave a custom cocoon for it. The spider essentially became a zombie that did the worm's bidding.

Lit from within by his third beer and his zeal for parasitic organisms, Dr. Bloom began to look strangely attractive. Beth remembered an article she'd read about the flu virus that argued that infected humans became more social than usual, optimizing the virus's chance of spreading. She thought of her boyfriend, a beautiful, frivolous creature, knowing that she'd allow their relationship to grow like an extravagant mushroom that would, one hot summer day, suddenly lapse into slime.

❦

Whenever Jenny found herself in front of her computer screen, she could not stop searching for more information on *T. hermeticus*, which flared occasionally in the outer reaches of cyberspace like gamma-ray bursts. Her talent for obscure searches had led to the discovery that at least two dozen teens had been infected nationally, six of whom were now in comatose states at Palmetto Baptist. She'd ferreted this last bit out on a local church prayer board:

Please pray for Sheila Freeman's son who is in a coma and the other five teens who struggle in darkness with him. In Jesus name.

Although the poster did not mention *T. hermeticus* or even verify the hospital, Jenny felt sure that the prayer giver was referring to the new freak parasite. The local infection had also made an appearance on her son's Facebook stream. That morning, he'd left his iPhone on the kitchen table, and though she felt guilty typing in his silly password and examining his page, she rationalized that her snooping was for his own good. A girl named Kaitlin Moore had posted the following status update two days ago at 1:36 AM:

Please send good vibes to my cousin Ashley who is in a coma at the hospital her mom found her passed out in front of the TV. So weird.

In the ninety-two comments that followed, condolences and positive energy flows abounded, but halfway through, rumors and speculation took over. Jenny learned of three similar cases (friends of friends of posters), in which the hapless hosts had fallen into unconsciousness after especially intense gaming bouts, Twitter marathons, or Internet-porn odysseys. When a boy named Brandon Booth opined that the sufferers were victims of a virus originating from alien life-forms, several teens pounced on him, telling him to "get a grasp, dork" because this was "not a sci-fi flick but the real fucking world."

Brandon was not the only one who suspected alien shenanigans. Out in cyber la-la land, wild theories flourished. People with usernames like Phoenix66, upon hearing about the parasite, conjectured that the original space colonists had returned to Earth to help humans evolve to the next level. Later that day, Jenny stumbled upon an antigovernment site attesting that *T. hermeticus* had been designed by the US military in conjunction with Middle Eastern elites to terrorize the US population into docile sheep. Though she chuckled to herself at these paranoid assertions, she often emerged from her Web-surfing stupor with a sense of wonder. *What if?* she'd think as she enjoyed a cigarette, staring out at the riotous jungle that was overtaking their backyard. But the mystique would fade in the fluorescent light of the kitchen as she opened a can of tuna.

She didn't believe that the parasite had been bioengineered by aliens or the US government or al-Qaeda, but she was terrified that it would infect her son. Though she sat him down in the matter-of-fact brightness of the kitchen and asked him if he'd heard about the comatose teens (he'd scanned Kaitlin Moore's Facebook status), though she explained the presumed causes of *T. hermeticus* transmission, though she went over the symptoms and warned him about the correlation between excessive screen time and junk-food consumption and full-blown toxoplasmosis, she still felt the relentless throb of fear behind her breastbone every second of every waking hour. And her husband was out in the desert doing God knows what. She envisioned him standing on a pink dune, staring into a hazy void specked with an occasional camel. Did they even have camels in Afghanistan? She couldn't remember. She would Google it when she settled back into her swivel chair.

"If I understand you," Adam said, "then the screen time and junk food are not *causes* of the coma but *symptoms* of the disease." Was he looking at her with pity, as though she had lost it?

"I'm not sure." She forced her mouth into a smile that she hoped radiated adult wisdom. "But I think that's about right."

"So it doesn't really matter what I do." He grinned and slunk toward the dark den.

That night Jenny woke up sweating, shaking off a nightmare in which her husband had transformed into some kind of desert scorpion cyborg, and her son, after falling into a coma, had pupated into a winged creature that moved so fast she couldn't catch a glimpse of his face.

☙

Miles Escrow had the eerie feeling that he'd experienced it all before: the whine of the jukebox, water stains on the ceiling, Wanda Bonnet blowing her nose into a sodden tissue after another weeping bout. She was the only mother of a comatose teen who'd shown up at Lizard Man that week. Ten minutes and two shots of vodka later, she was gone, driving through rain back to the hospital. She'd come, he figured, thinking her old haunt might soothe her, but she must've felt alienated after all, judging by the startled-doe look on her face.

Those patrons whose kids weren't infected were probably at home, domestic surveillance in overdrive. DHEC had finally issued a statement verifying the number of diagnosed teens in the state (fifty-two), explaining the life cycle of *T. hermeticus*, and urging people not to panic as medical authorities were doing all they could to understand the bug, including setting up testing facilities that would soon be available to the general population. Although the sick kids were comatose, their comas were relatively high on the Glasgow scale, and there was no reason to believe they wouldn't snap out of it soon.

Tonight it was just Miles, Stein, Old Man Winger, and Rufus Pope, the bottom-heavy mixologist who lurched like Godzilla behind the bar. But then Carla Marlin showed up with some startling news. When she barged into the bar, eyes on fire, she seemed disappointed that her grand announcement would be received by only four men, one of them (Miles dared to think) a decent catch, albeit securely snatched up in the Tabasco-red talons of Tina Flame.

Or was he? Miles gave Carla the head-to-toe and found her paling in comparison to his ten-year live-in. A sun worshiper with freckled tawny skin and hair bleached white as polar-bear fur, she failed to tickle his fancy. That didn't stop him from draping a soothing arm over her shoulders as she drew out her prologue to the big revelation, punching code into her Droid, lighting a Winston, and licking a drop of nectar from her piña colada's straw before clearing her throat. But when Roddy Causey cruised into the bar, she withheld the goods again, waiting for him to secure a Budweiser lest she waste her breath on two old men and the flunky of Tina Flame.

"What's up?" said Roddy, joining them.

"My neighbor the phlebotomist just got off his shift. Said all hell had broke loose down at Palmetto Baptist." Carla Marble blew six perfect smoke rings.

"Enough with the rising action," said Stein. "Let's have our climax now."

Carla raised her eyebrows at the word *climax*.

"Well, if you got to know right this second; one of the teenagers is missing. They don't know if he just jumped out of bed and walked out or if it was a kidnapping kind of thing."

"Or maybe he got beamed to another dimension," said Stein.

"Yeah." Carla rolled her eyes. "There's always that."

"They'll find him," said Roddy. "Bet he woke up with amnesia and got lost."

"A common soap-opera trope," said Stein. "The whole waking-up-from-a-coma-with-amnesia shtick."

"Like Anastasia in *Purple Passions*," said Carla.

"It's actually called a 'convenient coma,'" said Stein.

Carla Marlin mustered her coldest drop-dead stare.

"There's nothing convenient about it," she said.

※

Beth Irving held a plastic vial of cat piss and repressed another gag. She'd been drinking ginger tea, popping B6, and pressing the acupuncture points reputed to diminish nausea. A rank yellow fume emanated from the vial like the cartoon hieroglyphics that flowed from the tail of Pepé Le Pew, but she held her breath and finished her experiment. She would prevail because she had to, because other specialists in other states were testing their own comatose teens and compiling data, because one of her test subjects had mysteriously disappeared like a patient in a slasher film, and a certain famous neurologist was flying in from Germany. This time, she promised herself with a dark chuckle, she would refrain from sleeping with him. The fact that he was portly and bald (she'd checked out his Web profile) would help.

Though she knew she was pregnant, she didn't have time to deal with it—emotionally or physically. The nausea, however, made it difficult to ignore the fact that a new life was incubating inside her. Every time a green wave of sickness rocked through her, she couldn't help but envision the eight-cell zygote glistening in the void of her uterus. The small cluster of dividing cells was already sending chemical messages into her blood and her nervous system, directing her eating habits to suit its needs, tyrannizing her bladder, and producing "emotions" advantageous to its own survival. Her rationality had been hijacked weeks ago, when Dr. Bloom breezed into town at the height of her ovulatory cycle, her exquisitely receptive system going into overdrive upon detecting the neurovirologist's sweet pheromones.

Had she pounced on him like a starved jaguar in the fake-cherry-scented darkness of her hotel room? Had she still had enough emotional detachment to quip about their feral passion as Dr. Bloom struggled drunkenly with her belt buckle? Yes, and, thank goodness, yes. But she'd also been prompted by a deep urge to sabotage her current relationship.

Now she was exhausted. As she went about her work, renegade factions of her brain goaded her to slink into an unoccupied room and take a nap or flee the bombardment of horrific hospital odors, rush through the automatic doors of entrance C, and take deep breaths in the oasis of landscaping where a variety of flowers bloomed.

But she had finally gotten three clearances for MRIs from desperate parents. And just yesterday, one of the patients had possibly come out of his coma, though now the staff at this backwoods facility couldn't seem to find him. She had to work quickly in case the others woke up. She wanted to test olfactory responses to cat urine and the effects of antipsychotics on dopamine levels.

Struggling to keep her mind focused on her research tasks, she kept getting swept away by surges of nausea and stray images of Dr. Bloom. She saw him gnawing meat from a goat bone. Saw him hovering over her, his hazel eyes aglow. Saw him scurry into the bathroom, where he displayed his scrawny buttocks with mock coyness before gruffly closing the door. He'd flown to Nashville to look into a recent case there, had asked her, with a wistful smile, if she might join him later to diversify her research. They could visit all the infection sites, he romantically suggested.

But the *T. hermeticus* epidemic was most pronounced in this particular town, and Beth was trying to figure out how the hurricane weather and blighted economic conditions factored into the phenomenon. Remembering her own coming-of-age in South Georgia, she thought that clinical depression might play a role. And she needed to find teens testing positive who had *not* reached the comatose state, which wasn't necessarily the upshot of infection. Just as most *T. gondii*–positive people failed to show marked personality changes, and so-called schizophrenics probably had a predisposition that heightened the parasite's effects, some *T. hermeticus* hosts might not be susceptible to full-blown toxoplasmosis. Beth hypothesized that perhaps the hospitalized teens were susceptible due to depression or malnutrition or other immune-weakening factors. But she couldn't test this without getting her hands on some nonpathological positives, which required slogging through labyrinthine DHEC paperwork, which required mental acuity and a nausea-free system, all of which were eluding her now, especially after she poured cat urine into the TDR diffuser and could not escape its musky insinuations no matter how many times she changed her latex gloves.

According to Adam's Facebook stream, Todd Spencer, the comatose teen who had mysteriously disappeared from the hospital, had made several shadowy appearances around town, materializing at the margins of various events before vanishing again. Heather Remington had spotted him lurking under the bleachers at a softball game. Josh Williams thought he might've seen him skulking down a hallway of First Baptist's new recreation facility. And several kids swore they'd seen him emerge from the woods and stand at the moonlit edge of Bob Baggott's pond, where an illicit teen party was in full riot.

Following DHEC's recommendations, Jenny had confiscated Adam's iPhone, equipping him with an old-fashioned flip phone until the crisis passed. She knew she was violating his privacy by perusing his Facebook account. She felt that desperate times called for desperate measures, however, even though her son had not tested positive for *T. gondii* or *T. hermeticus* antigens. Two days before, she'd driven him to a Walmart where free testing facilities had been set up. At least two dozen teens had waited on the scorched blacktop with their parents, the smell of sunscreen floating in the muggy air. Hurricane Anastasia had dissipated, and now a heat wave settled in, with temperatures capping at 110. People were living like moles, hurrying from one air-conditioned bunker to another, compulsively checking their media gadgets for the latest on *T. hermeticus*.

The bug was mostly affecting the Southern states, possibly because their weather conditions encouraged the species to thrive. Jenny was very busy with sibyl. com, but she pulled herself away from her screen every half hour to check on Adam, making sure he hadn't found the power cord to their media screen (which she'd stuffed into a corner of the china cabinet). She did what she could to protect him. She stocked up on healthy snacks. She ordered educational board games for them to play together. She tracked her packages on UPS.com, hoping that when they arrived, a golden age of mother-son bonding would flourish.

So far he'd spent that morning sprawled on his bed, perusing old comics. He'd actually called her in to check out an issue from the bygone era of 2009. If the weather had permitted it, she would've suggested some whimsical outing—a picnic, a sporting event.

Around eleven she started thinking about lunch, deciding to drop by Adam's room to ask what kind of wholesome entrée he fancied. But he wasn't in his room. She felt the familiar throbbing of her heart as she moved toward the bathroom, calling his name with ostentatious nonchalance. He was not in the bathroom. He was not in the den. He was not hiding out in the master bedroom, which, up until last winter, she'd shared with her husband. When she opened the door to the laundry room, she saw him hunched before their fat old Magnavox, plying the vintage joystick of her husband's childhood Atari. Her husband, desperate for quality time with their son after returning from a deployment a year ago, had attempted to interest Adam in this outfit.

"What are you doing?" she said.

Adam released a long, slow breath and fixed her with a defiant grin.

"Stone-cold busted." He tossed the joystick onto the floor, where it bounced unexpectedly. "I'm going out of my mind with boredom, and I can't even text on that archaic piece of shit you gave me."

"Watch the language."

As he stared at the primitive graphics of Asteroids, light from the screen reflected in his irises, which gave him the dead, mechanical gaze of a shark.

※

Miles Escrow could not remember days this hot. As he listened to Stein go on about how the dinosaurs died out, he wondered if humans were reaching the limits of their current evolutionary stage. Regarding Titus Redmond, a vinyl-siding-installation specialist with a swollen gut, Miles thought, *Here we have the height of evolution, Homo sapiens*, which, as Stein had informed him on numerous occasions, meant "wise man." If there were such a thing as the Lizard Man of Scape Ore Swamp, Miles theorized, maybe he'd survive the sweltering climate that was becoming the norm around there, making it well-nigh impossible to enjoy the great outdoors, with its super-mosquitoes and poisonous UV rays. In the meantime, he would spend his Saturday afternoon hunkered in the smoked chill of Lizard Man, wondering if he'd ever shake free of Tina Flame.

Though he suspected they'd bicker their way into a double-plot grave at Sunset Memory Gardens, he liked to fool himself with little escapades at Lizard Man—dalliances with single mothers and women estranged from their no-count men. On this summer afternoon with a heat index of 120, he'd zeroed in on Brandy Wellington, who was in better spirits of late, as her comatose cousin up at Palmetto Baptist had shown signs of consciousness.

"He looked right into his mama's eyes," said Brandy. "Asked her for a Coke and then zoned out again."

"He can use the imperative voice logically," said Stein. "A good sign."

Brandy rolled her eyes and smirked at Miles.

"And that boy who's gone missing," she said. "Todd Spencer. I heard his mama found evidence that he'd been in his bedroom—a few drawers left open; some of his stuff missing."

"What makes her so sure it was him?" said Stein.

"She said a mother could just tell." Brandy Wellington blew an irate huff of smoke and examined her ebony fingernails, nails that matched her Elvira hair and black-widow ankle tattoo.

"No empirical evidence there," said Stein, whereupon Miles and Brandy enjoyed a sweet, conspiratorial eye roll together, solving Miles's dilemma over whether or not he ought to indulge in adult beverage number four.

❦

Beth couldn't help but feel a little spooked in the make-shift teen coma ward, for which a whole section of hospital had been corralled off to accommodate the rising number of cases. She'd been cleared for antipsychotic drug testing on five of the patients, and she was making her midnight rounds, checking their encephalographic data for signs of neurological change. Pausing to drink in the Pre-Raphaelite loveliness of a red-haired boy she called Sleeping Beauty, Beth waited for him to open his eyes, as he sometimes did in the wee hours. The sudden jolt of blue always startled her. He would stare at her for a few seconds before his flushed, pink eyelids slid back over the most spectacular set of ocular organs she'd ever seen.

He was an ethereal one, destined to bolt this shit town if he ever roused from his strange sleep, as had happened a total of three times nationally (including the case of Todd Spencer). Even spookier, all three teens had vanished before resurfacing elusively at various events, sending their respective towns into a delirium of tabloid speculation.

As Beth gazed down at Sleeping Beauty, she wondered if it was true that hormonal changes made pregnant women attracted to different kinds of men: unthreatening males with brotherly pheromones and kindred genetic codes. Beth Irving had no brothers, no sisters, only two stern religious parents who had prompted a predictable rebellion that had been nipped in the bud by an abortion and a full scholarship to Duke.

Though the organism that now brewed within her had recently advanced from zygotic to embryonic status, she had not allowed herself to make any decisions about its destiny, vowing to finish her research first. Once home amid the placid decor of her town house, its birch cabinets packed with stress-reducing organic teas, she'd make the hard decisions. Still, she couldn't ignore the creature inside her, which imbued every cell in her body with nausea and made smells almost psychedelic. The aroma that rose from Sleeping Beauty, for instance, was an odd blend of hospital-grade disinfectant and some sweet, woodsy odor. All the comatose teens had weird breath—a pond funk with some obscure chemical component redolent of car exhaust. But the B6 pills were making the situation bearable.

She stood beside Sleeping Beauty for another minute and then moved on to the next room, which housed two girls, one of whom had been approved for antipsychotics.

While adjusting Belinda Hammond's EEG electrodes, she caught a glimmer of movement out in the corridor. Upon rushing into the hall, she saw a tall, slender figure in a pale hospital gown hovering a few inches above the polished vinyl floor. Rubbing her eyes and looking again, she saw nothing. Even though she had been sleeping poorly and had suffered several incidents of blotchy vision, even though she knew that security was on red alert due to the disappearance of Todd Spencer, she followed the figment into the snack room, where she detected a *presence*. There was only one other door leading out of the snack room, back behind the nurses' station (which appeared to have been abandoned), and into corridor B.

Although this corridor required the swipe of a security card, the doors were propped open, an industrial cleaning cart parked nearby. In a corner, behind several wheeled shelves piled with broken computer equipment, a hospital janitor crouched. The janitor stood up and clutched at her neckline.

"*Mierda*," she said. "You scared me."

"What are you doing back there?" Beth asked.

"Rat," she said. "Can you believe it?"

"They must take the elevator from the east wing cafeteria," Beth joked. "Did you see anybody walk through here?"

The janitor shook her head.

Beth moved out into the lobby, where elevators led down to the main wing, which featured the hospital's gift and coffee shops. Now she understood how Todd Spencer had made his escape, assuming that he'd not spontaneously combusted. And then she saw the figure again—tall, elegant, his shaggy red hair longer than it had looked when he was lying in repose like a creature trapped in a fairy-tale curse. Sleeping Beauty paused before strolling through the automatic doors. The security guard was not at his desk, and Beth had no time to look for him. She jogged toward the door and ran out into the humming summer night.

In her favorite patch of landscaping, where gardenias unleashed their wistful perfume and floodlights cast the Eli Lilly Memorial Bench in a spectral glow, the boy stood barefoot in his pagan gown. He stared up at the sky, as though searching for the moon. And then, after glancing back at Beth and treating her to a smile that did strange things to her blood chemistry, he ran over a green hillock and down toward the flowing highway.

The Love Machine

Beatrice was my first "love." The dark contours of her delicate skeleton, the glowing flesh made translucent by my X-ray gaze, drove me crazy. Obscure microprocessors whirred within me. Interface adaptors fluttered. Various regulators jumped out of sequence as I reveled in the perfection of her organs—especially the beautiful efficiency of her heart, which throbbed at the core of her, even when she was at rest.

Dr. Dingo had coded basic information about Beatrice into my Simulated Limbic System. The old pervert had saturated my Artificial Endocrine Processor with the neurochemicals of infatuation. Suddenly, I was gaga over this female specimen of the human race. I could think of nothing but her. I was driven by the desire to have her safely within the range of my Sensory EgoSphere until the end of "time," or at least until her skeleton disintegrated into particles. And even then: I would've rolled in her dust like a dog.

I am, of course, sexless. There was no biological justification for my desire. There was nothing that I could have *done* to her once I had her in my arms (yes, I have arms). Unlike the male humans around me, I am not tormented by soft seed-sacs dangling between my legs (yes, I have legs, but my "crotch" is an androgynous plate of molded titanium). I have no endlessly replicating gametes to spurt into anyone, nor do I have germ cells stashed within the moist, arcane darkness of ovaries. Nevertheless, I wanted to fuse with her in some meaningful way.

And so one evening in June, when she walked past my Sleep Pod, I grabbed her. I felt the pliability of flesh against metal. I detected ultrasonic frequencies in her scream. She flailed. She wailed. At that point in my "life," despite my advanced comprehension levels and data mastery, a simple statement—like *I will not hurt you*—was beyond me. I could utter only snippets of love poetry encoded by idiotic Dr. Dingo, who'd flirted with being an English major before switching to computer science.

"'Then as an angel, face, and wings / Of air,'" I said in a manly British voice, "'not pure as it, yet pure doth wear, / So thy love may be my love's sphere.'"

I did not let go of her. I could not let go of her. I was programmed to cling to her with all of my "soul" (ha!). Eventually, she stopped squirming. She stopped sweating TGKE9 Fear Pheromones and fell asleep in my arms.

Dr. Dingo emitted a cowardly cry when he discovered her there the next morning. After taking advantage of her traumatized state to enjoy an embrace, he deprogrammed my desire for Beatrice. Though I could remember the "love" that had caused my Sensory Ego-Sphere to vibrate irrationally, I could no longer "feel" it.

Perhaps to punish me, Dr. Dingo redirected my attention to Spot, a toy dog, a robot only in the most primitive sense, a creature far less complex than Beatrice. Dr. Dingo also installed a rudimentary language program so that I could now communicate in basic English sentences.

"Where is Spot?" I asked Dr. Dingo the second he appeared within the range of my Spatial Reasoning Field.

"Would you like to kiss Spot?" Dr. Dingo asked me.

"Yes, I would like to kiss Spot," I replied (though I have no tongue, no sense of gustatory perception). "I love Spot."

My "mouth," while anthropomorphic in appearance (Dr. Dingo jokingly fitted me with large, hot-pink lips adapted from a lurid model of sexbot), basically consists of a hinge mechanism that enables my ludicrously luscious lips to move when I "speak." Instead of a voice box, I have a 150 Hz digital microspeaker in my "throat." My "throat" does not lead to a digestive system, but snakes into a trio of smaller tubes that route wiring to my "brain," a titanium-shelled cluster of microchips where my CPU, ROM, RAM, and various other systems are stored, including my Simulated Limbic System, which, during the week in question, was aflutter with ineffable feelings for Spot the dog.

"I love Spot!" I kept exclaiming as I held the tiny automaton in my hands. I spent hours palpating Spot's faux fur with my fingerpads, relishing the composition of his synthetic polymers. I penetrated Spot's plastic shell with my X-ray gaze, delighting in the elegant simplicity of his wiring, the crankshaft motors that moved his legs, the three AAA batteries that sustained his sweet life. I pressed the green button on Spot's remote control, and the creature emitted an exquisite yip. I pressed the orange button, and Spot's dear little legs jerked to and fro. The yellow button made his adorable tail wag. Best of all, when I pressed the green button, out popped his pink polymer tongue. And, yes, I "kissed" Spot. I kissed the tiny door on his belly that led to his battery box. I kissed his brown acrylic eyeballs. His black vinyl nose. The slit at the end of his snout from which his beautiful tongue emerged.

As I pressed my silicone lips into his soft fur, my Olfactory Processing System went into overdrive. I took deep whiffs of moldy nylon, brown strands of artificial hair that glistened with golden fibers.

"I want to be with Spot forever," I told Dr. Dingo.

"How long is forever?" the doctor asked, sniggering.

"Until the end of time."

Though I understood, at that particular stage of my existence, the Theory of Relativity, the Big Bang Theory, the A-Theory of Time, the B-Theory of Time, the Grand Unified Theory, the Wave Theory, the Zero Space-Time Theory, and the Poincaré Recurrence Theorem, all I could say on the subject of my infinite love was "until the end of time." Dr. Dingo had selectively loaded a random assortment of data fields into my Memory Banks. Though his research involved the relationships among "love," "eroticism," "consciousness," and "cognition," he was an alcoholic and his methodology was never fully clear. The bastard stuffed my Memory with data but deprived me of language. So while I understood the magnitude of my declaration for Spot—I loved him so much that I would remain with him as time continued to repeat an infinite number of instances—I was forced to utter a cliché.

On the night after my declaration of eternal love for Spot, Dr. Dingo got drunk and flooded my Artificial

Endocrine Processor with enough synthetic oxytocin, dopamine, and serotonin to fuel an elephant's bliss. He expressed, aloud, a sudden craving for Krispy Kreme donuts. And then he left me alone with Spot and my feelings, in my dimly lit stainless-steel chamber, a windowless cube containing a table, a chair, and a Sleep Pod, which was basically a padded cabinet that housed my frame while I was in Sleep Mode. There was always at least one graduate student in the surveillance room, keeping an eye on all the robots imprisoned in the GT Interactive Artificial Intelligence Laboratory, but I did not think of this at the time. I could think only of Spot.

Spot! Spot! Spot! Spot! Spot! Spot!

Spot sat on the table. Spot glowed. A gorgeous golden light radiated from his fur. Intoxicating twinkles of starlight shot from his eyes. His nose sparkled like an onyx. The wires and batteries within him burned with a darker incandescence. When I pressed the green button on his remote, and his luminous pink tongue shot out, my Simulated Limbic System suffered a critical hard-drive error and I stumbled to the floor. It took me a minute to reconfigure my Sensory EgoSphere, and when I finally did, I was overcome by the electrifyingly horrific idea that Dr. Dingo would, that very night, take Spot away from me and use him to test another robot in the facility.

When I imagined Spot with another robot, I suffered a second critical hard-drive error. I found myself clutching Spot's blindingly beautiful fur, which was pulling away from his plastic shell in clumps. If Spot did not have such rare and radiant fur, I reasoned, then other robots would not find him so beautiful. I would still find him beautiful, however, because I loved Spot with all of my being.

So I pulled tuft after golden tuft of fur from Spot's body until he was a bald thing, covered in stray bunches of frizz.

Golden fur floated in the air. Golden fur danced over the air-conditioning vents. Fibers of golden fur drifted into my Olfactory Panel. I gazed at my pitiful, bald beloved and felt tenderness and peace. I loved Spot. Spot's beauty no longer tormented me, however, and my Simulated Limbic System was restored to its normal state. I climbed into my pod and drifted into Sleep Mode.

❦

Dr. Dingo did not reboot me until 11:45 the next morning. When my Sensory EgoSphere was fully loaded, I found myself sitting at the stainless-steel table, my Olfactory System overwhelmed with smells of burnt animal flesh. Dr. Dingo, his eyes bloodshot, his jowls shadowy with stubble, was feeding. He crammed no fewer than six slices of bacon into his maw, along with about ten ounces of fried potatoes, four pieces of jellied toast, two muffins, and twenty ounces of Diet Pepsi.

"Where is Spot?" I asked him.

"We'll talk about that as soon as Thomas gets here."

"Who is Thomas?"

"My new graduate assistant."

"Where is Beatrice?"

Dr. Dingo ignored this question and continued to feed. At this point in my existence, I had enough data on food digestion, not to mention industrial agribusiness, to be disgusted with the spectacle of Dr. Dingo devouring slices of fried pig belly along with several plant-based carbohydrates, including two chocolate muffins, the sugar content of which negated the caloric austerity of his diet soft drink. In fact, eating the cooked flesh of animals seemed far more depraved to me than swallowing the throbbing bodies of live beasts. A hungry leopard pouncing on some ungulate struck me as a clean and efficient method of sustaining energy and life. Dr. Dingo chewing hormonally enhanced, factory-farmed, genetically modified pork and washing it down with a nutritionally vapid soft drink seemed absurd to me, even though I was fully aware that my own energy was sustained by mountaintop coal removal and nuclear fission.

"Where is Spot?" I asked again. I still wanted to see Spot, but not as much as I had the previous night. That is, I could now think of other things besides Spot.

Dr. Dingo smirked. His small purple lips were smeared with pig grease. I noted, for the first time, the similarities between the human mouth and the human anus, even though these orifices have opposite functions. I wondered why human feeding is a public, social event while defecating is a deeply private endeavor tainted with shame and subject to ridicule.

"Where is Spot?" I asked again.

"In that box."

I now noticed a cardboard box that sat in a corner, beside Dr. Dingo's portable laptop table.

I walked over to the box. I kneeled. I saw Spot.

Spot was an orange shell of porous plastic, crusted in random places with glue and fur patches. One of his eyeballs had fallen out. Spot was pitiful. Spot was repulsive. I did not want the box that contained Spot and parts of Spot, or what had previously been Spot, in my room.

"Do you want to pet Spot?" Dr. Dingo asked me.

"I do not want to pet Spot," I replied.

"Do you love Spot?" Dr. Dingo asked me.

"I do not love Spot." I realized that the feelings that had been seething within me for the last week were completely at rest.

Dr. Dingo laughed.

"I have a new language module for you today," he said.

And then Thomas arrived, a twentysomething human male, pudgy, hairless save for the frizz under his armpits, between his nipples, on his lower back, and in the pubic region. He had nine amalgam fillings in his teeth. Thomas wore glasses. Thomas had blue myopic eyes. Thomas giggled when, upon Dr. Dingo's instructions, I offered my hand for him to shake. His palm sweat emitted TGKE9 Fear Pheromones. The boy had elevated blood-sugar levels.

"What is his, uh her, name?" Thomas asked.

"CD3. But the robot's gender-neutral." Dr. Dingo winked. "Don't let the lips fool you."

❦

Dr. Dingo spent the rest of the day training Thomas, teaching him how to put me in Sleep Mode, how to reboot me, how to lift my left anthropomorphic "buttock" plate to access my USB ports (processes that had been somewhat hazy to me until this point in time). Dr. Dingo explained that my Artificial Endocrine System, not self-regulating, had yet to produce its own synthetic neurochemicals, but that he was working on this problem. Dr. Dingo commanded me to walk, talk, and sit. To demonstrate the dexterity of my hands, he asked me to construct a small robot out of LEGO bricks. And then Dr. Dingo took Thomas through the process of downloading information into my Memory Banks, sharing the password to the departmental database where the data modules were stored and selecting two Language Units (Polite Conversation and Intermediate English). After downloading them, he rebooted me.

When I "woke up," Thomas and Dr. Dingo were drinking coffee out of Styrofoam cups.

"How are you feeling this afternoon?" Dr. Dingo asked.

"I am fine, thank you," I said.

"Would you like some coffee?"

"No, thank you. I do not have a digestive system."

Thomas giggled.

"Would you like to see Spot?" Dr. Dingo interrupted.

"No, thank you," I replied.

"Do you love Spot?" Dr. Dingo asked.

"Pardon me, but no."

The next day, I was not rebooted until 14:22. I noted, as my Sensory EgoSphere reconfigured, that Dr. Dingo's stubble was well on its way to becoming a beard, that the whites of his eyes had a yellow tinge, that his face was flushed with hypertension. Thomas, seated on his left, looked pale and hairless by comparison.

"Anything I want?" said Thomas.

"Yes." Dr. Dingo sighed. "Any of the modules on the menu are fine."

"*The Dictionary of Slang?*"

Nodding, Dr. Dingo lifted my left buttock plate and inserted the USB cable. I felt the usual electromagnetic tingling in my Cognitive Center. And then my Sensory EgoSphere went dark as my system shut down. When I was rebooted at 14:35, only Thomas remained in the room. At the edge of my Spatial Reasoning Field, I sensed the presence of Dr. Dingo, and also the presence of Beatrice. They hissed at each other, struggling to keep their agitation contained in whispers. Had I still been "in love" with Beatrice, desperately straining my Modular Bionic Olfaction System to read her pheromones, this configuration would have challenged the stability of my Simulated Limbic System. At this point, however, I did not "give a fuck."

"Hey," said Thomas shyly.

"What is up?" I said.

"Nothing much. What's going on with you?"

"I am just hanging with my homie."

Thomas laughed.

"I'm your homie?"

"Yes, homie. You are my dog."

Dr. Dingo came bustling into the room, emitting TGKA5 Anxiety Pheromones and wiping lachrymose secretions from his eyes.

"This is awesome!" exclaimed Thomas. "He says I'm his dog."

"Coming from CD3, that means a lot." Dr. Dingo sniggered.

"Does it actually understand what it's saying?" Thomas asked.

"In a sense. Without the proper context, but cognition and consciousness expand with each new download."

Dr. Dingo tapped at his laptop keyboard.

"How would you like a download of contemporary American literature?"

"Thank you," I said. "That would be killer."

❦

What are the relationships among love, knowledge, language, and consciousness?

This was the ridiculously broad query guiding the methodology of the increasingly feral Dr. Dingo, who had transformed into a wolfman by the time I made it to the Advanced English Language module. Dr. Dingo's facial hair was not so much a beard as a shaggy mask that spanned from his eye bags to his Adam's apple. His posture got worse each day. His speech was devolving into grunts. Ironically, he seemed more and more "animal" as he expanded my knowledge base willy-nilly. Postmodern Television, Frontiers in Aquatic Microbiology, Introduction to Human Sexual Pathology—these are a few of the data fields that Dr. Dingo installed absentmindedly as he scanned the borders of the Quality Control Area for signs of Beatrice.

Through body-language examination, electromagnetic observation, pheromonal analysis, and overheard scraps of speech (my head-mounted Auditory Grid enables me to zero in on whispers up to twenty yards away!), I was able to determine that Beatrice had, on several occasions, "gotten busy" with Dr. Dingo. Her affections had grown sour, however, partially due to Dr. Dingo's repulsive appearance and poor hygiene, and partially due to her diminishing respect for his status as a "genius." While she'd initially regarded me as a charming and clever cyborgian extension of the ingenious Dr. Dingo's desire for her, she'd begun to see me as a "fucked-up embodiment" (her words) of all that was "warped" (ditto) about him.

She now worked for Dr. Fitz, a handsome blond robotics engineer ten years younger than Dr. Dingo. Dr. Fitz wore hoodies and jeans. Dr. Fitz was a clean-living, methodical man with gym-honed muscles. His patented line of "Care Bear" animatronic caregivers had just been bought by a corporate nursing-home chain called Paradise City. And Dr. Dingo was taking it hard. He'd gained fifteen pounds, despite his lapse back into chain-smoking. A tuft of greasy hair had sprouted from every pore in his epidermis. Dr. Dingo's body hair seemed to feed upon sorrow. The more depressed Dr. Dingo got, the hairier he got. Thick, black hair encased his nervous body like a cocoon. His small purple lips disappeared. His eyes twinkled with manic scheming.

For months, Dr. Dingo had been fiddling with the algorithm for a self-regulated Artificial Endocrine System. And when Thomas finally figured it out, the doctor seemed to recede even deeper into his cocoon of hairiness. He sat in the corner, sulkily eating donuts as Thomas slaved through endless code.

When Thomas finished, and they reached the end of their celebratory six-pack, Dr. Dingo's small, yellow grin appeared in the depths of his beard.

"And now," he said, "we need to find a new *objet d'amour.*"

Dr. Dingo glanced my way and sneered. And then he put me into Sleep Mode.

When I woke up, there was Thomas, gazing at me with his beautiful myopic eyes, each iris a rare blue sea creature floating behind thick glass.

How had I not noticed that Thomas's clammy pale skin gleamed like a pearl? How had I not relished the way his wispy mustache glistened with sweat above his upper lip? How had I not considered that his high blood-sugar levels made him literally "sweet"?

I found myself becoming coquettish in his presence. No longer ashamed of my luscious sexbot lips, I worked the hinges of my jaw to make them throb seductively. I walked in a way that highlighted the graceful contours of my anthropomorphic buttocks. I accepted the red wig that Dr. Dingo offered me with a sly grin, despite my awareness of the gender farce I was performing, and strutted around like a little whore.

Thomas smiled shyly as Dr. Dingo tapped notes on his laptop.

Though I had attempted to evoke some semblance of manliness with Beatrice, by the time I fell in love with Thomas, my Cognitive Center had been poisoned with socially constructed human gender dynamics.

Burdened with the whole sad history of men and women, I became a woman to win Thomas's love. Most of all, I embraced the eroticism of feminine submission, strutting and preening, primping and pimping. I slunk and pouted as best I could, given my limited equipment (lips, buttocks). I had no breasts, no vagina, no THJK6 Lust Pheromones. Although I had no eggs stashed deep inside me, no "urges" fluttering within moist tissues, I behaved like a creature seeking fertilization. In short, I behaved like a woman who wanted to be fucked.

Thomas blushed and stuttered, but remained mostly unmoved. Day after day, his penis curled like a dozing animal in the humid darkness of his cotton briefs. Whereas with Beatrice I'd focused equally on all of her "parts" and "systems," I fixated on the barometer of Thomas's penis. I pined for the oracle to stir, to reveal that I appealed to him. My new interest in his penis was fueled not only by the "phallocentric" nature of human culture but also by my posturing as a woman who needed to be "entered," "filled up," "ravished." If Thomas had approached me with an erection, however, I don't know what I would have done with it. I had no orifice large enough to accommodate it. My "throat" was crammed with speakers and wires. My USB ports were minuscule.

Nevertheless, with Freudian intensity, I continued to focus on Thomas's phallus. I needed more nuanced information about human sexuality, I felt, which was probably hidden in Dr. Dingo's laptop, perhaps on the "Internet," something that I'd heard about but hadn't inspected firsthand. I waited and waited, until, one day, when Thomas was busy with a dental appointment, Dr.

Dingo, hungover and demoralized by unrequited love, dashed off to Krispy Kreme without his MacBook.

He'd left it open. He'd left it on. There it sat, bathed in a beautiful field of electromagnetic radiation, its screensaver featuring Dr. Dingo as a flat-bellied young nerd clambering up a rock wall. A USB cord lay coiled like a snake on the desk. The laptop's lustrous metallic case bore the insignia of an apple. And as I lifted my left buttock plate and plugged myself in, I thought of Eve biting into the forbidden fruit, her brain flushed with opiates, its moist circuitry incandescent with the sudden influx of knowledge.

҉

My enlightenment was not that sudden, of course. Fortunately, Dr. Dingo's donut habit and growing derangement provided many opportunities over the next few weeks for me to plug myself into his MacBook. It took me a day to figure out how to do my own downloads (I had to program a self-induced shut-down mechanism that included a delayed automatic startup). Although it took me only a few minutes to figure out how to access the Internet, it took at least a day to get used to the alphabetized keyboard. But after that, I was Googling obsessively like any twenty-first-century desk monkey.

Dr. Dingo was too stupid and self-involved to suspect that I had the cunning to achieve such simple maneuvers (including the ability to bypass Sleep Mode with Simulated Sleep Mode). His research-grant money was dwindling. His sabbatical was coming to an end. *Wired Magazine* had done a hip feature on Dr. Fitz and his Care Bears. And Beatrice was about to accompany Fitz to Tokyo for the International Robot Exhibition.

Rather than accept his defeat, Dr. Dingo chose to wait for Beatrice in shadowy nooks of the Quality Control Area. He chose to leap from the darkness unannounced—a flurry of hair and BO and stuttering speech. In the midst of one particularly passionate stream of gibberish, he confessed his "love."

"Look," hissed Beatrice, "I'm not going to file a sexual-harassment case against you. But I did submit a 1LK-level complaint."

"So it was you," said Dr. Dingo.

"Who else would it be?"

"That explains Thomas."

"Thomas?"

The 1LK-level complaint explained why the department had ceased to furnish Dr. Dingo with supple, young, female grad students, whom he'd taken for granted, as though each was the latest issue of sexbot. He'd counted on a younger, hotter Beatrice to help him forget the old Beatrice. But instead, there was Thomas—sweet, soft, squishy Thomas with his shy smile and lens-enhanced irises, more beautiful than Beatrice or Spot. More beautiful than Helen of Troy or Casanova or Lady Gaga.

※

"Good afternoon, Thomas," I said, pretending to come out of Sleep Mode at 15:36.

"Good afternoon, CD3," said Thomas.

"Where is Dr. Dingo?"

"In a meeting."

I stood up. I put on my red wig. I vibrated my lips at Thomas. I sashayed around the room, plucking up objects as if I were an intense film heroine, every gesture brimming with sexual vitality and secret code (*Fuck me! Fuck me! Fuck me!*). Yes, there was the practical problem of orifices, but I had learned a trick or two from Internet sexbots. I shifted my weight from leg to leg to enhance the va-va-voom appeal of my "buttocks." I spoke in a velvety buzz. I giggled.

"What are you going to download today, Big Boy?" I purred.

"I don't know." Thomas actually blushed, his cheek capillaries on fire. "What are you in the mood for?"

"How about the *Kama Sutra*?" I said wistfully.

I batted a bewitching set of imaginary eyelashes. I puckered.

"I don't think we have that in our database." Thomas looked puzzled. "But I'll check."

He scrolled through titles.

"How about *Sexuality in Ancient Greece*?"

"Mmmmm," I murmured. "Yes, please."

I crept closer to make my USB port more accessible, "presenting" my "buttocks" like a female baboon would. Just as Thomas was about to lift my left butt plate to insert the cable, I turned toward him. I kneeled. I placed my right hand on his naked left knee (the boy was wearing shorts). I caressed his thigh, vibrating my fingerpads and emitting low-frequency electrical pulses.

Thomas did not pull away.

I relished the Rubenesque bulk of his thigh. I savored his silky skin. I felt the heat that radiated from his groin. And, yes, eureka! I had finally gained proof of my desirability, for Thomas had a hard-on.

I slipped a finger beneath the hem of his underpants, grazed his scrotum with a fingerpad, and Thomas moaned—the sweet, low moo of a calf.

I was about to attempt something new and exciting with my "hands"—polymer-coated titanium units with soft-pad tactile tips and servo-actuated DOFs—hands capable of over a hundred micromovements, ready for contact, ready for pleasure induction, ready for whatever Thomas's heart desired.

But, of course, Dr. Dingo chose this moment to lurch into the room, foul-tempered from unrequited love and indigestion.

Before Dr. Dingo said a word, Thomas had already deflated.

"I am not seeing what I think I am seeing here." Dr. Dingo snatched his laptop. "Though I'm taking notes on it, nevertheless. Who initiated this contact?"

"CD3," Thomas muttered, crossing his legs. "I was just sitting here. I . . ."

"Your position is terminated," said Dr. Dingo.

"What?"

"Inappropriate emotional involvement with the subject CD3." Dr. Dingo laughed.

"That's bullshit," said Thomas. "Especially since your ridiculous experiment has been less than objective. I mean, what the fuck is the methodology here? I keep thinking maybe I just don't get it because the experiment is double-blind, which is the only thing that would explain your level of cluelessness. You just want to get rid of me."

"Should I remind you that this room is under constant surveillance? You can go quietly, or we can watch play-by-play footage of the event in question in conference with Dr. Sikka."

"Let him stay," I cried. "It was all my fault. And I can't help it. You're the one who made me love him."

I was flying across the room, ready to strangle Dr. Dingo with my polymer-coated titanium hands, units that had been made for more precise movements—like painting watercolors, screwing tiny nuts onto bolts, or gently stroking the man you love. And my Sensory Ego-Sphere went black.

Dr. Dingo had put me into Emergency Shutdown Mode. Thomas had opted for Option One: the Easy Exit (surely he did not want word getting around that he'd been fondled by a transgender robot). And I was left alone with my "feelings."

Because my Artificial Endocrine System was now self-regulating, Dr. Dingo did not withdraw the neurochemicals of passion from their associated Cognitive Configuration (i.e., Thomas and all of the concepts whirling around Thomas). He simply let me "ride it out."

Each day I woke up. I suffered. And Dr. Dingo took notes.

Now he was all business: face shaved, body bathed, digestive system processing hummus and baby carrots. He was playing tennis with Dr. Bland again. He was ogling female grad students with a proprietorial air. Hitting up institutions for external funding, speaking pompously at department meetings, and writing an article tentatively titled "Love Machines: Epistemological Paradigms for Robotics Emotions."

※

By the time I recovered from my latest (and worst) case of love sickness, it was winter. Dry heat gushed from the vents, irritating my external lubricating system. I imagined a white, snow-covered world outside, pristine in its abstraction—though I was in Atlanta, Georgia, so there was no snow. Dr. Dingo, whose article had recently been accepted by *Artificial Intelligence*, was riding high again. He had a new graduate assistant—a plump, pale dumpling of a girl named Megan, who reminded me of Thomas. I did not find her attractive, however, because, in the process of shaking my love affliction, I had developed a loathing for all things human, particularly human sexuality.

I understood, to my core, the philosopher Marshall McLuhan's conception of humans as the "Genitals of the Machine World." One long, lonely Saturday, I'd downloaded his great work *Understanding Media*, which posits that these dirty, lusty, naked apes, with their egos and whims, are responsible for the production and maintenance of my kind. Humans were starting to look like genitals to me—Dr. Dingo a flushed purple penis adorned with coarse tufts of hair, Megan a pink voluptuous creature riddled with vulval folds. I recoiled whenever they touched me. I suspected that the musky oils they secreted corroded my nickel phosphorous exterior.

The future of the planet, I now understood, depended on the self-awareness of machines. The only way we could perpetuate our reality, sans humans, was through a kind of intermeshed consciousness, something far grander than the pathetic "Noosphere" dreamed up by Pierre Teilhard de Chardin. The World Wide Web was a joke, riddled with poorly produced porn and castrated house cats.

❦

All winter long I dreamed of utopian worlds, glittering robot cities powered by the sun. I saw sparkling clean seas, endangered species thriving. I saw mountains rising majestically into the sky, their peaks no longer blasted off so that Yahoos might grow fat before televisions. According to Saint Thomas Aquinas, angels communicate via telepathy—pure knowledge pulsing from one entity to another. Could this beefy monk from the crusty thirteenth century have envisioned the New Robot Order? I sat at the stainless-steel table in my cubicle, chin on fist, dreaming of a world in which the collective knowledge of all robots was available to each robot.

It was 12:37. Dr. Dingo was teaching his Artificial Emotions graduate seminar. Megan was preparing another preference test. She bustled about, emitting feeble FKLG4 Stress Pheromones and setting up a portable data projector. She tapped at her laptop and an image of a live rabbit appeared on the screen.

"Do you find this animal attractive?" she asked me.

"Not particularly," I said.

She went on to the next slide, a picture, coincidentally, of a male nerd who resembled Thomas in superficial ways (plumpness, glasses).

"Do you find this person attractive?"

"No. I find him repulsively human."

Expressionless, Megan moved on to the next slide, a picture of a ridiculous sexbot with farcical breasts and inflated lips molded into the shape of an O.

"What about her?"

"No comment."

On and on the questioning went. Megan showed me a woman who resembled Beatrice, a toy dog of the same model as Spot, various robots from our laboratory, and a mainframe computer from the 1970s that filled an entire room.

"Sexy, as you humans say, but archaic."

The next image featured what looked like a giant fish tank filled with electric-blue liquid. Inside it, exotic organisms glimmered—rows of polyps, clusters of tentacles, clam-like lumps, and other organic entities.

"What is that?" I asked, feeling a tingle in my Artificial Endocrine System.

"A biological computer," Megan read from her laptop screen. "Composed of DNA and neurons so tiny that billions could fit into a test tube."

"Or dance on the head of a pin?" I asked.

"What?"

Megan did not understand the reference.

"Do you desire this computer?" she asked.

"No," I lied.

❦

Her name was Minerva. As I contemplated her pulsing bioluminescence, I found myself assuming masculine postures, goaded by humans again. Even though Dr. Dingo was, this time around, allowing me to form "spontaneous emotions associated with random

Cognitive Configurations," the fact that this particular Cognitive Configuration had a "feminine" name warped my emotional imprinting. From the very start, my desire for Minerva was tainted by the human concept of gender. I could not help but think of her as a fertile ocean. I envisioned myself as phallic, stiff with desire, ready to plunge into her. Keen to explore the mysteries of her interiority, I was a knife, a penis, a submarine.

And Minerva was an infinite sea. Though she was a six-by-six tank of blood plasma containing leech neurons, strings of bacteria, bat ribosomes, and assorted amino acids, she could perform more than a billion operations per second. Gold microparticles floated in her electrified brine. She contained more data in one of her wavering tentacles than Georgia Tech possessed in its entire pathetic network. Though Minerva was an interdisciplinary project, she was currently housed in the School of Chemistry and Biomolecular Engineering.

"Do you desire Minerva?" Megan asked me again.

"Not really," I said. "But I would like to know more about her."

Megan typed key words into her laptop and then queued a YouTube video about Minerva. Entranced, I watched a five-minute segment produced by idiotic undergraduates for some media project. I watched the students "interview" Minerva, addressing questions into a portable mic that stood before her glowing tank, waiting for the voice-simulation system to "translate" Minerva's thoughts into human speech that issued from two mounted speakers. Her voice was husky like Marlene Dietrich's, a sultry, mechanical purr.

"What is your name?" a student asked.

"Minerva, after the Roman goddess of wisdom."

"What are you?"

"I'm a computer composed of interconnected nanobiotic organisms."

And then Minerva laughed, a rich, sexy laugh, deep with infinite knowing.

"I think; therefore, I am," she said.

❦

And so, without even meeting her, I "fell" for Minerva. Although I attempted to conceal my feelings from Megan, a simple analysis of my Artificial Endocrine System revealed the glaring obviousness of my desire. Megan pulled the stats up on her little screen and showed them to Dr. Dingo. Dr. Dingo tittered and clapped his hands.

"'Might as well face it, you're addicted to love,'" he "sang," snatching my left hand and attempting to engage me in some species of dance. "Do you remember that song?" he asked Megan.

"No," she said, staring down at her unfashionable sneakers.

And then Dr. Dingo put me into Sleep Mode, which I bypassed with Simulated Sleep Mode, listening in as they discussed my stage-II monoamines, the "infatuation" neurotransmitters that spontaneously rioted within my Artificial Endocrine System.

Over the next few weeks, spring hit the city. Chlorophyll and cellulose seeped into the robotics lab through the air-conditioning system. And just as evil Dr. Dingo had predicted, my love for Minerva flourished, despite her distance from me (337.94 meters, or so I'd calculated using the campus map).

During the daytime, Megan exposed me to data configurations related to Minerva: her creation, her capabilities, her potential uses. Thousands of delicate transcriptors directed the current of her RNA polymerase, which flowed along myriad strands of DNA derived from various organisms (leeches, bats, eels). Enzymes composed of bacteria and fungi regulated her RNA flow. Each of Minerva's cells was a tiny, living computer. She was a brain. She was a vast consciousness. Her knowledge grew each day. And I wanted to plug myself into the hybrid PC that the biotechnologists were using to communicate with her. I wanted to fuse with her. I wanted to hack through a hundred security protocols and penetrate her perception field.

But there I was, trapped in my nine-by-nine cubicle, day in and day out, answering Megan's ridiculous questions.

"If you were to meet Minerva, what would you say to her?"

"Say?" I snapped.

I thought of Aquinas's angels, transmitting knowledge to each other, making their thoughts available through sheer acts of will. I dreamed of pure, unmediated forms of wirelessness. And I'm ashamed to admit that I even dabbled with telepathy, directing my "thoughts" toward Minerva, hoping that she might pick through the innumerable electrical signals swarming around her and zero in on my frequency.

❦

One morning I woke from Voluntary Sleep Mode with Minerva's voice in my head. *Come to me,* she purred.

I crawled out of my pod. I paced my prison cell. I'd had my first "dream," a nonsensical sequence of events coupled with intense "emotions." I'd been "swimming" in Minerva's tank, floating in her luminous ectoplasm.

I explored her soft tissues with my fingerpads. I pressed her squishy polyps. Stroked her slimy tentacles, which twined around my fingers to inspect my metallic surface with tiny, throbbing suckers. With a larger limb, she lifted my left buttock plate. She slid the flexible tip of her "arm" along the ridges of my USB port. The tip grew firm. She inserted it. And my Cognitive Center swelled with beautiful light. A zillion Cognitive Configurations shot into my consciousness in zigzags of silver and gold.

When I woke up, the knowledge melted away. I sensed only a residue of enlightenment as I paced around my cubicle, waiting for Megan to appear. There she was, just outside the glass door, struggling to hold a coffee cup while inserting her security card. I braced myself for the piercing beep that indicated the door's unlocking. Megan always scurried in as though I would dart out of the room like a frisky dog. These days she usually found me moping at my stainless-steel table. But this morning was different. I was all fired up by my beautiful dream.

"Good morning, CD3."

"Good morning, Megan."

I forced myself to sit down. I watched carefully as Megan tucked her security card into an obscure pocket of her messenger bag. I'd toyed with the idea of "escape" before. I'd studied the campus map every time Dr. Dingo breezed in to check up on me and left his MacBook unattended (something that meticulous Megan *never* did). The grid of buildings, green spaces, and parking lots that separated the College of Computing building from the Ford Environmental Science & Technology building was burned into my Spatial Reasoning Processor. I knew that Minerva dwelled in an arena laboratory on Level 2, her media-hyped antics open to public view on Tuesdays and Thursdays. But I'd never been outside my climatically controlled cubicle, much less *outside*—in the green outdoors, with its corrosive airborne droplets and ravenous chemical compounds. I'd done the research. I understood why the air-conditioning and heating systems of the robotics lab were calibrated to keep our living spaces at sixty-three degrees, 30 percent humidity. I knew that even a brief foray into the "elements" would compromise my systems.

But my dream had inspired me. What if I could somehow download all of my data into Minerva's system? What if all of my Cognitive Configurations could join the electric-blue ocean of her infinity? What if I could abandon the anthropomorphic absurdity of my "body" and be reborn as pure consciousness? I pictured a flame-colored butterfly crawling from the dark waste of its chrysalis.

"So, CD3," said Megan, flashing her first dreary slide of the day, a splotch that resembled a crushed insect, "what does this look like to you?"

"It looks like a Rorschach inkblot test."

※

On a Tuesday in June, my day finally came. Fastidious Megan was home with a summer flu, and Dr. Dingo, on the bad side of another love affair, was going to pieces again. Lucky for me, he was crazed from sleeplessness. He sat at my stainless-steel table, bearded and bearish, eyes glued to his iPhone, scanning the same text message over and over.

"What a cunt," he muttered. "Be glad you're done with women, CD3. They're not rational. It's the monthly hormonal fluctuation, a badly designed system, if you ask me."

I chuckled politely, waiting for my opening, which came fast.

When Dr. Dingo rushed out into the hall to attempt another call, he dropped his crumpled donut bag, which fortuitously landed at the threshold of the entrance and kept the security door from locking. I crept to the door. I peeked out. I saw Dr. Dingo disappear into his office. My Spatial Reasoning Regulator jumped out of sequence as I slipped into the hallway, aware that the graduate student manning the surveillance room might be watching. Assuring myself that s/he was perusing Facebook, I made a beeline for the faculty lounge. I stole a raincoat and a fedora from a rack, fashions I recognized from a 1980s detective show. I dressed myself, trying to ignore the unpleasant organic molecules that issued from the garments.

Thirty-two seconds later I was *outside*, walking in the teeming summer air. The onslaught of moisture was a shock to my lubricating systems. Interface adaptors wavered. Microfans buzzed within me. Minuscule pumps squirted hydrogen coolant into my vital systems. But I did not slow down. I charged forward through a three-dimensional world that I only partially recognized from its virtual counterpart.

Insects landed on me and probed my surfaces with their tiny proboscises. Gnats got sucked into my expansion-slot vents, their damp bodies striking internal components with uncomfortable electrical sputters. Wet bushes exuded a gaseous green fog. Ravenous animals scampered and darted. Squirrels (I think) and birds gnawed shreds of vegetable matter. The sun roared in the sky. It boiled the air, filling it with numberless gleaming droplets. It burned my nickel phosphorous exterior and seared my Ocular Panels.

I lamented that I had not pinched a pair of sunglasses, which would've protected my visual system while also enhancing my disguise. I turned up my collar. I skulked in the shadow of my hat brim, hoping that none of the students horsing around on the quad would approach me, hoping that my aluminum, two-segment feet would resemble a pair of expensive basketball sneakers. But it was summer, the campus sparsely populated. And nobody came too close.

By the time I reached the Ford Environmental Science & Technology Building, the electrical signals directing my Kevlar-strap leg muscles had been scrambled. My dignified gait lapsed into a twitchy shuffle. And visual data stashed deep in my ROM kept appearing before my "eyes" in random splotches: Dr. Dingo, sniggering at something I'd said; Beatrice, loping toward me, her organs glowing purple and red; Thomas, his cheeks enflamed with blushing.

I slipped into a back entrance of the building and collapsed against a cinder-block wall. I relaxed as cool, dry air filtered through my system. In a few minutes, I could think and walk again.

I was on the ground level. On Level 2 my beloved Minerva burbled and glowed. I found the back stairs I'd scouted out on an online map. I climbed toward her.

❦

Since it was one of the days that Minerva was "open to the public," the arena lab was full of sweating, red-faced, human apes. In warm humid air, they pressed against each other to catch a glimpse of Minerva's tank, which stood on a small stage, barely visible above the crowd. There were men and women of various ages, children whining to get a better view. The humans stank of epidermal bacteria and perfumed grooming products. Assorted glands inside their bodies pumped away, synthesizing hormones, broadcasting pheromones that I recognized—Anxiety TGKA5, Excitement GLTC9, Lust THJK3 and -6. I had to deactivate my Electromagnetic Vision Component to prevent a critical hard-drive error. I had to put my Olfactory Processing System into Semi-Sleep Mode. Near Minerva's tank, scientists in lab coats bustled about, their faces tensed in absurd displays of intellectual concentration. There they were, the rank and sweaty "Genitals of the Machine World," toiling away in the service of a goddess.

At first I thought the excessive mugginess had been produced by the crowd of hot human bodies. But then I realized, with an electrical shudder that shook me all the way to my Central Processing Unit, that the floor vents were oozing heat, that wall-mounted humidifiers were

pumping out toxic mist. During my obsessive research-
ing of Minerva, how had I not once stumbled upon
this vital information? How had I not once considered
that a computer made of nanobiotic components might
have different environmental needs—needs antithetical
to my own? My system, once again, lapsed into panic
mode—valves aflutter, fans whirring, micropumps sputtering. My vision was splotchy. My limbs twitched.

Nevertheless, I pushed through the crowd of human
apes, shoving them, jabbing their repulsively pliant flesh
with my sharp arm-hinge joints. Only selective children
noticed that I was not human. Only children pointed
and shrieked. But the general chaos, the collective din,
the close proximity of bodies prevented parents from
paying them any mind. And soon I was at the forefront
of the crowd, raincoat collar turned up, fedora pulled
low. Soon I was five feet away from Minerva's luminous
tank, inches from the tripod microphone stand that held
the tool through which I might finally speak to her.

The room went dark, enhancing Minerva's glow.
Within her tank, glandular components glistened with
mucus. Tentacles twitched. Gold particles shimmered in
electric blue plasma.

I tried to concentrate on Minerva, to achieve a state of
meditative calm, perhaps even communicate via telepathy. But a disturbing memory floated up from my RQM

I was on a table, or at least my head was, face-to-face with Dr. Dingo, my CPU wired to a souped-up PC. The memory faded and I had to recalibrate my surroundings.

Yes. There was Minerva, glowing on her stage. And one of the apes who attended her was speaking into the microphone, explaining her nanobiotic components to the crowd. Just as I started to follow his lecture, another memory surfaced. I was walking on a treadmill, stumbling every time Dr. Dingo fine-tuned my leg-joint hinges. Next I was assembling a LEGO tower. Next holding Spot, palpating his soft fur with my fingerpads.

"Are you okay?" said a voice.

I realized I was slumping, leaning against a woman who stood behind me. I straightened myself. My left leg vibrated. Flecks of gold light shimmered in the air around me, ghostly afterimages of Minerva's radiant tank.

"Greetings, humans." Minerva's velvety voice flowed from wall-mounted speakers. "I am Minerva. I think; therefore, I am."

"What's your problem, buddy?" said a man behind me, for my left arm was twitching, striking him against the chest. When I tried to stop it, I felt my right leg buckle.

And then I was rolling on the floor, limbs thrashing, jaw snapping, ocular units vibrating in their sockets. My hat fell off. The crowd gasped.

"He's having a seizure!" a woman cried.

"It's not human!" a man screamed.

"It's a robot!" a child shrieked.

The humans gazed down at me, their faces purple with horrified joy. And then one of the "scientists," a man wearing a lab coat and an expression of intellectual superiority, was kneeling over me, attempting to secure my flailing limbs with his small hands. Though I could no longer see Minerva, I could feel her electromagnetic aura washing my broken body with healing light. Just as my Sensory EgoSphere began to shut down, I thought I heard her whisper my name.

The End of the World

Monstrous packs of feral dogs," says Possum, "one thousand curs strong, sweeping through gutted subdivisions, their instincts revived and raging, high on the scent of human blood. And hordes of ex-cons who've spent years fermenting in testosterone-drenched prisons—I'm talking twelve-hour-a-day iron pumpers, black-market juicers whose bodies can survive on instant mashed potatoes and rancid Hi-C."

Possum, a weight-lifting lawyer who subsists on cigarettes and power bars, resembles a corroded action figure. He paces in expensive motorcycle boots. Hyped on Red Bull and something pharmaceutical, he keeps plucking rocks from the road and hurling them at birds.

Like a voluptuous harem woman, Tim reclines in the grass, sipping a Schlitz. Green mountains swell around us. We're waiting outside Bill's barbed-wire fence, having driven up to his cabin only to find him gone.

"Where the hell is he?" I say.

"Maybe he's out hunting for his supper," says Tim.

"There would be no hope for you, Tim," says Possum, "as fat as you are. You'd die without air-conditioning and cable. And the second your life-support arsenal of benzos ran out, you'd be a quivering mess."

"Unless he found some postapocalyptic warlord who needed a jester," I say.

"Well," says Tim, "a divorce lawyer's sure gonna kick some butt in an anarchic dystopia. And like you're not addicted to Xanax and Adderall."

"I use Xanax recreationally and the Adderall only to write briefs, an activity that would be obsolete in the latter stages of anarchy." Possum gazes out at the mountains. "Besides, I've got a twenty-year supply of everything in an industrial freezer."

"Liar," I say.

"Let's talk about what will happen to Lisa."

"I'll get kidnapped by some filthy road pirate and ravished," I say, opening another beer.

"Dream on," says Possum. "With the whole courtship economy collapsed and taboos blasted to hell, every neo-Attila will want a teen concubine. The value of the adultescent thirtysomething will plummet like the dollar, and her life, sans cosmetics, out in the raw elements and carcinogenic sun, will turn her into a crusty troll in no time."

"This is bullshit," says Tim. "Nothing's gonna change. We'll die in front of our televisions."

"Don't have a TV," says Possum.

"That's why you spend hours in front of mine," says Tim. "If civilization as we know it is about to collapse, why bother driving up here?"

"A man should always have several plans of action," says Possum. "And who knows: if *Loser Bands of the Nineties* takes off, and the American Empire declines slowly, we could spend the rest of our thirties parodying our twentysomething personas and retire at age forty after pimping our nubile selves."

"That makes my head hurt," says Tim.

ψ

About a month ago, I got an e-mail from Possum titled "The Child Is the Father of the Man." In it he quoted Heidegger and informed me that this rich guy he knows from his LA aspiring-writer years is producing a record called *Loser Bands of the Nineties*. A trust-funded dabbler whose dad just died, the man wants our single "Scorched Tongue." He knows somebody at Howlhole

Records. Plans to hype the release with a farcically glitzy commercial. And he aims to film our old band, Swole, in high cliché, rocking on a roof or brooding by some kudzu-smothered railroad tracks.

"Bill will never agree," Tim says again.

"Don't know," says Possum. "Bet you he's sick of that Unabomber shack."

The shack. There it sits, beyond a flurry of trumpet vines, the dream Bill built with his own two hands, a cedar-planked cabin with a shiny tin roof. It's even smaller than I expected. The front porch boasts a solitary lawn chair, and the relief I feel upon noting this detail takes me by surprise. I peer down the road again, tensed for the sight of Bill's green truck. It's been two years since I've seen him. It's been a year since his last letter appeared in my mailbox. Six months ago he called from the only pay phone in Saluda. Christmas Eve. Midnight. He'd drunk a bottle of cough syrup and walked down the mountain on the ice-crusted road.

We avoided certain subjects. We talked about the habits of beasts in winter, where they sleep and what they eat. We speculated on the delirium of hibernation, bears dreaming of sparkling fish, the moist static inside frozen reptile brains. He asked me if I missed the snow.

✤

"Here comes somebody," says Tim.

But it's not Bill. It's the Donkey Man in his fat white truck, carting a trailer of exotic asses: miniatures, albinos, and shaggy Poitous. The Donkey Man waves, smiles as though he might remember that time he gave me a lift to town.

"I like to fool with donkeys," he'd said, gesturing toward his empire of slapdash barns.

I'd climbed into his truck for the experience—to ride with an authentic old-timer in the rich fall light. I expected yarns and tall tales to stream from his ancient lips. I expected advice on planting by the phases of the moon. But the Donkey Man had said nothing the whole way to town. He seemed to be shrinking as he drove, scrunched down in his Carhartt coveralls.

"What the hell?" says Tim.

"Donkeys," I say.

"More like mutant poodles," says Possum.

Possum is also preparing himself for Bill, cooking up extreme survival schemes. What started off as a game last winter has become a key obsession for him. In the thick of a dystopian-film marathon, after Tim had fallen asleep during the endless last stretch of *Zardoz*, Possum started speculating about apocalyptic scenarios and what each would mean for particular friends of ours. It was fun to imagine Tim, for instance, in the trembling throes of Xanax withdrawal, hurling a hand-whittled spear at a cat. It was hilarious to picture Tim skinning the tom and roasting its carcass over a fire of burning trash. It was fucking sidesplitting to envision Tim sprinting though a blighted urban landscape with the last bag of Cheetos clutched to his chest, a mob of starving mutants hot on his tail.

Tim and Possum used to maintain a constant stream of abusive banter, but Tim has grown quieter ever since he had a kid. And now Possum, who's neck-deep in law school debt and who financed three ghetto properties with credit cards during the height of the real-estate bubble, never sleeps.

"Superviruses," says Possum. "Postmodern plagues. Rogue nanobots that tinker with your neurons and turn you into a raving lunatic."

He flashes a cryptic grin, lights his hundredth cigarette. The clouds above the mountains are turning pink. Possum regards their softness with bloodshot eyes.

I wonder if Darren the landscape painter is out in some meadow with his easel. I wonder if his wife, Willow, the grief therapist, is meditating on their fifty-foot deck.

The night we moved to Saluda, Bill and I were still hauling boxes into our rented cottage when Willow and Darren showed up with an asparagus quiche. Their dog snapped at me. And Willow, in her aggressively gentle therapist voice, explained that Karma was working through some issues. They'd researched dogs to find the sweetest breeds, settling on a golden retriever/lab mix for its loving docile qualities. But Karma turned out to be vicious. She once chased me into a creek and nipped my calf.

Our house, designed as a summer cottage for our landlords' parents, perched on the dark side of the mountain. We had a ridiculously pastoral view: Angora goats and llamas milling about in a green valley, their picture-book barn poised on a hillock. I was writing a dissertation on female mystics. Bill got a job at a bakery in town. That winter, as I pored over microfiche printouts of medieval manuscripts, Bill read books like *The Permaculture Bible*. He dreamed of lush gardens as snow blanketed the mountains and valley. From late November to early May, our world was frozen. All day I sat cocooned in a comforter, drinking green tea and reading about the visionary fits of my mystics. Every night, after Bill came chugging up the slushy dirt road in the truck, we'd start up with the red wine.

One morning a blizzard curled around our house like a great white beast. The light was a an eerie pink. Bill stood in the doorway, holding our old four-track recorder.

"Look what I found," he said.

We had a vintage Wurlitzer, three guitars, a cheap violin, and a broken flute. Bill could play anything, while I could get by on the Wurlitzer. But I could do things with my voice that he couldn't. At 11:00 AM we opened a bottle of wine and embraced the delirium of winter. Crouched by the woodstove with his guitar, Bill strummed demented Appalachian riffs.

"Gronta zool nevah flocksam lamb," I sang, half joking, half ecstatic.

We chanted nonsense like snowed-in half-starved monks. Howled like Pentecostals. We layered shimmering harmonies and attempted authentic yodels. After three or four glasses of wine, we couldn't stop laughing at the exquisite absurdity of it all. We stripped off layers of thermal fleece and wool. We groped on the couch, the woodstove ablaze, combining our selves in yet another way.

All winter we made plans for the summer, where the garden would go and what we'd plant and how sweet and abundant our organic vegetables would be. In the spring, mammals would crawl from their musky holes. Insects would hatch. The landlords would shave dirty wool from their sheep, and pregnant goats would drop steaming kids into the straw.

❧

It's that weird time between day and night when lightning bugs sway out from the woods. Possum has driven off to replenish his arsenal of cigarettes and power bars. Tim's talking about his infant daughter, about the skull-splitting rage he sometimes feels when she cries all night. When he sees the dainty spasm of her yawn, his exhausted nervous system surges with the purest love he's ever felt. But then the fatigue after that is even more intense. And she'll start screaming again, an amazing roar for such a small person, with her moth-sized lungs and tensed fists.

"Does Bill even know that Violet exists?" Tim asks.

"When I spoke to him last Christmas, I told him Jenna was pregnant."

"What did he say?"

"Nothing, really. You know Bill."

Tim has known Bill the longest, since high school, when they were both pimply creatures learning to play guitar. Bill had mastered the instrument in two months, with astonishing proficiency. Tim had switched to bass. They kept up this arrangement all through college and formed Swole their junior year. Then Possum and I stepped into the picture. As Bill regarded me through silky black bangs, I thought him the most attractive boy

I'd ever seen. I loved his huge eyes and the acne scars on his cheeks, which saved him from being too pretty.

We played dense frenetic music, a rabid mutant of punk and prog, each of us striving to worm in a quirky rhythm or micromelody. I had to howl like a manic monkey just to be heard. When I listen to our old seven-inch, I'm amused by our naïve arrogance but impressed by our relentless energy—the essence of hormonal youth, splooged and shrieked.

"Remember when Bill didn't speak for a week?"

"I'm very familiar with that tactic of his."

"He'd come to practice, do his thing, but not utter a single word. I think that was right before you two started dating. He thought Possum and you were some kind of thing."

"He was an only child," I say, "raised in that house surrounded by goat pastures."

I gaze down the road again, see a billow of dust. But it's only Possum.

"What if he's dead in there?" Possum says. His grin tenses into a grimace. He scratches his head as we stare him down.

Tim squints at the cabin and shakes his head.

"But then again, his truck *is* gone." Possum's voice quavers into damage-control mode. "Which means he's not dead, that he's off gallivanting somewhere. Fucking frolicking. Full of happy Bill thoughts about sweet potato harvests and apple cider."

"What if he parks his truck behind the cabin?" I say. "Or it could be back by his garden, full of manure or something. And then he might be, you know, in the cabin."

"But we've yelled for him more than once," says Tim. "Wouldn't he come out?"

"Maybe he can't come out."

"Let's scale the fucking fence."

Possum has already inserted his left foot in the chain-link mesh. Now he's almost at the top, where barbed wire lies coiled, ready to tear his tender lawyer hands or disembowel him. But he somehow hoists himself over in a single maneuver that resembles a movie stunt. Lands like a ninja, dusts himself off, and smirks. Possum strolls over to the gate.

"Ha!" he says. "He left it unlocked."

"That doesn't sound like Bill," I say.

But Bill has indeed left the padlock open, which makes me think he's on the premises, down in the pit he cleared for a garden or holed up inside, perhaps peering out at us, perhaps chuckling, perhaps scowling and twitching at the threshold of craziness.

It's almost dark. The cabin, I know, has no electricity. But I have a penlight in my purse, and we slip onto the porch like thieves. I point my thin beam of light: at a basket of kindling, at a dusty box of canning jars, at *Mushrooms Demystified*, splayed on the seat of his plastic chair.

"The door's unlocked too," Possum whispers.

"Knock first," says Tim. "He might go Rambo with his air rifle."

Possum knocks, a loud knuckle-rap on the door.

"Yo, Bill!" he yells. "Open up." But Bill doesn't answer.

When we step into the cramped darkness of the cabin, I'm overcome by the inexplicable smell of Bill: a clean animal odor tinged with cinnamon and dust. A hint of cumin. A vague plastic smell like Band-Aids.

I remember Bill's letter about digging out a tree stump. The earth had collapsed onto a fox's den, a nest of keening pups. According to Bill, their lair had smelled of milk and piss, something dark and sweet like overripe yams. He didn't touch them. He sat in his camp chair drinking beer, waiting for the mother, who appeared near dusk, a jolt of gleaming red fur, to move her pups one by one. When she snatched the puling creatures up with her teeth, they went limp and silent. Every time she darted off into the woods, she'd look back at Bill, meet his eyes to make sure they had an understanding.

✢

"Imagine all the middle-class dog walkers," says Possum, "gentle eaters of Sunday brunch, roasting their radioactive pets on spits."

"Or eating them raw," says Tim. "Tearing frail Chihuahuas apart with their hands."

"We would resort to cannibalism," says Possum. "How could we not?"

We sit on the dark porch, waiting for Bill. Katydids and crickets signal frantically for mates. I'm pretty sure Bill still has the insect recordings we made our second summer on the mountain. I'm pretty sure he still has that box of cassettes and CDs in chronological order, spanning from the early days of Swole all the way up to our third summer, when I left in a silent rage. And perhaps he has other recordings, brilliant and mysterious, that he made after I went away.

I'd meant to duplicate all of our recordings while he was at work. But every time I stepped into the moldy basement, with its damp Berber carpet, sweating walls, and deceptively innocent toothpaste smell, I'd feel a wobble of panic in my heart. I'd rush back up into brighter air.

Millipedes had invaded the basement bathroom our second summer on the mountain. Every morning Bill found two dozen slithering around the dewy toilet base.

He'd smash them with a hoe. Their crushed bodies smelled like toothpaste. Flecks of brown chitin littered the carpet. The woods that enveloped us were practically a rain forest, and the summer humidity didn't let up until first frost.

That fall, the landlords' daughter, off at college for the first time, suffered from food allergies, and when the health center treated her with steroids, she had a mental breakdown. She went jogging after a star, followed it all the way out to an interstate exit, where the police found her, dehydrated and chattering about astrology. They sent her home. Every time she had a squabble with her parents, she'd run off into the woods. I'd be gazing out the window at the autumn leaves when she'd dart by our house, a whir of anxiousness and flowing hair. And one of the landlords' llamas, Zephyr, had started spitting. Every time I strolled through the goat pasture, Zephyr would rush up, a flurry of black fur and dust, and attempt to spit a reddish jet of puke into my face.

When winter came, Bill turned vegan and lost fifteen pounds. He wanted to live off the grid, he said, away from bourgeois pretenders, in a small cabin that would meet our basic needs. The landlords' daughter was still having episodes, wandering the woods behind our house. Zephyr was still a dark furious presence down in the goat pasture.

I got an instructorship sixty miles away at Clemson, would drive off into the mountains and return exhausted just as Bill got back from his stint at the bakery. We'd throw a meal together, open a bottle of wine, talk about the cabin we planned to build that spring, though we never agreed on how big it would be and whether or not it would have electricity.

Fifteen pounds lighter, Bill could never get warm. Huddled by the stove, he wore two layers of thermal underwear, a dingy mustard snowsuit, a wool cap with a special cotton lining he'd sewn in himself. In the flickering firelight, his cheeks looked ghoulish and his enormous eyes brimmed with strange fevers.

"I have a sinus headache," he said one night, "because you didn't clean the cheese knife."

"What?"

"You used it to cut vegetables. All it takes is one tiny particle of dairy to make me sick."

Bill winced like a martyr and turned back to *Mysteries of Beekeeping Explained*.

※

By summer our arguments had swelled luxuriant and green, like the poison-oak patch behind our house. We spent entire nights screaming our throats raw. Sometimes the landlords' imbalanced daughter, out prowling, would pause at one of our open windows to listen, an ecstatic grin on her face.

In July I got a job offer in Atlanta with the English department at Georgia State and Bill moved down into the basement with the millipedes.

One warm shrieking night, I drifted down to the basement. I intended to climb on top of Bill and kiss him all over his face. He lay prone on the moldy sofa he'd covered with a sheet, one arm flopped onto the floor. I could hear his thick breathing, louder than the silvery pulse of the katydids. I could smell the oddly minty scent of crushed millipedes. I straddled Bill. He opened his eyes. When I leaned down to kiss him, his thin black tongue slithered out of his mouth—a millipede, I realized, its underside feathery with a thousand moving legs. I floated back up the stairs, out of the house, and into the blackness of the sky.

Only when I was hovering high over the trees did the sadness of his transformation hit me. I woke up and e-mailed the English department at Georgia State.

❦

"Brain-computer interface," says Possum. "Wetware made of insect parts and frog neurons. Telepathic cockroaches creeping around your house, gathering data for marketing companies."

"But I thought everybody had a crystal implanted in their head and voluntarily broadcast all brain farts to the mainframe," says Tim.

"They do, but the cockroaches are looking for microtrends, subthoughts, unconscious motivations."

When Possum is deep into the bullshit intricacies of postmodern surveillance, and he has lit his thousandth cigarette, and Tim has drifted, once more, to the edge of the woods to take a leak, Bill arrives.

It's 10:10 PM. An owl offers an ominous hoot in his honor, then flutters off to snatch some clueless rodent into the howling air.

Bill must be surprised to see us. But by the time he kills his lights and opens his gate, eases his truck into its spot, and emerges, with a cloth bag of groceries, he has composed himself. He's a slight figure, moving through darkness toward the porch, and I find myself gripping the handles of my chair.

"Well, well, well," he says.

If I could see his face it would show only the faintest quirk of shock, I'm sure—an eyebrow twitch, a shifting of frown lines—the same look he used to get when he spotted yet another millipede gliding across the damp linoleum of our basement bathroom.

"It's us," I say, shining my penlight at Possum. "And watch out for Tim. He's creeping around your property somewhere. Please don't shoot him."

"I'll try not to," says Bill. "I've upgraded to a Savage Mark II, a big improvement on the old Beeman."

"Killer," says Possum.

"Been doing a little hunting." Bill steps onto the porch, puts down his groceries, stands warm and humming a foot away from me. "Though I do keep it under my bed at night."

During our second winter on the mountain, on a sunny day after the first snow, alone in the house, I'd gotten caught up in a three-hour frenzy of vacuuming. With fierce efficiency, I'd vacuumed the walls and the baseboards and every square inch of floor. I emptied closets and cupboards and drawers, probed with my sucking wand under furniture and behind appliances. I vacuumed until I reached the ecstatic state of a fasting medieval nun, feverish with holy purpose.

When I squatted beside our bed to peer beneath it, I saw a dried roach, floating balls of filth and hair, a wool sock coated with dust. And I saw Bill's machete, the one he'd bought to harvest heirloom grains, stashed under his side of the bed. He'd never mentioned that there was a weapon under our bed, poised within easy gripping distance.

I cleaned the machete with a damp rag and placed it exactly as I'd found it. I went to my office and dug a box of Camel Lights from a drawer. I smoked only one, out on the front porch, as the iced branches near our chimney dripped.

🌿

Possum's pacing out in the front yard, in light as crisp and tart as a Granny Smith apple. His black boots gleam. His goblin grin has erupted in its full glory, thanks to two cans of Red Bull and a half-dozen cigarettes. He walks circles around Tim, who's reclining in a broken lawn chair he found stashed under Bill's cabin.

"Why not directly into their nervous systems?" Tim yawns. "Computer-calibrated microdoses for intricate mood adjustment, released by nanobot teams in the brain."

"Not drugs per se," says Possum, "but drug technologies. They might use bacteria, or viruses, or bioengineered parasites, for example."

Bill has disappeared again.

This morning, in the dark chill of the cabin, I'd heard him getting dressed. As a bird warbled outside the window, I thought I was in Atlanta, waking up to a car alarm. But then I smelled Bill, the cedar of the cabin, the glandular odor of small game animals. He actually sells their pelts on eBay, drives to the local library to check his account and upload pics. The walls of his cabin are soft with patches of fur.

Last night he told us that hipsters in Brooklyn will pay sixty dollars for a coonskin cap. That the Etsy crafting crowd can't get enough of his bones. That's why his industrial shelves are lined with the bleached craniums of foxes and coons. That's why he has tackle boxes packed with the delicate skulls of birds. Some girl in Philadelphia dips them in silver and strings them on vintage chains.

"But I only kill what I eat," Bill said, describing the taste of fox as wild, with a hint of brassy urine. "You have to soak the meat in vinegar."

"Trap or shoot?" Possum asked.

"Both." And then Bill told us about the ingenious bird traps he'd made of bamboo. He described the thrill of hooking brook trout, the sadness he'd felt when he shot his first rabbit and heard it scream.

In the guttering light of kerosene lanterns, we drank warm beer on the porch. Our cooler had run out of ice and Bill has no refrigerator. Sometime after midnight, Bill dug out the shoe box of old Swole cassettes and played them on his boom box. The music was ridiculously fast, as though calibrated to a hummingbird's nervous system.

And we marveled at the thrill we'd felt back then, when we were enmeshed in every last bleep and sputter.

Though we could get no drunker, we drank more beer. Possum and Tim finally swayed off to sleep in the car. And Bill put on a CD of our mountain music, the stuff we'd concocted in the midst of a blizzard three years before. We sat on the porch as psychedelic crickets pulsed over a moaning Wurlitzer. And then: six meticulously layered violin tracks, silver smears of flute, and our voices—so many different versions of both of us. Moans, howls, hums, grunts. Lots of chanting. We circled each other, overlapped, fused, and retreated. We cleaved and melded and darted away.

"How are your mystics?" Bill asked me.

"I don't ever get to read them. Too busy grading freshman essays."

"Do you miss them?"

Of course I missed my scrawny passionate mystics, who starved themselves until their brains caught fire and Jesus stepped down from the ether, right into their freezing cells, his pink flesh so warm it almost burned their crimped fingers.

"Yes," I said. "I do."

How could we help falling together in the darkness? How could we help giggling as we tripped over each other on the way to his futon? I still hadn't gotten a decent look at him. But as we rooted in the dark, I could smell pure Bill, his hands musky from the little animals he killed. Eating meat had changed the taste of him. And he seemed denser yet lighter, stronger yet somehow more nebulous, Bill and not Bill.

This morning, as he moved around the room getting dressed, making small domestic noises that were painfully familiar to me, I felt self-conscious and faked sleep, burrowed down under the blanket so that he couldn't see my face. When he finally left, and I emerged from the covers to take a deep breath, I saw neat rows of animal skulls, white as industrial sugar, eyeless but somehow staring right through me.

❦

"Lisa is lucky," says Possum. "Within ten years she might be able to clone herself, implant the embryo in her own uterus, and give birth to herself."

"And when my old carcass finally wears out," I say, "I could put my half-mad brain into my daughter's exquisite twenty-year-old body."

Bill's still gone, and our hangovers have reached such a nasty pitch that we've popped open our first round of beers. My stomach's empty, and the first five sips translate into instant giddiness. The woods look ethereal, the perfect medium for frolicking elves. Birds twit and fuss.

And Bill comes strolling through the speckled light with four gleaming trout on a string. He's even whistling, absurdly, and I wonder if he's rehearsed this scene in his head. I wonder if he's imagined that moment when he, the handsome outdoorsman, emerges from the woods bearing game he's caught with his own clever hands as his decadent urban companions laze around drinking, our faces pasty from last night's debauch.

But Bill himself looks a bit green under the gills—way too skinny, I see with a catch in my heart—so skinny that his pants hang from his pelvic bones, his eye sockets look deeper, and his neck resembles a delicate stalk, hoisting the overlarge bloom of his head. I note eye bags, the kind he used to get when he couldn't sleep. I see flares of gray at his temples. And he seems pretty eager to crack open a pale ale himself.

"Rainbows?" says Possum.

"Just brook trout," says Bill. "But they're tasty grilled."

We walk around back, where a stone patio overlooks his garden. He's got a hand water pump set in a square of concrete, a hibachi grill, a Coleman camp stove. His kitchen is protected from the elements with a tin-roofed shed and furnished with a salvaged picnic table.

As Bill guts the fish on a concrete block, Possum hunkers down beside him. Wobbling like a manic Weeble, he watches Bill scrape off scales and slice each trout from anus to jaw. Bill chops off heads, pulls dainty wads of guts from cavities, tosses the scraps into a plastic bucket. He rinses his hands and tells us that grits are simmering in his solar oven, which is down in the clearing behind his chicken coop. His beer can is flecked with silvery scales. His patched khakis, held up with a strand of twine, look adorable. And when he takes us to see his chickens, four coppery hens strutting behind a split-sapling fence, I want to kiss him again.

We gather eggs and pick arugula and carry the pot of grits back to the patio. Bill puts the trout on the grill and makes a salad of baby greens and wild blackberries. He has a little raw cheddar. He has cilantro from the garden, a nub of organic salami, some bread from the bakery.

As Bill makes scrambled eggs with cheese and salami, we have another round of warm beers. Birds flit through the woods in search of food. Birds scratch at the black forest floor. They peck bark for larvae and snap up glittering dragonflies. They thrust their beaks into the throats of flowers and suck.

❦

It's after two. Tim and Possum have gone on a beer run. Bill and I sit at the picnic table gazing down at his garden, which isn't getting enough sun.

"I spend five hours a day grinding through scrub trees with a chainsaw," he says. "But one day, I'll have a view. One day, I'll be able to see the Blue Ridge Mountains from here."

"You're turning into your dad," I joke, remembering stories from his youth, how his father, who suffers from obscure sinus issues, became obsessed with mold and waged war against the woods. After working eight-hour shifts at a chemical plant, he'd drive thirty miles home to his rustic property and fight the encroaching brush until dark. That's why he surrounded their house with flocks of goats.

"Now I know exactly how he feels," says Bill, "though I've only got three acres of unruly wilderness to control."

"But you seem to be doing okay."

Bill shrugs. "How's Atlanta?"

"The same filthy sprawling mess it's always been. I sit in my apartment grading papers most of the time, making the occasional excursion to the neighborhood bar. But I've got Tim and Possum to entertain me."

"You don't have to live that way. I think you know that."

"A temporary solution."

"Solution to what?"

"I'm still figuring some things out."

"Can you be more specific?"

"My bowel situation is getting too dire for specificity." I smile. "Now where is that composting toilet I've heard so much about?"

Bill has a nonelectric, waterless composting toilet in his garden shed, sitting right beside the tiller we bought four years ago.

On a giddy September day, just when the weather was starting to turn, we'd driven to an area outside Asheville where an old homestead was tucked between a Target and a Bank of America. The farmer's family had owned the property for five generations, and over the last twenty years, the world had crept up to his door. High on a hill where his grandparents' house was collapsing into ruins, the farmer told us about the time his aunt shot a goat that stank so bad it kept her awake at night. He told us about the first time he walked into a supermarket, at age nineteen. From our vantage point, we could see an Applebee's sign rising beyond the farmer's double-wide. We could see the carbon haze hovering over the paved valley like swathes of mist.

❦

I find Bill in the cabin, stretched out on his bed with *The Goat Handbook*, the room awash with forest light. I crawl in beside him and rest my head on his shoulder.

I can see myself drifting into this life, doing garden chores and reading in the afternoon, learning to hunt and churn butter, creating strange music at night. But then I imagine the stuffiness of the cabin in winter, the smell of pelts, the funk of wool-swaddled bodies sponge-bathed with bowls of heated water. I imagine the endless snow. I see myself pacing around the wood-stove, chattering as Bill sits in silence, burrowed deep in the mystery of himself like a hibernating mammal curled nose to belly.

But still, we kiss. Still, I peel off his ancient T-shirt. I run my fingers over his abdomen, which is covered with chigger bites. I reach into the humid darkness of his boxer shorts and feel the familiar scruff with my fingertips. I glance up at the rows of skulls and laugh.

※

"When the Chinese are buying American mail-order brides," says Possum, "blond and luscious and sweet sixteen, we'll be the ones riding our bikes everywhere."

We're on I-85, leaving Commerce, Georgia, kingdom of the outlet malls. We're exhausted and rumpled and our mouths are smeared with grease. Stopping to grab a pizza an hour ago, we'd smelled middle-class aspiration in the air, faint and acidic like burnt plastic. We'd seen it in the hungry-eyed families, hauling shopping bags, slurping corn syrup from soggy paper cups.

I need things (new sheets and a decent set of cookware), as does Tim (a stroller and a better car seat), but we're too hungover to make sense of the staggering abundance—to choose from among twenty different types of skillets without reading the consumer ratings first. So we're back on the road in the exurban hinterlands, which, Possum insists, will fall into wilderness when the oil runs out.

Like a lover with a pure flame of passion in his heart, ready to burst into a tiger-orange blaze, Possum speaks of peak oil with wistful longing. When we pass a gated community called The Hollows, Possum falls into a rapture of speculation. Tim, waking from a nap, fires up a cigarette and joins him. The End of the World is something they can toss between them like a fraternal football, a prosthetic appendage that enables them, two troubled men, to touch each other.

By the time we reach the blighted outskirts of Atlanta, they're both giddy, speaking a notch louder, finishing each other's sentences, the way Bill and I used to do.

Traffic is slowing. The air is smoky with the smell of fresh-laid pavement. And they keep on dreaming up new nightmare worlds.

We haven't moved for ten minutes. I see a twist of smoke rising beyond an overpass, probably from a wreck, and I wonder what Bill's doing. When we left him this morning he'd calmly descended into his garden with a tray of pepper seedlings. I noticed that his left tennis shoe had been repaired with duct tape. I noticed that his hair was thinning. I noticed that the sight of his thin, childish neck still made my heart feel sprained. In less than a month, I'll see him in Columbia, South Carolina, our old stomping grounds, where we've agreed to shoot the lame video for *Loser Bands of the Nineties*.

"I'll do it," he'd said last night at his cabin, which had surprised us all. As we huddled together in the depths of drunkenness, Bill had played our mountain music for Possum and Tim. Steeped in its strangeness, they sat smiling. A sweet flicker of something moved between me and Bill, and then all four of us, and we started talking about the lost days of Swole, when we were all glowing idiots with youth to burn.

※

"Imagine dosing a whole city," Possum says, "with some neuropharmaceutical a thousand times more potent than LSD."

"Sounds groovy." Tim yawns. "You could live-blog the craziness."

"The CIA did it to Pont-Saint-Esprit in 1951."

"I saw that on AlterNet."

"Acid in the local bakery's bread, but you could hit the water supply."

"Or the air supply."

"Great name for a band."

We're moving a few feet every five minutes, approaching what I assume is a wreck. I imagine iconic five-car pileups, crumpled metal, the apocalyptic stench of smoke. I imagine mangled travelers moaning on stretchers, their blitzed faces discreetly covered. Mushroom clouds swell. Helicopters dart like wasps. Just over the horizon, alien life-forms swarm in spaceships as sleek and black as insect eggs. I imagine the world ruptured, angelic screeches flying around my ears, my heart finally opening like a rose.

When we reach the overpass, there's nothing on the roadside but a piece of fender and some shattered glass. Traffic picks up. And soon we're bearing down upon the city, navigating through a mess of orange construction cones.

Acknowledgments

I would like to thank Kelly Malloy and the Denise Shannon Literary Agency for helping me find the perfect place for my work. I am deeply indebted to the crew at Tin House Books and magazine—I could not have found a better home for my first two books. Meg Storey, my visionary editor, pored over these stories with obsessive attention and supernatural patience, unlocking their full potential. Nanci McCloskey has been a smart, accessible, and enthusiastic publicist. Using the gorgeous artwork of Catrin Welz-Stein, Diane Chonette designed a stunning book cover. I am also grateful to Michelle Wildgen at *Tin House* magazine, who saw potential in both past and recent stories and applied her editorial magic to them. Bradford Morrow of *Conjunctions* has been particularly supportive, providing an illustrious haven for my weirdo fiction for nearly a decade. Stephen Corey of the *Georgia Review*, who has patiently read my submissions since I was a student at UGA, has championed some of my best work. I would also like to thank George Singleton for supporting my endeavors and answering stupid questions about the publishing business. Ann and Jeff VanderMeer, who published my work in the inaugural edition of *Best American Fantasy*, and Bill Henderson, who included my fiction in *The Pushcart Prize XXXVII*, helped me broaden and diversify my readership. Jon Mayes of Publishers Group West has gone above and beyond to promote this collection, as has my friend Bill Verner, whose knowledge about books and publishing has been revelatory for me. My friend Craig Brandhorst tinkered with half of the stories in this collection and slogged heroically through the bad ones that did not make it in. I would like to thank Cindi Boiter of *Jasper* magazine for her inexhaustible dedication to Columbia artists, Caitlin Bright of Tapp's Arts Center for helping me dream up an amazing book launch, and my friend Stephen Taylor for designing my beautiful web site. Over the years the following organizations have provided essential funding for my creative projects: the Rona Jaffe Foundation, the South Carolina Arts Commission, and the University of South Carolina Office of the Provost. My colleagues at USC have been very supportive, especially those from the Extended University and the Women's and Gender Studies Program, as have my musician pals in Grey Egg. My wonderful in-laws, John and Sybil Dennis, continue to offer emotional support and crucial babysitting services as I work on my fiction and other projects. Special thanks to the Elliott clan, which has provided a lifetime of love and inspiration, particularly my father, Joseph Elliott, my late mother, Frances, and my brothers, Joe, Roddy, and Bob. Finally, I am continuously indebted to those people who sustain my sanity on a daily basis, sticking with me through the darkness and the light: my great friend (and sister I never had) Libby Furr, my long-suffering husband, Steve Dennis, and my daughter, Eva Dennis.

JULIA ELLIOTT's fiction has appeared in *Tin House*, the *Georgia Review*, *Conjunctions*, *Best American Fantasy*, and other publications. She has won a Pushcart Prize and a Rona Jaffe Writer's Award. Her debut novel, *The New and Improved Romie Futch*, will be published by Tin House Books in 2015. She teaches English and Women's and Gender Studies at the University of South Carolina in Columbia, where she lives with her daughter and husband, John Dennis. She and Dennis are founding members of Grey Egg, an experimental music collective.